BLACKWOOD CROSSING

A British Agent Novel

MK McClintock

LARGE PRINT EDITION

Published in the United States by Cambron Press.

Originally published in trade paperback by Trappers Peak Publishing in 2014.

LARGE PRINT PAPERBACK EDITION

McClintock, MK
Blackwood Crossing; novel/MK McClintock
ISBN-13: 978-0-9965076-1-5

Cover design by MK McClintock

PRAISE FOR
The British Agents

"Ms. McClintock weaves a thick tapestry of mystery and romance in her historical setting . . . Multiple twists and unexpected alliances hook the reader into her complex tale . . . Bravo Ms. McClintock!"
—*InD'Tale Magazine*

"Ms. McClintock succeeds in masterfully weaving both genres meticulously together until mystery lovers are sold on romance and romance lovers love the mystery! —*InD'Tale Magazine*

"This is a wonderful book with suspense to keep me on the edge of my seat and surprises to keep me guessing." —Verna Mitchell, author of *Somewhere Beyond the Blue*

"*Clayton's Honor* is utterly enticing and captivating!"
—*InD'tale Magazine*

BOOKS BY MK MCCLINTOCK

MONTANA GALLAGHER SERIES
Gallagher's Pride
Gallagher's Hope
Gallagher's Choice
An Angel Called Gallagher
Journey to Hawk's Peak
Wild Montana Winds
The Healer of Briarwood

BRITISH AGENT NOVELS
Alaina Claiborne
Blackwood Crossing
Clayton's Honor

CROOKED CREEK SERIES
"Emma of Crooked Creek"
"Hattie of Crooked Creek"
"Briley of Crooked Creek"
"Clara of Crooked Creek"

WHITCOMB SPRINGS SERIES
"Whitcomb Springs"
"Forsaken Trail"
"Unchained Courage"

SHORT STORY COLLECTIONS
A Home for Christmas
The Women of Crooked Creek

MCKENZIE SISTERS SERIES
The Case of the Copper King

To learn more about MK McClintock
and her books, please visit
www.mkmcclintock.com.

For my editor, Lorraine.
You continue to amaze me.

———————•◦•———————

I would also like to thank Karen C. for
the idea of Keswick.

AUTHOR'S NOTE

Dearest Reader,

Sometimes a story comes along that you want to write but it's a struggle. Your characters take on lives of their own, and no matter how much you want to control them, you can't. Rhona and Charles are unlike any other characters I've written. Their personalities took some getting used to, I'll admit, but when I did, I came to love them as much as I have any others. In some ways, they are the strongest "people" I've ever known and certainly written. They're fierce and uncompromising, and if they were to walk this earth, I would be honored to call them friends.

I hope you enjoy their tale of romance, mystery, and adventure.

Happy Reading,
-MK

One

"You cheated!"

"You're too slow." Rhona's laughter grew as her brother dismounted. "What were you thinking taking an untrained horse against my Mador?"

"That creature you call your pet is a beast. I don't know how you manage him."

Rhona smoothed a gloved hand over Mador's muzzle and placed a kiss between his eyes when he lowered his head to nudge her. "Oh, all right." She slipped half an oatcake from her cloak pocket and fed it to the horse.

"Spoiled, that's what he is." Wallace slapped the dust from his trousers and handed his horse to the groom.

Rhona pressed her head against Mador's neck and grinned at her brother. "Your horses live like kings, brother."

"Yes, but they bring in hefty purses from the races." Wallace stepped up to the tall black Friesian. "He is a beauty. What a marvel he would be at the tracks."

Rhona hugged the horse and stepped away, giving the animal one more kiss before handing him to the groom. "Mador will not run a course so long as I'm around." She slipped her arm through her brother's.

"Come. Let us go in for tea and discuss your plans for the new racer."

Warmth from the fires welcomed the pair when they walked into the stately home. They'd both been born within the stone walls of Davidson Castle. It had once been a peaceful and enjoyable place to live, but over the years, the younger Davidsons had learned to create their own joy. The eldest, Alistair, had spent the past five years at university and traveling the continent. All that Rhona knew of him was from the letters he sent once a month. She longed for him to return, for he was the only one who managed to please their father.

Wallace's deep laughter mingled with her own as the butler removed their coats.

"Is tea ready, Graham?"

"It is, my lady."

Rhona turned and looked up at the butler. "Whatever is wrong?"

"Your father has been looking for you."

Rhona's smile faded, as did her brother's. With a light touch, she set her hand on Wallace's arm. "It's all right."

"He's been in a mood for weeks. Let me come in with you."

"No, it's my turn." Rhona removed her long gloves and handed them to Graham. "Wish me luck." She turned with a glance and grim smile cast over her shoulder and walked to the study. It was the one room in the house where she was prohibited to go unless her father summoned her, even though it remained empty most of the year. Rhona waited immediately outside the study door to listen curiously to her father and another man. The door pushed open and Rhona stepped aside to let her father's guest pass. Her gaze followed him as he walked down the hallway.

"Ye kept me waiting."

Barely inside the door, Rhona turned to her father, searching for any resemblance between them, but she felt no kinship. His disdain always reminded her that a third son would have been preferable to a daughter who served him no purpose. She detested the man, even as her heart ached for the father she'd always hoped he would be.

"I didn't realize you'd returned or that you had company."

"He's a business associate and of no concern to ye."

Rhona pressed the door closed. "We weren't expecting you to return from Edinburgh until Christmas. Wallace and I were testing his new racer. He's no match for Mador, but he'll be a fine addition to the stables."

Her father studied her as though he had heard nothing she had said. "Sit down."

Curious, Rhona did as her father bid, though she remained silent, unwilling to cower or beg for a speedy departure from his presence. The silence continued as tea was brought into the room, a consideration she would not have attributed to her father. It did not bode well, for the tea service meant she could be here longer than she would like.

When the footman departed, Rhona prepared a cup for her father and set it down on his desk knowing he wouldn't touch it. She helped herself to a cup and a small sandwich to help appease her hunger, but she soon grew weary of the quiet.

"I am grateful for this chance to speak with you alone. I've finished making arrangements for my holiday to the continent, but I did want to ask about taking Wallace. He'll be off to university in a year, and I do think he—"

"Ye'll not be going. I have made other arrangements for ye."

Rhona stood now, the tea forgotten. "What arrangements?"

"Marriage."

She shook her head with such force she felt a pain in her neck. "You have no right." She reached for the bell pull, but her father grabbed her arm before she could. "Let go of me."

"Ye'll marry, Rhona, and ye'll do as I say."

She pulled against the force of his grip, but her strength did not match his. "I have means enough to make my own plans and to live comfortably. I neither need nor desire a husband."

The heat of his breath touched her skin when he pulled her closer, but it was anger, not fear, which slowly consumed her.

"Ye'll do as I say." Her father spoke the words with enough force to make her believe she might comply. "I'll ruin ye from here to the far reaches of the continent. Ye'll not find peace so long as I live. Ye will do this, Rhona."

Rhona looked into the hardened face of Calum Davidson and pushed him away, almost falling over from her effort. He returned the favor with a slap across her face, and the weight of his strength sent her toppling to the carpet. She lifted a hand to the cheek that burned and looked in disbelief at her father. He had treated her with indifference throughout the years, but he had never struck her. He lowered himself until he could speak in a whisper.

"Ye'll marry Laird Crawford."

"No." She raised herself to her knees. Rhona knew she should call out for someone, but doing so would only force Graham or Wallace into a confrontation. "Crawford killed my mother. I'll never go to him. I will leave by week's end."

"Ye dinna hear me."

"I did, and I don't care if you ruin me. I'll leave this place. I'll leave Scotland forever if I must." Rhona spoke the words, even though it bruised her spirit to say them. She rose to her feet, her determination now fierce. "I love my brothers, and I love this land. I've stayed for them, but I will leave this soil for all my days if I must. I will not marry a man who you, yourself, told me was responsible for my mother's death."

He reached for her once more, though this time she skirted away and managed to ring the bell pull before he caught her. "You will never see me again, I swear to you."

"I dinna care, but ye will marry Crawford. I've promised ye to him, and if I have to force yer cooperation, I will."

"You're my father, and I've always honored you, but did you truly believe I'd do this?" Her one last desperate hope for him to understand the cruel enormity of what he was doing had failed.

"I never wanted ye. A daughter is

of no use to me."

Rhona choked back the tears threatening to fall and jumped at the sound of a gentle knock at the parlor door. "Come in."

"Miss Davidson, I . . ." Graham watched her, and she wondered if her damp eyes or red face had caught his attention first.

Her father glanced at the butler then back at her. "This land, and everything on it, including ye, belongs to me."

"And when the week is over, you will never again see my shadow cast upon your home." Rhona remained behind her chair, grasping at any barrier to keep between her and her father. She found the strength to walk toward the door.

"Ye'll have the week to pack, and then ye'll go to Crawford." Calum closed the distance between them and leaned over the chair. Rhona held up a hand to prevent Graham from interfering, and then looked directly into her father's eyes while he spoke. "The world is dangerous for a woman alone. Ye dinna want to live in fear."

"Why do you insist on this marriage? I'm of no consequence to you, and I am no burden. I live in this house, but we both know that you have never supported me."

"Yer mother was a fool to leave ye with such a fortune."

"A fortune you could not touch. Is that what angers you?"

"There's more at stake than money. Will ye defy me and risk yer brother's life?"

"What do you mean?"

"Ye love yer brother."

Rhona endeavored to remain

calm. "You would threaten Wallace? I matter nothing to you, but he's your son!"

"I will do what I must."

The weight of her father's veiled message became painfully clear. Do his bidding and marry Crawford, or live in fear every day. Rhona did not fear for herself, but she would not risk her brother.

"Rhona?"

She ignored the light rap on the door, not wishing for Wallace to see the results of her father's anger.

"Would you like me to send him away, my lady?"

Rhona looked across the room at Emsley, her maid of three years. Her brother knocked again. "No, please let him in."

"I'll return later."

"That won't be necessary, Emsley.

I prefer quiet tonight, but thank you."

Emsley gathered up the dress Rhona had worn that day and answered the door. She glanced back at Rhona before stepping aside, allowing Wallace to enter. Rhona waited until the door closed behind the maid before speaking.

"I thought Father would have you occupied all evening."

Wallace stepped toward the fire and lowered himself into the chair opposite Rhona. She kept her face turned. Though it didn't appear it would bruise, her cheek still bore the redness from her father's strong hand.

"He only just released me, but then I spoke with Graham." Wallace leaned forward and using a gentle touch, turned her face. "You should

~ 14 ~

have told me."

"It would only have angered Father to have you caught in the middle."

Wallace's face tightened. "Has he ever done that before?"

"No, but it was bound to happen. Father and I have been at odds for years."

"I know you stayed for me, Rhona."

She smiled at her brother. Wallace had started at Eton when he was thirteen but returned home during all of his breaks. Rhona never wanted her brother to find himself alone for too long with Calum Davidson, but now that he was eighteen, Rhona knew she could no longer protect him.

"I've never regretted that decision."

Wallace stared into the low-burning flames. "I want to go to university, but I can't imagine returning here after. Alistair will inherit, and I have a chance to make a life for myself."

"You've decided on a course?"

"I want to study the law."

Rhona slowly shook her head. "If you told Father that, I can't imagine he's pleased."

Wallace grinned. "Irate is what he is. He forbade it, of course, and promised to cut me off, but I don't care."

Rhona scooted forward in her chair. "You'll make a fine solicitor one day. Don't worry about Father. Mother's money is not for me alone."

"I cannot take anything from you."

"You won't. I'm giving it to you. Mother left you enough to pay for Oxford."

Wallace sat forward. "You never said anything."

"I couldn't, not as long as you were beholden to Father. You can make your own decisions now, without interference."

Wallace leaned back, his lips forming a wide grin. "Father won't like this."

Rhona laughed, then covered her mouth. "No, he won't."

Wallace sobered, his eyes studying her cheek. "Promise me you won't stay here any longer."

Her brother's fierce words brought her reality to the surface. She would be gone, but she would not marry Crawford. The only way to ensure that her father could not force her was to act tonight. Her plan would require her brother's cooperation.

"Wallace, listen to me. I need to ask something of you. It won't be easy, and I can't explain why."

"You're worrying me."

Rhona reached out and covered his hands with her own. A few moments ago mirth had filled her mind, but now desperation clouded her heart. "Will you trust me?"

Two

Blackwood Crossing, Keswick, England

"It is with great joy to share the most wonderful news with our closest friends." Tristan smiled at his wife, and Charles experienced a small twinge of envy at the happiness Tristan had found with Alaina. "Alaina and I will welcome our second child in the spring."

Charles raised his glass. "That is something we can all celebrate." He drank, then stood and walked around the table to congratulate his friend with a strong embrace and

Alaina with a light kiss. "No wonder you look even more ravishing than usual."

Alaina beamed her beautiful smile up at him, and for a fleeting moment, Charles's memories faded back to another time and another smile. "Tristan's retirement has been a blessing for us." Alaina leaned toward him with a conspiratorial smile. "Though I do believe he misses it at times."

Charles glanced at his friend who was accepting hearty congratulations from Devon. Of the three, Devon had managed to go through life unscathed by heartbreak. He'd also avoided giving his heart to one woman. Charles envied that freedom almost as much as he envied Tristan and Alaina. "He loves you more than the work,

Alaina. He always did."

"I know that, but still, I wonder if a quiet existence at Claiborne Manor is what he had in mind for the rest of his life." Alaina turned her face up toward him. "Do you ever miss the work, Charles? I know Tristan has done his best to remain in retirement, but I thought you might return to it on a more permanent basis."

Charles studied Alaina's delicate features and wondered why she worried. He instead asked a question of his own. "Has Tristan mentioned returning to the agency?"

"No, he is devoted, but have I been fair in expecting him to sit quietly at home with me and our son? He has estates to manage, but that must bore him terribly."

Charles had his own reasons for his absence from the agency and for refusing to accept the request Patrick, their supervisor, sent almost two years ago. Unlike Tristan, he believed he had lost his chance at love and family and blamed the work. However, he recently considered returning to the agency with Devon.

"Tristan's only duty now is to you and your family. I cannot believe he would be happier anywhere else."

His words seemed to calm her worries, for she smiled brightly, thanked him, and returned to Tristan's side.

Charles drew the attention of those in the room back to him for another toast. "To Tristan and Alaina and their growing family." He suggested they retire to the study for drinks. Alaina excused herself to check on her son, Christian.

Once settled, with drinks all around, Charles grinned at his friend. "Tristan, you do make a man wish he'd chosen a different life. You're a lucky man."

Tristan raised his glass and then nodded to Devon. "I do miss the adventures, but we can live vicariously through Devon and his brothers. Did not the three of you return from an assignment before coming here?"

Devon looked uncomfortable when he nodded. "We've only returned from Scotland. I almost missed your invite, Charles. Derek and Zachary apologize, but they were sent immediately on another assignment. It is different with you both gone."

"You're still alive, so you must be doing something right." Charles wore a smile, but he studied his friend. "Devon, I feel your anxiety from here. Did something go wrong up north?"

Charles caught the glance Devon shared with Tristan, piquing his curiosity even more.

"Nothing wrong exactly, but news you may find difficult."

"What news?"

"We were up north to gather information on a Braden Crawford, a laird of some wealth and consequence, both in Scotland and England."

Tristan leaned forward in the chair. "I know of Crawford. One of my estates borders some of that British land you mention. What has he done to warrant the attention of the agency?"

"Nothing that we can tie directly to him, but he is suspected of conversing with someone on our watch list."

Charles listened, but since he didn't know Crawford, and agency business no longer concerned him, he failed to see how the news would be difficult. "What has this to do with me, Devon?"

"I learned of a wedding to take place between Crawford and a Miss Rhona Davidson."

Charles's breath nearly stopped. He tightened his grip around the near-empty glass of whisky until he felt it tremble in his hand. "You're certain?" Charles had searched for Rhona after his initial retirement. After having been turned away by both her father and a cousin in Skye, he had written to her. His only response had been a request to stay away.

"When is the wedding to take

place?"

Tristan stood now. "Wait."

"No, I won't wait. Devon, when?"

Charles watched him look everywhere in the room except at him. "When?"

"Less than a fortnight."

"You have to wait, Charles. There's more."

Charles crossed his arms. "Well?"

"Patrick's asked me to return and escort Rhona to Crawford."

Tristan crossed the room and sat across from Devon. "Why would he want an agent escort for Davidson's daughter?"

"The assignment is to gather information on Davidson and his eldest son, Alistair. They believe there is a reason why Davidson arranged the marriage, but they haven't been able to uncover the motive."

Charles stared out the window overlooking the bleak winter landscape. "I'm coming with you."

Devon didn't turn in his chair when he replied. "Patrick has asked for both of you."

Charles nodded. "Then it's done, though Tristan should remain here."

Devon nodded. "Agreed."

Tristan glanced at Devon, then at Charles. "I'm going."

Charles recalled his earlier conversation with Alaina. "Your wife won't understand, Tristan. Remain blissfully in retirement. I don't have that luxury—not any longer."

"Alaina will understand. I'll speak with her tonight, but I am coming with you."

"Tristan—"

"I saw what losing Rhona two years ago did to you, Charles. I'm coming."

Charles nodded, unwilling to argue. Anything he might say to contradict his friend would be a lie. "What exactly is being asked of us?"

"Ah, yes, well that is still somewhat unclear. Patrick is sending a dispatch with the final orders." Devon sat back in the leather armchair. "The request was for at least three agents. Officially they are concerned about the lady's safety. Davidson has received legitimate threats on his family in this past, but that is merely a cover for this assignment."

Charles finally sat in the other leather chair facing the desk. "Many of the landowners are still in poor favor after the forced displacements. Traditional clan systems may no longer exist, but as we well remember, that doesn't stop both the old and new gentry from trying to glean the best of both the old world and the new."

"It is unfortunate that for some at least, barbarism is not dead in Scotland. Most of the lairds are historic remnants of their ancient counterparts, tolerated by current dukes and earls so long as they remember that their world has changed. So much for progress and civilization, though I do find it difficult to believe that is why his family has been threatened." Tristan turned at the sound of a knock at his study door. "Enter."

The butler walked grandly into the room. "Your Grace, a dispatch has arrived. The messenger said it was most urgent." He held out a tray to Tristan, upon which a thin envelope sat.

"Thank you, Henry." Tristan nodded and smiled when he departed.

Once the door was closed, Devon turned to Tristan. "Does the man ever smile?"

Tristan broke the agency seal on the envelope. "A word of advice, don't ever ask a butler if he smiles." Tristan's own smile vanished as he read the short missive. "We'll be leaving tonight. Laird Davidson's youngest son is missing."

Three

Davidson Castle, Northwest Highlands, Scotland

"In all my years, I have never had the misfortune to be this far north in the winter." Devon shifted slightly in the stiff saddle and pulled his wool cap down lower.

Tristan rode between Devon and Charles on horses that had been waiting for them at the train station in Inverness. A carriage would have been more comfortable, but the horses afforded them convenience.

"I'll suffer through all manner of cold, ice, and wind these Highlands bring, so long as I am home with

Alaina and Christian before Christmas." It was decided before they left England that Tristan would be the point agent for the mission considering Charles's history with the Davidson family. It was no secret that despite gaining allies in the British government, Davidson detested the English. They hoped that Tristan's title would afford them more cooperation.

"It would seem, Devon, that your suffering will soon be at an end." Charles reined in his horse and twisted the leather straps in his hands to loosen them up from the cold. The animal appeared to be as anxious for a warm stable as the men were for a hot meal and a bed. "It's unfortunate that rest and pleasure are not on the menu." Charles lowered his scarf until it rested only around his neck. His lungs filled with icy air, and his green eyes narrowed against the cold to take in the view.

The home of Laird Davidson was a seventeenth-century castle, originally built by the family of the laird's great-grandmother, who had been a Kendrick. The present laird's grandfather managed to escape with his mother to her family's home in the North, after his father was accused of Jacobitism and shipped to the colonies. Calum Davidson would have inherited land and clan had history been kinder to his family. As far as Charles had learned, the Davidsons managed to live a semi-peaceful existence, though Charles was under the impression that not everyone wanted it to remain peaceful.

They approached the castle steps,

where a butler and footman waited to the right of the entrance. To the left stood Calum Davidson, a man Charles remembered well. The laird was a shrewd man, a trait which had allowed him to avoid conspiracy charges. Though the mission had proven to be unnecessary and Davidson cleared of any treason against the crown, the memory of those two weeks had remained with Charles as though they had happened only days ago.

The men dismounted and handed their mounts' care over to two stablemen. Laird Davidson hesitated before walking at a stiff and deliberate pace down the wide stone steps. He didn't stand on ceremony any more now than he had nearly three years prior when Charles had first met him. He didn't like Rhona's father now any more than he did back then, either. "We expected ye this morning. Wiser tae have come by carriage."

Tristan, a greater diplomat than his two fellow agents, smoothly replied. "Our primary goal was to arrive today, and we feared the wheels of a carriage would have fared worse than the horses."

The laird's eyes narrowed before the lines around his eyes smoothed out, and he motioned them to follow him inside. Once the heavy wood doors closed behind them, the butler passed their outer garments along to a footman. "Graham will see tae your needs while ye are here." Davidson indicated the butler who had stood outside when they arrived.

"We appreciate your hospitality while we are in your country." Tristan removed his gloves and handed them to the butler. "We understand the urgency of your situation and your concern for your son. If you have time now, we'd like to discuss our plans."

"Ay, ye're me guests, but I dinna have much choice." Laird Davidson's eyes met each of theirs, but Charles noticed that Davidson's anger was focused solely on him. Davidson would not have forgotten Charles's pursuit of his daughter and obviously didn't care that he had lied two years ago when Charles came north to find her.

"I have matters tae attend tae briefly. Graham will show ye into my study." Without ceremony, Davidson left their company and disappeared down a hallway.

Graham cleared his throat, drawing their attention. "If you'll follow me," he said, surprising them with a British accent, and began to walk, expecting them to follow.

Charles caught Devon and Tristan's shared amusement, but his focus centered on Graham's back. Charles didn't recall the butler from his previous visit. Graham showed them into a spacious room, bereft of ostentatious furnishings. The heavy wood desk dominated the room, flanked on either side by shelves filled with not only books, but stacks of rolled parchments and old bottles.

Graham remained near the door and informed them that a light refreshment would be sent in. "Dinner is served half past six o'clock."

Charles stopped the butler before he left the room. "You're English, are you not?"

Graham's body stiffened.

"Proudly, my lord."

"Have you been with the family long?"

Graham straightened until his body grew another inch over his already tall frame. "More than twenty years, my lord."

"A loyal man." Charles nodded once to the butler. "Forgive me for keeping you."

Graham bowed and left them alone. The door remained opened.

Tristan looked at Charles. "What was that about?"

"I feel as though I've seen that man before." Charles walked across the room to the window, his eyes scanning what was visible of Davidson's vast estate. Darkness slowly covered the snow-dotted landscape.

Tristan glanced into the hallway

and lowered his voice. "I expected him to be more concerned about his missing son."

Charles shrugged. He knew firsthand that not all fathers cared about their children's well-being. "Alistair is the heir, not Wallace." Charles turned back to his friends. "I'd as soon complete our business with Davidson and leave at first light."

Devon contemplated whether or not to pour himself a drink from the sideboard since one was not offered by the butler. "I thought you rather enjoyed Scotland. She certainly treated you well enough."

Tristan grinned at Devon. "Let us spare the chap a reminder of his regrets and a broken heart."

Charles turned back to the window. "I do not regret, nor should we speak of it here. There's little chance we will—"

"Miss Davidson." Tristan's voice may have interrupted Charles, but it was his words which caused Charles's hesitant move to face the room.

Rhona Davidson stood just beyond the threshold. Her blue eyes deepened to gray during times of anger or sorrow. At the moment, anger evidently consumed her. The long red hair her maid had plaited that morning now fell in soft curls down her back, loosened by the wind during her walk. She brushed aside a loose lock as she stepped forward. "My father told me you had arrived."

Charles remained rooted by the window, staring at the woman he'd betrayed and then lost. Tristan had been right. She was his only regret. Her eyes narrowed, staring at him briefly before moving on.

Devon finally stepped forward. "Your youngest brother is missing. You do not believe that is reason enough to seek help?"

"I do not believe that Englishmen can find him any faster than Scots. Though we all know you did not come here only to find my brother."

Charles found his voice. "For a woman who speaks without the barest hint of her country, your opinion of Englishmen is laughable." Charles could barely believe he spoke the words, and if his friends' glances were any indication, neither could they. He remembered exactly why she sounded more British than Scottish. He remembered everything she ever told him.

Rhona's eyes narrowed. "I've neglected my manners, but I will not feign pleasantries for I do not wish you here, though I have little say in this matter." She quickly looked toward the door before turning her eyes back on the men. "I know what happened to my brother."

Tristan stepped toward Rhona, careful with his words. "Why then have we been summoned? It is no small thing, this favor your father asked to bring us here."

"Stop the farce. My father hates the English and would not welcome you willingly. You are here to deliver me to a church, are you not? Is this before or after you find my brother?"

Charles stepped away from the window, his green eyes studying the woman who had changed little in appearance in two years. "Forgive me my earlier rudeness, but if you know the truth, tell us now."

Rhona shook her head.

Charles stepped forward until he stood between Tristan and Devon. "Pray tell, what is the truth?"

Moisture threatened to coat her gray eyes. "My brother is dead."

"Rhona!" Davidson stepped into the room. "Ye shouldn't be here."

"They should know the truth, as I know it, and as you refuse to believe it." Rhona's words belied a calm she did not feel.

"Forgive me daughter. She's heavy with grief over her brother's disappearance." Calum stepped between Rhona and the men.

Charles watched Rhona stiffen, her palms pressed flat against her sides.

Tristan chose that moment to interject. "Davidson, if you'll allow me to be blunt, we all know why we are here. If you truly believe your daughter has no knowledge of your son's whereabouts, then we will proceed without prejudice, escort her south, and be done with it. However, if there is a chance she is correct in her assumption, it might be prudent for us to confirm her belief."

"How dare ye! You are here tae—"

"We know why we are here." Charles drew their attention. "You have important friends in our government—that is the only reason why you have been granted our services to escort your daughter," Charles said, and then spoke as an aside to Davidson, "though you may have wished it hadn't been me." He turned back to the group. "I lack my friend's diplomacy, but what I have to say is best not spoken in mixed company."

"How dare you."

"Rhona, enough. Calum gripped his daughter's arm. "Nae more will I allow ye tae disgrace me with yer behavior. Go now."

Rhona remained where she stood after her father released his grasp. Her eyes followed a path from one man to the next. Charles hated what he had done to her. He longed to hear her strong laugh and watch her eyes brighten. Instead, he watched her turn and leave.

Davidson faced the men but did not speak until the door closed. "I was tae understand there is noble blood in your veins, Yer Grace, yet ye behave this way."

"In our line of work, truth comes before nobility." Tristan stepped aside so that Calum could walk to his desk. "It is important for Rhona to trust us, but we were informed that your children do not know of the threats to their lives, and we were instructed to distance them from that. Your daughter is on her way to a wedding, and she does not need to concern herself with these matters."

Calum looked at them with disbelief. "Ye mean tae say that was intentional?"

Devon nodded. "They are to know as little about our involvement as possible. However, from your daughter's reception, you have already told her more than is necessary."

Calum sat down in his chair and motioned for them to occupy the other chairs in the room. "I spoke only of English here tae help find her brother and see her safely to her new home. I didn't want ye tae come."

"With respect, you gave our government little choice in the matter when you sent your son to spy in England." Tristan leaned forward. "Yes, we know about Alistair's activities. Your daughter believes her younger brother is dead and that is a worry to us. If he has gone to Alistair, and you did not tell us, you will suffer for it."

Charles vacated the chair to stand directly in front of Calum's desk. "Our original assignment was to escort Rhona, but your son's activities have altered our plans. Our superiors are concerned only with locating Alistair and by any means necessary. We will also ensure that your youngest is returned home, so long as he's not involved. We have no reason to suspect him of any wrongdoing."

"Wallace is a disgrace tae me." Calum pushed away from his desk and stood to face Charles, though the laird stood a few inches shorter. "He spends all his time with Rhona or his blasted horses."

Tristan and Devon rose, flanking Charles. Tristan said, "It is imperative that we locate Alistair and return him to England. Your . . . acquaintance with our government is on an unsteady precipice. They are affording you the opportunity to correct this, shall we call it, misunderstanding."

Calum puffed himself up in an attempt to stand as tall as the other men. He walked grandly around the desk until he stood between them and the door. "I'll be comin' wi' ye."

Charles shook his head. "Out of the question."

"I was nae asking."

Devon held up a hand to divert the laird's attention. "What my friend means to say is it would be prudent for you to remain here in the event either of your sons returns."

Calum looked carefully at each of them. "Then ye have a plan?"

Tristan nodded. "We do. We will continue with our original assignment."

"Ye mean tae escort me daughter to Crawford."

Charles's jaw clenched. He didn't trust himself to speak.

Devon said, "Yes, and we will leave at first light. Will you ensure your daughter is ready?"

Calum appeared to consider the matter. "She'll be ready. Now if ye'll excuse me. Graham will be in tae show ye tae yer rooms and then tae supper." Without ceremony, Calum walked from the room.

Now that they were alone, Tristan said, "We'll need to alter our plans."

Charles shook his head. "No."

Devon glanced at the door. "Charles, you risk too much if you alone escort Rhona. We've been ordered to separate if we confirmed that Wallace was indeed missing. He may not be suspect, but we cannot risk that he's gone to join Alistair."

"Bloody hell, I know that." Charles swiped his hand through air, his frustration mounting. "She's to be married, and I'll be damned if I . . . what do we know about this laird Rhona is to wed?"

"I told you, I found him to be honest, despite the stories." Devon looked at his friend. "I spent weeks looking into him, and nothing suspicious ever came to light."

Tristan drew Charles's attention. "You have to consider that she wants this marriage."

Charles had considered it and dismissed it. "I'll let it go." He addressed both men. "If she tells me herself that she wants Crawford."

Charles listened to the howls of wind beyond the glass window panes and contemplated Rhona's glances. When she had first set her eyes on him in the study, her gray eyes expressed no emotion beyond the anger directed at them all. Davidson had joined them for supper, but Rhona had remained absent throughout the meal.

Now he lay on a bed in one of many rooms gracing the interior of Davidson Castle. Unable to find solace in sleep, Charles, still clothed, removed himself from the bed and looked around the dark interior of the room. Charles and the others had discussed everything they knew about Davidson and his family, including his wealth, as a possible motive for whatever happened to his son, Wallace.

None of them believed that Wallace Davidson had been kidnapped. That he found himself in dire circumstances because of his older brother's illicit actions remained to be seen. Using Rhona as a cover did not sit well with Charles, but to refuse the plan would be to give her father a reason to question their true motives.

"Bloody hell!" Charles's whispered frustration dissipated in the quiet of the room. Resolved that he would find no peace on this night, he slid his feet into boots, lit the lantern Graham left for him earlier in the evening, and halted. The faint knock at his door led him to believe that either Tristan or Devon had been of the same mind to go downstairs. He turned the lantern up and walked quickly to the door. The soft hand reached out and connected with the side of his face.

"Bastard!" Rhona's whisper wasn't much of a whisper, and she looked down both halls before pushing past Charles into his room.

"I wondered how long that would take." Charles leaned into the hall to ensure himself that no one had heard her. He gently closed the door, the resounding click making them both fully aware that neither of them should be there.

"I assume you are not here for the reasons we enjoyed on my last visit."

Rhona closed the distance between them, her palm once again meeting his cheek.

Charles immediately regretted his nastiness. "I deserved that."

"That and more." Rhona turned abruptly and walked past the edge of the light's reach. "I want to know why."

"Not that I don't enjoy your lovely company, but I do like my head where it is. If your father or anyone else caught us—you want to know why what?" Charles walked toward her. The past two years and his deception created a barrier that stopped him from reaching out for her.

She turned to face him. "Why come back? I'd almost let myself believe I felt nothing for you."

"I didn't choose . . ." Charles

reached for her, ignored her efforts to tug her arm loose from his grasp, and pulled her out of the shadows. "I came back now for the same reason I left—orders."

"Everything was an order. Get close to me and make me . . . betray my family. Those were your orders?" She pulled at her arm and his fingers reluctantly loosened their grip.

Charles shook his head. "Nothing between us was an order, and I won't apologize for what I told you back then." Charles expected to see tears or regret in Rhona's eyes, but the grayish-blue orbs revealed nothing.

"I shouldn't be here. My maid doesn't sleep soundly and at times wanders the halls." She hesitated. "We were close enough to . . . I thought you would come back."

Incredulous, Charles stepped toward her. "I wrote letters, and I returned once I resigned. Your father said you visited a cousin, but I went north to Skye, and they'd not seen you."

"You came back?"

Charles slowly nodded and traced her smooth cheek with his finger. "Given my line of work, I should have been able to find you, but I contacted your other living relatives. None claimed you'd been there."

"I wasn't. I spent six months with a distant cousin on my mother's side. I was in Caithness, and I never saw your letters." Rhona pulled the edges of her shawl close to her body and walked toward the door.

Charles deemed her last letter now irrelevant, certain it was not she who told him to stay away. "Why did you never to return to England?"

With one hand on the door handle,

Rhona slowly turned around. "How do you know I didn't?" Her hand slipped from the handle. "You watched for me?"

Charles remained silent.

Rhona closed her eyes and breathed deeply. "There was nothing for me there. When you saved me that day on the road, did you know who I was before you came north?"

"No, it wasn't until I saw you again here. When I learned you were Davidson's daughter, I tried to forget you, set you from my thoughts, but nothing I did worked. It was never my intention to cause you pain."

"And yet, you did, but I made my choices, too." Rhona steadied her eyes on his. "My father hates your people with such passion. He would not have told either of us the truth. If I had known you came back . . ." Rhona's hand reached once more for the door.

"He hates the British, but you had an English tutor."

"That was my mother's doing." She pressed down on the handle, but Charles stilled her movements.

"Did you ask for the marriage?"

Rhona attempted to push Charles away. When she failed, she turned angry eyes on him. "It does not matter because the deed is done."

"When was it decided? Not when we were—"

She shifted and leaned back to look into his eyes. "No. There's never been anyone else."

"Then when?"

"A few days ago. It's not uncommon."

Charles could have left it alone, asked her if she wanted to marry Crawford, but he let seconds pass.

Rhona leaned toward him briefly, and Charles wondered if she might stay. He prayed she would. She smelled of heather and lavender, and the fragrant scents sparked memories of a night years ago when he held her in his arms as they lay in a blanket of heather near the woods.

"I'm sorry." Her whispered words barely reached his ears before she quietly exited the room.

Charles found his way through the darkened hallway and down the stairs, his lantern turned low so as not to awaken anyone beyond the doors he passed. He didn't believe Davidson would appreciate him using the study without permission. He remembered passing a library when Graham showed him through the house and walked down the long corridor to that room. A dim light shone beneath the closed door. Charles pressed the door open.

"We wondered how long it would take her to leave your room." Devon motioned Charles over to where he and Tristan stood around a long table.

"How did you . . . never mind." Charles set his lamp down next to theirs and slowly extinguished the wick. "You've been busy." He reached across the table to move some of the documents in front of him, each one of the papers containing information carefully written in the shorthand used by the agency. "I see you met with the dispatch?"

Devon nodded. "Under the pretense that I needed a walk. Graham wasn't inclined to believe me since it began to rain when I left."

Tristan handed Charles the papers he had finished reading. "Patrick has been busy since we left. One of our agents on the border located Wallace, and then lost him again. Patrick also learned of Miss Davidson's betrothal and has instructed us to continue with our previous assignment and then meet him in Langholm with Rhona."

Charles swore because he knew what Tristan wasn't saying. "You still want to use Rhona to carry out the new mission. And while we're on the subject, how did Patrick learn of her betrothal? Rhona told me she learned of it only a few days ago."

Devon held up his hands. "He didn't hear it from us. News travels too fast these days. You know that."

"There." Tristan leaned over and pulled a sheet of paper from beneath the stack he had handed Charles. "He only learned of her betrothal the day he dispatched the messenger. Apparently, there are certain parties interested in seeing that this marriage takes place."

Charles examined the document carefully but found no information about Crawford. "What value does our government place on this laird, and why did Davidson choose him specifically?"

Devon and Tristan looked up from the papers and exchanged a rather telling glance. Charles knew that look as he had shared it with them many times. "I know we still have orders and that Alistair Davidson is the priority." Charles walked across the room to a sideboard and helped himself to a glass of whisky.

"Devon, is there anything else you

can tell me about Crawford?" When Devon failed to answer, Charles continued. "I ask because, regardless of our mission, if Rhona is set on following through with this marriage, I have to be assured of her safety."

"I do believe the reputation is worse than the man." Devon lowered himself into one of the chairs. "I take it you didn't ask her."

Charles shook his head and settled into the chair opposite Devon. "Do we believe Alistair has acted alone?"

Charles was finished discussing Rhona, for now, and was grateful when Tristan helped turn the subject. "That is precisely what we were discussing prior to your arrival. Devon believes he found a connection between Alistair and an earl in the North, in fact, not far from Blackwood Crossing."

"Oh?" Charles leaned forward. "Who?"

"Lord Kitchener."

Charles's father had dragged him to hunts with the earl, even though as a young boy Charles had no interest in hunting or spending time with lords older than his father. Charles had learned to admire the earl. Lord Kitchener lived his life apart from society, and any lord who managed that feat was admirable in his eyes. "I happen to know that Kitchener is well past eighty years. His only claim to espionage is an attempt to sneak up his nurse's skirts."

"Does he have a son, nephew, brother?"

"His land borders mine, and in all my years, I never saw any evidence of family. No wife, no children—no one. Only his nurse and the occasional visit from his doctor. I don't think he's your man, Tristan."

"We have more than half a dozen letters to Alistair from someone who signs his name as Lord Kitchener." Tristan began to gather up some of the loose papers. "If not him, then someone wants us to believe it's the earl."

"Well then, let us uncover the culprit. We've taken on missions with less than mediocre reports." Charles downed the remaining Scotch in his glass, allowing the warm liquid to settle before speaking. "First, we have a bride to deliver." He set the glass down and helped gather up the remaining documents and toss them into the hearth, where a fire still burned enough to offer warmth and incinerate the papers.

More than two years had passed since Charles had crossed the border into Scotland. The journey would have been a few days, but the memories the land held proved too painful and uncomfortable. After Tristan and Alaina settled into nuptial bliss at Claiborne Manor, Charles accepted a solo assignment that took him into the Northern Highlands. His assignment had been simple—learn all he could about one Calum Davidson, a laird with too much power and wealth, especially since no one admitted to knowing how he came by the money.

Charles learned that Davidson's ancestral money ran out years before, but everything he discovered proved Davidson's business dealings to be legitimate. The case eventually returned him to England and an associate of Davidson's who was unable to claim the same innocence. Charles still believed Davidson was guilty, but he was reassigned after the government had a man on which to lay the verdict reserved for traitors to the crown.

His assignment had been straightforward, but the reality was far more complicated. Davidson's daughter, Rhona, had captured his heart. Her long, curling hair the color of autumn leaves and blue-gray eyes that turned, depending upon her mood, had remained in his thoughts since the day he left her behind. Her sharp mind and desire for adventure never failed to bring a smile to his lips. Their conversations often lasted late into the night, a less than difficult undertaking with her father in residence elsewhere. She embodied everything in a woman he desired, and Davidson never knew what had transpired between them. In fact, Davidson had left for Edinburgh two days after Charles's arrival, unknowingly leaving time for Charles and Rhona.

Rhona assured him she understood his duty to country and his reluctance to accept the gift of her heart and body, but neither of them was able to resist the magnetic pull that brought them together. When his assignment brought him back to England, after months searching the continent for the traitor blamed for Davidson's actions, he sought out Patrick, his supervisory agent, and resigned his commission with the agency. His only thought was to begin a new life with Rhona. Nearly a year had passed, and all the while Charles waited for a response to his letters, but Rhona never wrote. When he was free of his duties, he returned to her home, only to find her gone. Now he knew why, but it did not lessen his guilt or anger at losing her.

Four

Charles had managed nearly two hours of uncomfortable rest before a footman knocked on the door. Used to managing on his own in the field, Charles dispensed with the use of a valet at home and had no desire to utilize a footman's services. He noticed a fire burning low in the hearth and the drapes pulled open, but he couldn't recall if he had heard the maid come into the room. *Blast the Scottish and their whisky.* Never one to over imbibe, Charles thought back to the hours in the library with Tristan and Devon but could not recall consuming more than the one glass. He blamed his inability to sleep on the shoulders of a beautiful Scottish woman.

"My apologies, sir, would you like me to return later?"

Charles stared at the footman over heavy blankets.

"One of your companions asked me to wake you, but—"

"No, it's quite all right." Charles pushed the blankets off his body and swung his legs off the bed where they met with a cold rug. Charles watched the footman gather the clothes he had pulled from his valise the evening before and run a brush over the sleeves of the coat. "I won't require your assistance for dressing, but perhaps you wouldn't mind seeing that fresh water is brought up for a bath."

The footman walked across the room to a closed door. Pushing it open, he looked back to Charles. "A private bathing chamber, sir, with a bath prepared."

"Thank you. Your name?"

"Garth, sir."

"Thank you, Garth. I can manage well enough now."

The younger man bowed his head, backed out of the room, and closed the door quietly behind him. Once again alone, Charles walked naked across the room to the bathing chamber and made use of the facilities and bath. A quick glance out the window told him that the snow may have stopped falling, but the sun would not win its battle with the clouds.

The clock on the mantel told him that he'd wasted enough time. Three quick raps at the door confirmed it. "I'm decent."

The door swung open and Devon

sauntered in.

"Not that my state of dress would have halted your entry."

"Not at all." Devon smiled and walked directly to one of the windows. "It's a ghastly morning for travel, but Tristan is adamant about leaving within the hour. By the by, you look awful."

Charles slipped into his jacket and ignored Devon's remark. "You appear to have managed a few hours of sleep."

"Slept like a newly born babe at his mother's breast." Devon grinned. "Never mind your appearance. If we're to breakfast before we leave, we'd better find our way downstairs."

Charles packed his few remaining items into his valise and buckled it closed. When on assignment, the agents had learned to make do with minimal necessities, which often included only one change of clothing carefully packed. On longer assignments, they traveled by coach in order to accommodate a trunk or two. Charles stepped into the hall and closed the bedroom door behind him. "Have you seen Rhona this morning?"

Devon looked at Charles, brows raised over blue eyes. "I haven't had the pleasure, but I did see the servants gathering an impressive collection of trunks in the foyer."

Charles halted at the top of the stairs. "Were our travel arrangements not explained to her?"

Devon laughed. "Apparently not, but I for one will gladly leave the explanations to Tristan. Breakfast first, Rhona's tantrum after."

Tantrum? Hardly. Charles had the

misfortune to know that Rhona Davidson did not throw tantrums—*that would certainly be simpler.*

"You're not fooling me, Rhona." Emsley considered the lack of space in each trunk.

Rhona and Emsley had long ago dispensed with formalities when they were alone. "Whatever do you mean?"

"He's the same one, is he not?"

Rhona tossed a cloak onto the bed. "How could you know that?"

"It's not him, it's you." Emsley shook her head and closed the top of a trunk and moved onto the next. "The way your eyes and expression change when you speak of him."

"I've been such a fool." Rhona lowered herself onto a closed trunk.

"Not a fool, just someone who

loved a man."

Rhona faced her maid and friend. "Have you ever loved a man?"

Emsley slowly nodded. "It was a long time ago."

Rhona smiled. "You're a year younger than I am. How long ago could it have been?"

Emsley didn't return the smile. "I was eighteen. I can't know if it was real, but I hoped it was real."

"You never speak of the years before you came here."

"England was another life. I've loved my time here in Scotland." Emsley filled another trunk and waved at Rhona. "You're sitting on the last trunk."

Rhona stood and reached for the last pile of dresses. "You know I want you to go with me, Emsley, but you don't have to. I can speak with

Father."

"I've already packed my things in with yours."

"I can't promise I know what comes next."

Emsley stopped her task and looked directly at Rhona. "What comes next? Your father has planned everything that comes next, and your new husband will plan the rest."

Rhona sensed Emsley studying her.

"What are you not saying?"

"Nothing." The lie fell easily from Rhona's lips.

"You said yourself that Laird Crawford was a good man."

Second lie, Rhona thought. "Yes, I did. Never mind any of that. I suppose it is leaving home I do not wish to contemplate."

A light knock drew Emsley to the

door. After a few seconds of speaking to whoever stood on the other side, she closed the door and looked grimly at Rhona. "It's time."

Rhona had spent nearly twenty minutes longer than usual at the morning meal and endured the curious glances sent her way by Graham, as she was more often the first one to leave. Concerned that her father would return looking for her, Rhona left the dining room. She had to speak with Charles.

Her father had pulled her aside that morning to discuss travel plans and what was expected of her. She believed there would still be time to find a way to dissolve the betrothal to Crawford, but her father gave her no explanation why expediency was necessary. Her father dislodged her last hope when he explained she would be leaving that morning and would be wed within the week. She only prayed Wallace was safe because she did not have as much time as she originally thought.

Rhona waited with inward impatience in the foyer for her remaining trunks to be loaded. The cool air from the open doors threatened to chill her skin, but the hood on her heavy woolen cloak fell to the back where she preferred to keep it even when outside. Emsley stood beside her, an encouraging smile on her face.

Rhona's impatience grew when she noticed the servants return some of her trunks to the foyer. She watched her father walk into the house through the front door with one of the men who arrived with

Charles, Tristan Sheffield.

Charles's friend bowed slightly. "I am sorry, Miss Davidson, but we will be unable to accommodate all of your trunks. We face delays with the icy roads, and we cannot risk more with additional wagons and stock." Tristan informed them both that he and his companions would be ready momentarily and left them alone.

Rhona whispered aside to Emsley who stepped away with an excuse that she must speak with Graham. When Rhona was certain they were as alone as they could be, she stepped closer to her father. "Haven't you made enough demands?"

"It canna be another way." Calum reached out as though to grasp onto her arms, but Rhona stepped back. "Ye know what's at stake."

"You won't let me forget. I wonder though, Father. If Wallace is gone, how do you suppose to leverage him?"

Calum reached out and pulled her closer. "I'll find yer brother, make no mistake. He'll be safe so long as ye marry. After the wedding, I don't care what either of you do." Calum directed the servants to return the trunks to Rhona's bedroom. "Ye'll nae dishonor yer family or risk yer brother's life, will ye?"

Rhona's eyes lifted, but she suffered nothing but disgust. "No, Father, I won't risk his life." She heard heavy footsteps coming down the hall behind her, but she did not have to turn to see who walked toward her. Emsley came up beside her and drew her attention with a gentle touch.

"It's time."

Rhona sensed his presence not far behind her but could not bring herself to acknowledge him. If she was to survive this, she didn't want another reason to be angry with her father. Instead she forced a smile. "Yes, Emsley, it's time."

Mindful of Rhona's unexpected silence, Charles followed the women outside. Her maid slowed in order to speak with the head housemaid, and Charles silently thanked his good fortune and trailed Rhona down the steps to the coach. She hesitated in accepting his offered hand for help but relented.

Charles always had difficulty reading Rhona, yet she was now more of an unbendable mystery than before. He hated seeing this side of her and vowed to find a way to bring back the woman he once knew and still loved. "The winds have stopped, but it will be a cold journey. We will stop at an inn this evening and board the train tomorrow afternoon. You'll have relative comfort for most of the journey."

Rhona merely nodded, increasing his concern. Her maid watched them, but she slowed her pace to the coach. The laird was in conversation with Tristan, and Charles would have only a minute before the others were close enough to hear their conversation. "Are you well, Rhona? You led me to believe last night that you didn't want this."

Gray eyes moved slowly until Charles saw the desperation Rhona had thus far kept hidden. "How I am matters little to my father."

"I'm not asking your father, I'm

asking you." Charles heard a light cough behind him—a warning that his time was near an end. "Do you want this marriage?"

"I never wanted it." Rhona's whisper died under the power of her father's words.

"Ye'll be happy and married ere long."

Charles stepped away from the coach when Davidson approached. Rhona's father closed the coach door and rested a hand on the open window.

"Yes, Father." Rhona's eyes passed over her father's face briefly.

Charles rode alongside the coach, occasionally looking at the windows, but Rhona kept the curtains drawn throughout the first few hours of the drive. More than once he noticed Devon or Tristan looking behind them, but neither moved back to rotate, as they normally did when an assignment required escorting duties. Had it not been for the few stops along the route to allow Rhona a minute of rest and refreshment, Charles would have not seen her the length of the journey.

They had all been introduced to Rhona's maid prior to their departure, and it was Emsley alone who attempted to keep communication open. With a few words, she managed to convey what was happening inside the carriage. From what Charles surmised, Rhona either said little, or her maid was too loyal to repeat what they discussed.

Nearly twenty miles on questionable roads brought them to The Horse and Iron, a century-old inn Davidson had assured them would provide clean rooms and hearty meals. Charles chose to reserve judgment. The coach pulled to a stop near the entrance, but it wasn't until Tristan had ventured inside to see after the accommodations, that Charles dismounted and knocked gently on the coach door before pulling it open. He nearly spoke her name, but his eyes settled on her gentle and relaxed features, and he watched as her chest rose slowly with each soft breath.

"They have . . ." Tristan quieted when he saw Rhona's sleeping form. He moved away without sound or word and motioned the coachmen to help unload Rhona's trunk.

Charles watched Rhona for as long as he dared, then turned to Emsley and motioned for her to wake her mistress. Never having the pleasure of seeing Rhona wake, Charles did not know what to anticipate, but the quiet moan and slow opening of her eyes were not expected. Neither was the reaction those slight actions had on him.

Her eyes fluttered once and remained open. "We've arrived?"

Charles nodded. "Rooms have been secured. I'll give you a minute." Charles moved away but left the door open. When they were ready to step down, he helped first Emsley and then Rhona, both of whom he moved quickly into the inn. Devon and Tristan stood inside speaking with the proprietor.

"Miss Davidson, may I introduce you to Mr. Duff, our host for this evening." Tristan indicated the stout man with graying hair standing next to him. "His wife will see that you have everything you require."

Rhona was ready to speak, but a curious look from Devon changed her mind. Instead she nodded, offered a quiet "thank you," and allowed Charles to guide her and Emsley across the main room of the inn and to the stairs, where an older, skinny woman waited to show them upstairs. Charles waited in the hall while Mrs. Duff explained to Emsley where everything was and what to do if they needed anything else. When Mrs. Duff excused herself and returned downstairs, Rhona stepped into the hall.

"Is something wrong with thanking the innkeeper?"

Charles glanced over Rhona's shoulder. Emsley made no move to pretend she wasn't listening. "It's best if we keep to ourselves as much as possible. Our mission is to ensure your safety. Everything we do is out of concern for your welfare."

"Do you truly believe Alistair is a spy?" Rhona backed into the room, her hand on the door.

"How did you—"

"I'm not above eavesdropping."

Charles smiled briefly. "Good to know."

She returned his smile, enjoying for a few seconds the ease they had once known together.

"We won't know until we find him, but the evidence is damning."

"He's been good to me and Wallace. Were it not for him, life at Davidson Castle would have been far less pleasant."

Charles slipped his fingers around her upper arm, then up and over her shoulder. She did not push him away but welcomed the memory his soft touch invoked. His deep voice caressed her mind as his fingers warmed the skin beneath her clothes.

"I promise you that I will confirm his guilt before any action is taken."

"That's all I can ask."

"Rhona?"

She looked up at him.

"What happened to Wallace? You're not a very good liar."

Of all the things she could have done, smiling seemed out of place. "Thank you for noticing." Quietly she closed the door and left Charles standing mere inches from the wood portal.

Tristan walked down the hall toward him. "Trying to make this more difficult for yourself?"

"Seems to be unavoidable. I believe she knows what happened to Wallace."

"The only reason to say he is dead would be to give him time to get away. We must ask ourselves, 'Is she helping because he's guilty or because he's in danger?'"

"That, my friend, is what I plan to find out."

Tristan nodded toward the bedroom. "We'll sit in shifts outside her room tonight and leave at first light."

Charles nodded. "Is the dining room empty or should we have their meals brought up?"

"Devon didn't like the state of a few of the patrons. He'll eat downstairs with the coachmen, and I'll take first shift up here."

Charles indicated the door. "I'll have a maid bring up their dinner."

Tristan placed a brotherly hand on his friend's shoulder. "In three days' time, one way or another, this will be over."

Charles said nothing. He put his own hand on Tristan's shoulder and walked reluctantly down the hall.

Five

Charles studied each man in the dining hall. Mostly hunters and drovers, they appeared to be a quiet lot. A pair of men in the center of the room talked quietly with each other, barely glancing at the servant girl when she set bowls of stew and a platter of biscuits on the table. The coachmen opted for a table of their own, leaving Charles with his own thoughts until Devon sat down across from him.

Charles took in Devon's red face. "Anything amiss?"

Devon smiled at the girl who brought their meal to the table. She winked at Devon and scooted coyly away. Alone again, Devon erased the smile. "Only the bloody winters here. I swear I'll never get used to them."

"Tupping with a maid in the stables?"

"Nothing that interesting." Devon reached into his jacket pocket and pulled out a slip of paper. "Patrick sent a courier."

"Foolish to send someone out in this weather and unusual." Charles plucked the paper from Devon's fingers, and carefully read over the message. "And now understandable." Charles held the paper over the low candle on the table and waited for the ash to fall into the candle bowl. "Did the courier stay?"

Devon nodded. "Mr. Duff said the inn was full, but he'll set up an extra cot in the coachmen's room."

"Enjoy the meal and warm up. I'll update Tristan." Charles left his unfinished stew and made his way out of the noisy room and up the stairs. Tristan sat casually in a wooden chair in front of the ladies' room. His eyes were scanning the pages of a book when Charles walked down the upstairs hall.

"Patrick has changed our destination." Charles leaned up against the doorframe.

"These doors aren't much for privacy." Tristan stood and set his book on the chair. He motioned for Charles to follow him a few paces away. "Where?"

"Inverness."

"Patrick's coming with us to Crawford's? We expected he might."

Charles nodded. "Apparently the situation has worsened, but he gave no details. Crawford is quite obviously not the man we believe he is."

Tristan glanced at Rhona's door. "I spoke with her earlier as you'd asked, but I can't help but feel sorry for her. She's unhappy."

Charles smiled, though it didn't reach his eyes. "She was always difficult to unravel, but you're right. Unfortunately, I can't do anything about it until she asks for help."

"Arranged marriages aren't as common as they once were. A woman with her strength . . . what reason would she have to go through with it?"

"I've been asking myself the same thing since I saw her again, and I'd wager it has something to do with Wallace." Charles stood straight. "I'd hoped to speak with her privately."

"If our mission included your

resolving your differences with the lady, then I would gladly suggest we delay, but as things stand, it's better to let her go."

"If it was Alaina on the other side of the door, under similar circumstances, would you walk away?"

Tristan lifted the book from his chair and sat down. "We still have a mission to carry out." Tristan handed the book to Charles. "You can take over the watch. And Charles? When this is over, you know I'll support whatever you decide to do, but right now—"

"Mission first." Charles's gaze swept over the door to Rhona's room. "Have you thought about leaving again? Making retirement permanent, never to return for any reason?"

Tristan nodded. "But we all know

that retirement would never be permanent. We've both tried it. They've invested too much into us." Tristan set a heavy hand on his friend's shoulder. "If caring about her doesn't hurt anyone, don't let the work stop you."

Charles looked directly at Tristan but said nothing.

Tristan stepped back. "Unless there's something we don't know."

"There's plenty I haven't told you or Devon, and I didn't think any of it would be a problem."

"Why is it now?"

Charles shook his head. "I don't know exactly, but something about Rhona's behavior when she came to see me. There's more to this marriage than what she or her father revealed."

"We have three days before we

meet Patrick. If you haven't learned the truth by then—"

"Then I have to let her go."

Tristan nodded. "Will you?"

Charles pressed his hand against the closed portal, his silence answer enough.

Charles held the silver watch in his palm, watching the seconds and minutes pass. Devon would arrive to relieve him in half an hour. Until then, his thoughts would continue to be plagued with images of Rhona in the room behind him. If she had met him, Charles Blackwood, Viscount and British agent, and not Charles Pearce, the common man who saved her life a little more than two years ago, would they have found a way to stay together?

Keeping their identities secret was

one of the reasons why both he and Tristan had quit the agency. Had the last assignment, which pulled them back into service, been for anyone other than a friend, they would have remained retired or at least tried to. That matter was easily solved, but then another case arose, and then another, until they found themselves once again at the top of the agency's assignment list. They had managed for nearly two years to avoid accepting assignments, and Charles appreciated that Tristan was here for him.

He also knew there wouldn't be another woman in his lifetime, and he was prepared to make his life a solitary one, but he never imagined escorting the only woman he had ever loved to another man. Charles recalled Rhona promising him that one day he would regret his choice to leave her behind.

"My father will never let me marry a commoner, but I will run away with you." Rhona pressed her gloved hand against Charles's face.

Charles turned his face inward and kissed her palm. "Nothing would please me more, but I can't stay."

Rhona pulled away. "I don't understand."

Charles ignored the heavy ache in his chest. "As you said, I'm a commoner, and England is home. It's where my work is."

"Then work here."

"Too many are leaving Scotland. You know it's not possible."

Rhona stood from the bench they'd been sharing inside the walled garden, now left dormant with the heart of winter settling in. "It would be possible if it's what you truly wanted."

"Rhona, it's not a simple thing for me to stay."

"When do you leave?"

Charles stood beside her and reached out, but she backed away. His hand dropped to his side. "I have to leave in the morning."

"One day, Charles, you will regret this choice." Rhona walked quickly, frost and leaves crunching under each step as she moved farther away.

"I already do." Charles's whisper was carried away with the wind.

I already do. Charles shook the memories from his mind and listened to the subtle creaks and groans of the old inn. Most of the patrons had retired some time ago, some passing him in the hall, but none who stopped to ask why he was there. Devon would have remained downstairs until the last of the patrons retired, and Charles knew from his earlier visit to the dining hall that two men were still unaccounted for.

He stood and pulled the watch from his pocket, then turned at the sound of movement on the stairs. Devon stepped onto the landing and walked toward him.

"Is anything wrong?"

Charles shook his head. "I'm not sure. I was waiting for the two men we saw in the dining room. Something about them . . . but they must have left the inn."

"They went into a back room nearly twenty minutes ago. I looked for them, but they went into a closed room." Devon automatically looked down the hall in both directions. "No one is left downstairs except Mr. Duff and a serving maid."

"That's not poss—" *It would be possible, if it's what you truly wanted.* His memory of Rhona's words came back to him but held a different kind of dread. He walked over to the door and gently knocked. After a minute of silence he knocked louder and then pulled the spare key from his pocket and unlocked the door. Devon entered two steps behind him.

Rhona and her maid lay in the center of the large bed, their backs to one another. Charles could barely see their faces beneath the pile of quilts.

Devon stood beside him, his voice a whisper. "What did you expect to find? We secured the room."

"I know." Charles stepped as quietly as he could to the window, his eyes never leaving Rhona until he turned his head to look outside. The wind and rain threatened to shake open the locked window, but he could see nothing beyond the immediate darkness. He moved slowly back to Devon who motioned him back out of the room.

"She's safe, Charles."

He said nothing.

"Trust your instincts. You stay here with them and I'll wake Tristan."

Charles nodded and watched Devon slip into the next room. The door beside him opened.

"Did something happen?" Charles looked past the maid to the bed where Rhona slept, barely noticing that she stood in her nightgown and robe.

"Miss Davidson sleeps through anything. However, I do not." Emsley pulled the edges of her robe tighter together. "I heard you come into the room."

Charles shook his head. "Forgive me, Miss Hargrave. Rest assured you may sleep without worry."

Emsley watched him closely until she finally nodded and quietly faded into the darkness of the room.

Devon and Tristan emerged from their room, and without words the two men walked away. Tristan searched the upstairs halls and Devon returned downstairs. Charles remained in front of Rhona's door, feeling useless. Always a man of action and decision, he preferred effective involvement and actions, which brought about end results. He knew how to wait patiently when an assignment required it, but it was not his strength.

Tristan approached him first, but he shook his head as he moved toward him. "There's nothing amiss up here, Charles. I've never questioned your intuition before, but could this uncertainty be more about whom we're protecting rather than a true threat?"

"No." Charles had never been more certain about his intuition than he did in that moment.

"Then wake them. I'll rouse the others."

Rhona stared up at the man beside her, but only when her vision had adjusted to the darkness, did worry replace fear. She nodded and the large hand lifted away from her mouth. The space beside her was empty.

"Emsley? Is she—"

"She's safe." Charles moved aside so that Rhona could see her maid. The young woman was frantically gathering the few items they'd unpacked for the night. "I need you to hurry and stay quiet."

Rhona pushed aside the blankets and reached for her robe. She did her best to ignore the quick perusal Charles gave her before averting his eyes.

"What's happened?"

"We need to leave."

"What time is it? We can't possibly travel in this weather at night."

"I need you to trust me."

Rhona moved past him to help Emsley. "You ask . . ." She lowered her voice. "You ask for a great deal of trust."

Charles reached out and lightly grabbed her arm. "Rhona, please."

Rhona studied him for only a few seconds, nodded, and pulled a dress from the top of the pile. "We'll hurry." She moved quickly behind a dressing screen in the corner.

Charles turned at the touch of a hand on his sleeve, a hand which quickly pulled back when she had his attention. Emsley looked up at him from her petite stature. "Will she be safe?"

"You have my word. Now go and help her. We don't have much time."

Cold air filled his lungs, but he gave little thought to the discomfort the night chill brought. Charles once again rode alongside the carriage, but this time Devon rode to the other side while Tristan rode beside the team of horses. The animals breathed heavily and created white puffs of air that could temporarily be seen in the darkness. Two lanterns at the front of the carriage barely lit the road in front of them. They traveled cautiously over the unpredictable roads. Anyone with a purpose would have caught up with them by now, but Charles's relief was short-lived. The unmistakable sound of riders was not far behind them. Devon gestured that he had also heard them.

Charles softly whistled, and Tristan turned in his saddle. Charles indicated to Tristan who nodded, then Charles and Devon slowly fell back and moved their horses off the road. They waited nearly ten minutes before the riders were close enough for Charles to see that they were the same men from the inn. The men rode without light other than what moonlight the snow reflected, giving Charles and Devon a slight, though brief, advantage. They remained off the road until the riders were directly beside them.

"This is not a fight you want." Charles held his pistol steady on the rider closest to him and moved from the shadows.

"Ye canna shuit us both."

"But we can." Devon walked his horse forward on the other side. "Slowly remove your guns and toss them to the ground."

Charles watched them closely, and when they didn't comply, he shifted his horse until he stared directly at both riders. "My friend will assist, but I promise you don't want that. Drop them, now."

Slowly the men pulled the guns

from their belts, but it was the loud report of Devon's revolver that drew Charles's eyes to the man slumped over in the saddle.

"Your friend chose wrong." Charles watched the handgun drop into the snow. "Good. Now, I'm willing to let you live, but you'll first explain why you're following us."

"Don't care none about ye blokes. We's wants the lady."

Charles eyes narrowed. "Curious. You thought we would simply hand her over? Who hired you?"

"I'm not sayin.' Ye'll go and kill me anyhow."

"I won't, actually. You have my word as a gentleman."

The man appeared to consider his options. His eyes darted back and forth between the two pistols pointed at him and his dead companion. "I don't know the bloke's name. Artie met 'im."

"Your name?"

"Dyson."

Charles lowered his gun. "What were you to do with the lady?"

"Take 'er to Moulin Kirk."

Charles slid his pistol back into the fine leather holster and grabbed Dyson's horse. "Remember what happened to Artie. If you happen to meet your employer, tell him to stay away from Miss Davidson."

Devon motioned for the man to get off his horse. "You'll want to walk quickly or you will freeze to death."

"Ye can't leave me here without me horse."

"Be grateful you're leaving."

Six

Tristan kept the entourage moving, but Charles and Devon caught up with them after a little more than two miles. They traveled much slower than Charles would have liked, but the occasional encounters with ice forced them to keep the sedate pace. Charles tied the men's horses to the back of the coach.

"I'll ride on. I remember a country house a few miles ahead. Perhaps we'll find a place to rest and warm the horses until dawn." Devon moved off the road and urged his horse into a quicker pace.

"Have you spoken with them?" Charles indicated the coach.

Tristan nodded. "Once when Rhona asked for you. She heard the gunshot. Who were they?"

"The men from the inn. They were to take Rhona to Moulin Kirk."

"The village from Davidson's file."

Charles nodded. "Alistair Davidson has been spotted there on numerous occasions."

"And you believe he would attempt to kidnap his sister."

"I believe that Alistair is unpredictable and that our superiors want him for reasons they haven't shared." Charles rubbed his gloved hand over his cold nose and face in an effort to keep the blood flowing to those outer extremities.

"Reasons we won't know about if we have to keep going much longer in this cold." Tristan glanced at Charles. "What happened to the two men?"

"The one who lived should be back at the inn soon." Charles remembered Dyson staring up at him from the ground. The low-born Scotsman had seemed far more dangerous and worrisome at the inn. "We can't know that they were alone. I couldn't risk keeping her there."

Tristan slowly nodded. "You don't have to explain your reasons. We're beyond me acting as supervisor for this assignment. You and Devon know the people involved better than I do. I need to ask how involved you became with her."

"We were intimate."

"Did she show fear or sound worried about anything when she spoke with you?"

"Nothing unusual, but—"

"Wait." Tristan rode up next to one of the horses. "Hold up, man, this lead mare is limping."

"Nae surprising with this weather." The driver, selected by Davidson, carefully pulled the team to a stop and climbed down. "Dinna know what nonsense coud hae drove us out at night."

Tristan looked over at Charles, who only smiled. He did understand the man's frustration, for the roads were difficult to navigate in winter without benefit of the sun. Charles held up a hand for Tristan to remain on his horse, and he dismounted to help the driver with the mare.

The coach door swung open and Rhona stepped down. "Is something wrong?" Rhona's dark hair fell from beneath her hat.

"You should remain inside, Miss Davidson."

"Thank you, Agent Sheffield, but I prefer to know what's happened. Is

Charles—"

Charles said something quickly to the driver and walked over the icy ground to Rhona. "We can tell you while you're inside." He held out his hand to assist her. "One of the horses may be lame."

"Are you positively certain that leaving in the dark was necessary?" She narrowed her eyes. "What happened before? I heard the gunfire."

He wasn't going to lie to her. "We've been tasked with ensuring you're safe. From time to time, that may require unpleasantries."

Rhona's gaze trailed his long body, and Charles's body reacted. Her eyes stopped at his. "You weren't injured."

"No one, except one of the men who came looking for you."

"They asked for me?"

Charles pulled her back a few feet from the carriage. "They did come for you, though we don't yet know who's behind it."

"Do you suspect my family?"

"Your older brother—"

"Is on the continent. He's been at university these past years. He writes to me every month. I cannot believe Alistair is guilty of what your government accuses him."

Charles held her face between his hands. Her red cheeks and nose attested to the cold, which for some reason he no longer felt. "I made you a promise, and I will keep it. Nothing will happen to your brother until we have proof."

Her hand came up to rest on his forearm. "I believe you. I won't doubt it again."

Charles lowered his hands to her

shoulders. "Have you ever been to Moulin Kirk?"

"No, but my mother spent much of her childhood in Pitlochry. My uncle lived there, though he passed when I was a child." She stared up at him, her eyes conveyed worry and curiosity. "Why do you ask?"

"The men were to take you there."

"I don't understand."

Charles guided her back to the coach. "Neither do we—yet. Will you remain inside this time?"

Rhona managed a nervous smile. "Promise."

"We shouldn't be long." Charles closed the coach door and returned to help the driver. Tristan was now on the other side of the coach, staring into the darkness. Charles knelt beside the driver and lifted the horse's leg into his own hands. He ran his hand along the sole, noticing the redness. The mare jerked her leg when his fingers pressed down. Charles turned to face the driver and explain that they would have to switch out the mare with one of the other horses, but the other man's hand swung a blade toward Charles's gut.

Charles fell backward and rolled away. He grabbed the driver's arm as he bore down once again and flipped the driver over until he had him pinned. Charles pounded the man's arm into the ground over and over until the blade fell. His right fist swept across his body and connected with the driver's face, bloodying the man's nose and cutting his cheek. The driver remained conscious but subdued.

"I almost thought you would need help."

Charles took long and deep breaths and glanced up at Tristan. "Perish the idea."

Tristan secured his pistol, dismounted, and lifted the driver to his feet once Charles had released him. Charles swiped his hand across the bloody lip he received from his scuffle.

Tristan twisted the driver's arms behind him and dragged him toward the back of the coach. Charles followed. "How long have you been working for Davidson?"

The driver shook his head.

"What's your real name?"

Charles stepped forward and grabbed the driver's jacket. "If you prefer, I can tie you to a tree in the woods and let the cold and wolves kill you."

"'Tis Murray. Me name is Murray!"

Tristan pulled Charles a few feet away. "We can't stay here, Charles. I'll switch the mare with one of the other horses. Were you injured?"

Charles shook his head and looked back to the way they had come. Instinct told him that they were right to leave the inn, but that didn't stop him from questioning the decision. "I'll drive. It shouldn't be long before Devon returns, and we can only hope he's found shelter." Charles waited for Tristan to walk away before moving back toward Murray. The smaller man stared at him, his eyes dark and unrelenting. "You aren't afraid of me, are you?"

Murray ignored the question.

"I believe you are, Murray. It would take a hefty purse to be willing to do what you've tried tonight. You're Davidson's man. Did he hire you to do more than just drive or is something else behind this?"

Murray spat at the ground and turned away. Charles yanked Murray's head. "You're perilously close to a slow death."

Charles tied him to the back of the coach and checked his person for anything he could possibly use to cut the rope. "Somehow I don't believe Davidson foolish enough to hire a daffy. Any reasonable assassin would have waited until we reached our next destination."

"Ye niver left her alone."

Charles looked around the carriage to check on Tristan's progress. "Have you seen reason, Murray?"

"I canna go back!"

"Back to whom?"

The driver hesitated and his eyes darted back and forth in an attempt to see around Charles. "You'll find no one out there willing to help you."

"He said he was a packman. Me kin needed the money."

Charles considered the driver. "A peddler would not have the coin to hire you."

"He dinna say who sent 'im."

Tristan walked around the back of the coach leading the lame mare. "She won't make it far."

Charles pointed to Murray. "He claims not to know the man who hired him by way of a peddler."

Tristan tied the mare. "Yet it was you he tried to kill, not the lady."

"And he must have known you would have returned the favor."

Tristan nodded.

Charles stepped forward, his eyes looking down at Murray. "Was Miss Davidson your target?"

Murray looked away, but Charles drew his head back around, his strong fingers gripping into the sides of Murray's neck. The driver shook his head rapidly. "Ye were."

Charles released him and stepped back. To Tristan he said, "Let's finish here and move on."

Tristan slowly nodded and walked the gelding away. Charles checked the security of the ropes once more, then followed Tristan. "He would not have attacked if he thought no one else was coming." Charles helped secure the straps while Tristan worked on the collar.

"I agree, but we aren't going anywhere quickly without risking another lame horse." Tristan finished connecting the harness.

"I'll drive. There's room for our friend up with me." Charles patted the rump of the gelding and walked to the door of the coach. He opened it enough to see only Rhona.

"We'll be moving on now.

Rhona dropped the edge of the curtain that covered the coach window. She turned her attention to the embroidery on her lap. Not a single stitch had passed through the wool tartan since their departure from Davidson Castle.

"You worry for him."

Rhona pulled the curtain back once more, her eyes scanning the darkness. The black of the night was interrupted by the moonlight, giving Rhona a brief glimpse of familiar trees. "I worry for us all."

"You've never left home, have you?"

"Only once, a long time ago." Rhona let the curtain fall. "When we first met, and you told me of your travels, I envied you."

Rhona smiled at the tilt of Emsley's head, knowing that particular habit led to a question.

"Why did you not travel? Excuse my impertinence, Rhona, but your father has the means to send you anywhere in the world."

Rhona smiled, but it was a falsehood. Resources were not an issue. Rhona never spoke of her own fortune with the servants. Graham is the only one who knew, for her mother had trusted the loyal butler with her life. Lara Davidson believed that her daughter would need an advocate. As it turned out, she had. Graham had been her friend and closer to a father than her own. Her father did once have the resources, but not the generosity, to let her travel.

Her father may have orchestrated the marriage, but by doing so he had unknowingly presented her with another opportunity. It was the chance for justice that Rhona used to fuel her now. Charles's unexpected return into her life made the execution of her new plan all that more difficult.

"I wanted to be home for my brother."

"Wallace?"

Rhona bowed her head once, her eyes avoiding Emsley.

"I am sorry, my lady. You must miss him terribly."

"Yes, I do."

"You'll have a new start now."

Rhona nodded. "Perhaps."

Tristan held the reins of the other horse confiscated from one of the culprits. Upon the horse sat Murray, whom Charles would have preferred to see tied precariously to the luggage.

"We need him alive."

Charles nodded and put the team into motion. Their silent journey continued nearly four miles more before Charles pulled the team to a stop. The whistle reached them despite the blowing wind. Seconds later, a rider slowed and used the snow to safely stop the horse.

"I expected you to be farther along." Devon rubbed his gloved hands together and pointed to Murray. "What happened?"

"More than we would like," Tristan said. "Did you secure lodging?"

Devon nodded. "Lord Allen's summer residence."

Charles considered that. "Is he the

lord who had the missing daughter four years past that you and Zachary found?"

"That is him. The butler remembered me and said we were welcome. Only he and a maid are in residence, but I assured them it would be for only one night. Devon turned his horse around. "Come, it's not far."

Two additional miles of travel brought them to the gates of Lord Allen's estate. A modest home by many standards, but the house contained more than enough rooms for everyone. Charles jumped down from the driver's seat to help the women from the coach. Rhona barely touched his gloved hand with hers, but it was enough to leave him wanting more contact.

The butler stood at the base of the house steps. "Do you not travel with footmen?"

"We had a bit of trouble on that score," Tristan said from atop his horse. "I apologize for the impropriety, but this man must remain with us tonight. We can sleep in the servants' quarters."

The suggestion elicited a quick denial from the butler. "I would not consider it, Your Grace. You do what you must."

Seven

Once Tristan had secured Murray in one of the spare rooms, thankfully one with a lock on the outside, he met up with Charles and Devon in the parlor, where they waited for the ladies. The only way for Murray to escape would be to leap from the second-story window.

"I'd rather keep the chap alive, but if he's determined to fall to his death, so be it." Tristan patted the pocket holding the key provided by Graham. "By the way, Charles, do you know who might want to kill you?"

"Could be anyone from our past who knows who we are, but in this case, it has to be someone from within our circles."

"I agree." Devon crossed his arms and watched the doorway. "Someone close. Only a few people were aware of our course."

"I only informed Patrick," Tristan said, "but anyone in his confidence could be the leak."

Charles shrugged. "It's possible, but Patrick is careful. If someone did indeed infiltrate, they're damned good." Charles looked to Devon. "You know the men from the home office better than we do these days. Anyone new?"

"My brothers would know best. They've been to London a few times in the past months. I've always met Patrick or his aide, Jameson, in the field."

Charles watched the door for signs

of Rhona, but when he heard someone approaching, it was the butler who stood in the doorway.

Addressing the highest ranking member of their group, the butler looked first to Tristan. "Dinner is served, Your Grace. We have simple fare this evening, what with the cook in London. The maid, Margritte, does a fine job."

"Quite all right. I fear we've inconvenienced you," said Tristan.

"Not at all, Your Grace." The butler walked forward and handed a small square of paper to Charles. "From Miss Davidson, my lord."

Charles read the two lines and folded the paper into his pocket. The butler led them to the dining room. Once the meal of cold meats, cooked winter vegetables, fresh bread, and hot spiced cider was served, Tristan insisted the butler go and enjoy his meal. Charles wondered for a moment if this English butler would be the first in history to defy a duke. Apparently not, because the butler nodded once and existed the room.

"She's angry," Devon said once they were alone.

Charles nodded. "She's justified. I haven't told her everything yet."

"It might be prudent to tell her the full truth."

"I've considered that many times, Tristan, but it could risk her life even more." Charles set his fork and knife down. "You didn't tell Alaina everything in the beginning."

"No, and I was wrong." Tristan finished the wine in his glass. "Had Alaina known of the dangers, she might have been more careful."

Charles smiled. "I think your wife handled herself quite well."

Devon's deep laughter broke most of the tension in the room. "Kidnapped three times by the same people. Would it have happened if she'd known everything from the start? Perhaps, or not, but I'll have to agree with Tristan on this."

Charles considered this, his own thoughts filled with memories of the case involving Alaina's family. She went through hell, lost her family, and yet was one of the strongest women he'd ever known. Charles believed Rhona to be Alaina's equal in every way, and he did owe her the truth and the best chance at remaining safe.

The meal over, Charles immediately retired to the room situated next to Rhona's. Lord Allen's estate was gated and far from anything of consequence, which is why none of them believed it necessary to guard Rhona's bedroom door. Yet, Charles remained awake. He listened for any whisper, creak, groan, or other sign that someone else might be wandering the halls. Howling winds occasionally rattled the window, but no sound came from within. Charles's insomnia soon grew into boredom, and he could no longer stare at the ceiling or listen for something that wasn't there.

He sat up and swung his legs over the edge of the bed. Still fully clothed, he pulled on his boots and quietly left the room. A soft glow in the hall drew his attention.

"I didn't expect anyone else to be awake."

Charles's gaze drifted over Rhona's white dressing gown and heavy plaid robes. He smiled at the short boots pulled over stockinged feet. "Are you coming or going?"

"I honestly don't know." Rhona's hand remained on the door handle. Charles hoped she would let go. She said, "It would be far too improper for us to be seen . . . that is, if Emsley wakes and finds . . ."

"Sharing a cup of warm milk is hardly scandalous." Charles stepped to the side and held out his arm in invitation for her to walk in front. He said a silent *thank you* when she nodded and walked down the hallway ahead of him.

They found the kitchen, and with the skill of a man used to spending time on his own and in oftentimes remote places, Charles found a heavy pot and a small pitcher of milk in the icebox. He deftly lit the fire in the stove and poured a healthy portion of the creamy liquid into the pot.

"You've done this before."

"My culinary talents are limited, but this I can manage."

"I can't do even that."

Charles sat in the chair opposite of Rhona at the table. He noticed for the first time that the braid in her hair was longer than he remembered. "You don't have to know how. You'll go from your father's home to your husband's, and surely he'll more than provide . . . Rhona?"

"Is that what you believe I desire? The chains are only being passed from one man to another."

Charles watched her face for signs of any emotion, but she had become too adept at hiding her feelings. "You are not in bondage. It is an insult to those of this world who are to compare your life with theirs."

Surprised, Rhona's eyes widened. "You've changed less than I first believed. Not a man or woman, before or since, has spoken to me that way. It's a relief."

"I deserve your anger." Charles stood to check the milk. He found two cups he assumed were for the servants' use and filled them both. "Here, this should help you sleep."

"I am not angry with you." Rhona wrapped her fingers around the warm cup. "My mother used to drink warm milk with me nearly every night of my childhood." Rhona sipped her milk while her eyes wandered. "I don't understand everything you've had to do for your work—your country, but I believe you're an honorable man. I cannot fault you for that."

Speechless, Charles watched her

eyes as they stared into his. No guile or pretense.

"Why did we not stay at the inn?" Rhona asked. "It looks as though we spent a good deal of time on the road at night for no apparent reason. The driver—"

"The driver was not the greatest threat to you." He held her stare. "The coach went ahead. Devon and I stopped two men on the road, two men who had been at the inn. Their intentions were quite obvious."

"Would it not have been easier to subdue them at the inn?"

Charles waited until she once again met his eyes. His gaze held her eyes, and his tone softened. "Not if it meant explaining their deaths. Killing can be a loud and messy business."

Rhona pushed the milk away.

Charles watched the rise and fall of her chest. Her eyes never wavered. "You killed them? I wasn't certain when I heard . . . I thought perhaps you only scared them."

Charles shook his head, more to himself than to her. "It did not end the way I had hoped, but they won't be coming for you again."

"I see." Rhona stood and pulled the edges of her robe closer together.

Charles left the table and hurried around to her side. "Would you rather I had lied?"

The sound Rhona made could have been confused with laughter had Charles not been so close to her. "No. I'm not upset." Rhona put distance between them and shook her head. "I regret that you had to kill a man on my behalf."

"Harbor no regrets. I would do it again." Charles finished his milk and set his cup aside. "I need to ask you something, and I hope I don't insult you when I say I'd like the truth."

"We both deserve more truth. What do you need to know?"

"Why did you agree to the marriage?"

"It is my father's wish."

Charles reached out and pulled her close to him. "The woman I once knew would not agree to a loveless marriage or a life not of her choosing."

Rhona gently pulled her arm free. "I won't tell you a lie, but I cannot tell you why." She backed up slowly, then turned and walked from the room.

Charles rode alongside the coach, keeping his thoughts and words to himself. Devon volunteered to drive. All three men agreed that it wasn't worth the risk to hire a new driver in the nearby village. The frost-covered road crunched under the wheels as mile after mile passed. They crossed paths with tenant farmers from neighboring country estates. No one spoke to them, and anyone who saw the coach moved to the side of the road to let them pass.

On the following day, country roads soon met with better-preserved streets as the group made their way into Inverness and finally into the railway station where the agents' supervisor waited with an aide.

Charles dismounted first, handed his horse to a porter, and shook hands with Patrick. Patrick indicated the coach. "You're earlier than we expected. I sent a runner out to meet you, but he returned with news that you weren't far behind."

"We dealt with a bit of trouble along the way, but we didn't meet with a runner."

"Is she safe?"

Charles nodded and walked toward the coach. A porter opened the door before Charles could reach it, then stood aside. Charles held out his hand, and after a few seconds, Rhona slipped her gloved hand into his and stepped onto the raised platform.

"Miss Davidson, may I introduce you to my supervisor, Agent Ashford."

Patrick's brow rose, and he looked directly at Charles.

"She knows what we do, Patrick."

Patrick bowed his head. "Miss Davidson, I do hope your journey was comfortable."

"Quite, thank you." Rhona stepped aside to make room for her maid.

Charles introduced Emsley to Patrick.

"I expected you'd travel with a companion. I've secured her passage with the—"

"I prefer she rides with me, Agent Ashford."

"That would not be appropriate."

"Then I won't be on the train when it leaves the station." Rhona met Patrick's stare with one of her own. Charles decided if there was a moment to intervene on her behalf, this would be it.

"I imagine the railway won't mind the purchase of an additional first class ticket."

"Of course not."

Charles caught the almost indiscernible expression Patrick

wore, as did Tristan, who had secured the cargo with a porter and now approached them. Charles inclined his head to Rhona, and Tristan nodded before turning his attention to the ladies. Charles followed Patrick a dozen feet down the platform.

"She's headstrong, Patrick."

"So I've seen. Did she prove difficult?"

Charles shook his head. "Quite the opposite. You'd know her kindness had you met under different circumstances." Charles briefly looked back over his shoulder. "We need to talk."

"About what? Your history with the girl?"

"You know about that?"

"Of course I know." Patrick reached into his pocket and pulled out the tickets. "I've decided to accompany you to Crawford's."

"We expected it."

"I planned to travel to Davidson Castle first. The agency has business to conduct with the laird. However, we have received new information and have every reason to believe that Miss Davidson's brother will make an appearance."

"At Crawford's? Why?"

"I would presume to interfere with the wedding."

Charles wasn't ready to believe it, his promise to Rhona in the forefront of his thoughts. "What reason would her brother have to stop Rhona's wedding?"

"We don't know." Patrick lifted a round watch from his pocket. "I've had men on it since you left, but they aren't you and haven't uncovered anything. It would have helped if the three of you separated as originally ordered."

"We weren't willing to leave her unprotected. As it happens, one alone may not have managed it." Charles ignored the doubting look Patrick gave him. "When does the train leave?"

"We have until half past the hour."

"The ladies will want some time for themselves and something to eat."

Patrick nodded toward the door of the train station. "There's a cart inside. We can get something more substantial on the train."

Charles nodded and turned away but was halted by Patrick's hand on his arm. "There's something more to discuss before you rejoin them."

Charles watched Tristan lead the small group into the train station and turned back to Patrick. "What is it?"

"I need to know that you're able to follow through with the assignment."

"You doubt my objectivity?"

Patrick shook his head. "I trust you, as I trust Tristan and Devon, but you have a personal past with Miss Davidson. I know what can happen when the work interferes with the heart."

Charles refrained from asking Patrick about his own experience but made a mental note. "I won't do anything to jeopardize the assignment, but I must know she is safe and that this is what she wants."

"The betrothal contract has been signed."

Charles ran a gloved hand roughly over his face. "Davidson demanded a contract? It's archaic and surely not—"

"It was Crawford who demanded the contract. He's paying a large purse to marry Davidson's daughter. He wanted insurance."

Charles rooted his legs and fought the urge to hit Patrick, not because he was angry with his superior but because he wanted to rail against someone. Instead, Charles pivoted and walked briskly away.

Rhona and Emsley rested in the comforts of the private car Charles had managed to procure. Simon Caulfield, whom Charles knew from the House of Lords, was attending to business during a week-long tour of Scotland and kindly agreed to lend them the use of his family's rail car. Charles sat with Devon and Tristan in the dining car, opting to leave the ladies their privacy. It was with great relief to Charles that both doors on the borrowed car locked.

Tristan swirled his brandy, his eyes on the passing landscape outside the window. "Once my retirement is official—again—I'll be ordering up one of those cars for myself. Alaina would like to travel more now that our son is old enough to join us for short trips."

"Will you be able to stay away from the agency next time?"

"Your time will come, Devon, when a fair-skinned beauty will capture your notice and your heart. I assure you retirement will be foremost in your thoughts."

"Perhaps. You're quiet, Charles. What did Patrick tell you earlier on the platform?"

"Nothing that I liked, and some of it made no sense."

They paused long enough to place their meal orders with instructions for two additional services.

"Was either of you aware of a betrothal contract?"

Tristan leaned forward. "Between Miss Davidson and Crawford?"

Charles nodded. "According to Patrick. Devon, is there anything about Crawford that might shed some understanding on this?"

"I know him but not well enough to know his character. As I said before, my first judgment of him was favorable."

Charles studied the amber liquid in his glass, still as full as when Tristan handed it to him. "Patrick did say something else curious. Does either of you know about a possible romantic conflict in his past? In few words, he implied that he knew the perils of mixing work with pleasure."

Devon shrugged. "I've always assumed Patrick was a self-imposed bachelor."

Tristan poured himself another drink. "There was a woman once. I'm not sure he realized I knew. It happened shortly after I first joined up. The situation was similar to what you're facing now."

"What happened?"

"He chose the job."

Charles had chosen the job once already. He wasn't going to make the mistake again.

The server returned with their meals and a tray bearing the additional services. Charles thanked the server, who insisted he was capable of delivering the meals. One silent look from Charles led the young man to release the tray, bow, and walk away.

"I won't be long."

Tristan and Devon watched Charles walk through the door, awkwardly carrying the heavy tray.

Tristan said, "The agency is playing us for pawns and Charles worst of all. Patrick used him."

Devon nodded. "Charles knows it, and it's why Patrick hasn't reassigned him. Using Charles's relationship with Rhona is a risky gamble." He faced his friend and sliced through the meat on his plate. "We've known from the beginning that this was not a standard case."

Tristan nodded. "True, but curiosity is a powerful motivation to keep going. When I disregarded orders when it came to Alaina's case, Patrick was supportive."

"Your relationship with Alaina helped that assignment. This one between Charles and Rhona could be detrimental."

"Does that bother you?"

"Of course not." Devon grinned.

"The question we must answer is: Why did Patrick want us when he could have sent anyone? If it is merely because of Charles's history with the lady, that's more of a reason to keep us off the assignment."

Devon lifted the crystal glass of wine. "Then we shall do what we do best—uncover the truth."

"You'll send for your brothers?"

Devon laughed and sipped his wine. "I already have."

Charles lightly rapped on the door while balancing the food-laden tray. A man of many skills and talents, serving was not among them. The short curtain covering the window was pulled back. Emsley dropped the fabric and quickly opened the door. He stepped inside, and his eyes immediately searched for Rhona, who sat quietly in a quilted chair, her legs curled up beneath her.

"I thought it best not to send anyone else." He glanced around for a clear table. Emsley moved an oil lamp from the center of one, and he deposited his burden. "If you require anything else, I'll return later for the tray."

Rhona stood and walked on stockinged feet toward him, then lifted a lid from one of the plates. "Your talents extend beyond warming milk, I see."

Charles watched her lips lift up at the edges. He admired her willingness to try and find normality given the situation.

Rhona set the lid down and

motioned for Emsley to excuse them. Without many options, the maid moved to the back of the car and set about rummaging through a trunk. "Thank you for the food."

Charles lifted his hand slightly, but retracted, sensing the maid's gaze on him.

Rhona lowered her voice. "Will we have a chance to talk again?"

"Would you care for a walk through the cars?"

Rhona glanced over her shoulder. "Yes, but I don't want to leave Emsley alone right now."

"Then I will find a way to get you alone." Charles discreetly squeezed her hand. "If there is anything else you need, let us know. We're in the car next door. One of us will be by the door at all times through the night."

Rhona reached out when Charles

walked toward the door, but she did not touch him. "What happens tomorrow after we arrive?"

He studied her soft features and followed the faint lines of worry and determination from her eyes to her brow. "Crawford's estate is half a day's journey by coach from the rail line."

"You'll travel with us, all the way?"

Charles glanced at her, then at Emsley, who seemed to have forgotten what she was meant to search for. His gaze settled back on Rhona. "Our orders are to deliver you to Crawford. The assignment doesn't end until we've done this."

"And my brother? Your promise . . ."

He held her stare. "It stands. You'll want to eat while the food is warm," he said and walked out the door.

Charles watched the passing landscape from the train window, both his body and mind impatient. Soon he would be back on his horse, moving at a pace more his speed. He'd never forgotten the beauty of Rhona's Highlands. The countryside spanned acres of hills and valleys. Meadows and farm fields stretched beyond the confines of the cities, reminding him a little of home. Unlike England, this land felt wild, and Charles realized how much he missed the scent of pine and heather intermingling. Gray clouds filled the sky, and powerful winds blew small passing trees in unnatural directions, but still they remained strong, their roots buried deep.

When the train rolled to a stop at the station in the small market town of Langholm, Charles disembarked before going to the back car where Rhona and her maid waited. He would not leave her the evening before until she promised not to leave the train unless he, Devon, or Tristan came for them.

The quaint town reminded him of Keswick, the village near his home in Cumbria, though the harsh winter weather kept the streets clear. Only the brave dared to venture out into the chilling wind. Charles pulled the fur hat, a gift from a Russian whose wife was kidnapped while in England, lower and scanned the platform. Two porters fought the cold and hurried from the warm station to assist passengers. Patrick had spent the entire length of the train ride in a card game, and they had not seen him until now. Charles waited, but only their small group stepped down.

He ducked his head, pulled himself back up, and knocked on the door to the private car.

"You shouldn't be opening doors, Rhona." Charles stepped inside. "Crawford has arranged for his private coach to deliver you to his estate."

"I see." Rhona stood in front of him, her body stiff, her hands agitated. "We're ready."

"Rhona . . ." Charles glanced behind her to Emsley, who stood only a few feet away. "Come, the weather will slow our progress."

"Would it not be better to remain here for a night?" Rhona leaned toward the window. "Where exactly are we?"

"Langholm." He reached out to steady her when she appeared to falter, but Emsley rushed up from behind. "Are you well?"

"My lady." Emsley tried to help Rhona into a chair, but Rhona shrugged away the effort.

"I'm quite well. Thank you."

Charles narrowed his eyes and focused on the change in pallor and tightness of her lips. "Wait here until the coach is ready."

Emsley let go of her mistress. "But the train, won't it leave?"

"No. Wait here." Charles left them and found Patrick and Tristan standing on the platform beside the car.

"Where's Devon?"

"He's passing Murray over to another agent."

Charles looked at Patrick. "The agency sent more men?"

"We had a man stationed here.

He'll deliver the driver to London, where he can be interrogated properly."

"He won't talk, not to them. If you gave us some time with him, Murray would talk."

"Those are the orders, Charles. Anyone connected, or suspected of cavorting with Alistair Davidson, is to be sent to London."

Charles watched as Patrick walked into the station. "I couldn't quite place what bothered me about this assignment until now."

"Rhona was never the assignment," Devon said.

"She's the distraction, and someone expected us to be a part of the diversion."

"Devon and I are of the same conclusion." Tristan turned until the winds blew against his back, and no one from inside the station could see him. "He sent for his brothers."

"Wise." Activity picked up on the platform. "Will you . . . never mind. The coach is here."

Charles moved a few steps away, then pivoted and returned to stand beside Tristan. "I will gladly play the fool, but as far as I'm concerned, our assignment is Rhona. Everything else, and I mean everything, is secondary."

Eight

The Borders lacked the wildness of her Highlands. Gone was the familiarity of land, which had surrounded her since childhood. The thick pines and carpets of heather were replaced by low hills and scattered trees. A heavy fog marred most of the landscape surrounding Langholm, but the snow and wind had dissipated since their departure, allowing for an easier journey over the winter roads.

"Will you tell me what has your brow creased and your mind to wandering?"

"Nothing important. It's been a long time since I've ventured this far from home."

Emsley pulled the curtain aside to gaze out the window. "It's lovely, perhaps different, but still lovely. You could be happy here, Rhona."

"I could be happy at home."

"Without a husband or a family?" Emsley returned her attention to her stitching. "You think this now, but we are not so different. I would be truly blessed to have the chance your father has given you."

Rhona studied her companion, younger only by two years. "I do not mean to sound ungrateful, Emsley, yet I would give you leave to marry the laird in my place."

"Rhona!" Emsley cringed inwardly and glanced out the window to ensure herself that no one had heard the outburst. "I am sorry, but you should not make light of such things."

"I'm not making light. Were it possible, I would be drastic."

"Is it really awful for you?"

Rhona slowly shook her head and gave the only lie that held some measure of truth. "It could certainly be worse."

Laird Crawford's estate displayed the wealth that Rhona's father sought. Though not grander in size than Davidson Castle, Crawford's mansion was a not-too-subtle reminder of his fortune. A fortune that Charles was certain interested more than Davidson. Charles knew the value of wealth, especially to those who lacked it and those who placed a premium on it.

Charles was no stranger to fortune, but it was a convenience that allowed him to live his own life on his own terms. Crawford, he knew, was in a similar position, but that position could be dangerous. Without family, who would miss the man should anything happen to him? All of the personal information known about Braden Crawford indicated that he was possessed of no living family, was twenty years Charles's senior, and rarely spent time in London or Edinburgh.

The men flanked the coach up the long drive and stopped next to the wide stone stairs.

Patrick dismounted and walked to stand beside Charles's horse. "We must take counsel with Crawford once the ladies are settled in."

Charles set foot on solid ground. "Tristan is the lead agent on this assignment. Should he not be the only one to join you?"

"Not this time."

"Your motives won't insult me, sir."

Patrick smiled. "No, I don't imagine they will. This alliance is important and not only for Davidson. I must ensure that no one interferes."

"You'd like to keep me by your side until the vows are spoken."

"You understand me well." Patrick pulled him aside. "Should I ever find myself in your position, I would not hesitate to stop the wedding. Unfortunately, I cannot allow it."

Charles nodded, walked around his supervisor. He saw that Patrick may not have succeeded in dissuading him, but he did delay him long enough for someone else to help Rhona from the coach. He watched as Rhona slipped her hand through a stranger's arm, a stranger who could only be her betrothed.

"He's handsome, and I don't mind being impertinent." Emsley walked back and forth between the trunks and the bureau where she neatly hung Rhona's clothes.

"You are impertinent." Rhona stared out the window from the bedroom on the second level of the spacious mansion.

"You will try to be happy here, yes?"

"A person shouldn't have to *try* to be happy." Rhona sank into a chair and stared while her maid unpacked garment after garment. Pieces of her slowly disappeared into a strange closet in a strange house. She would not be able to take them with her when she left.

"If you don't try, then how does one become happy?"

Rhona laughed at the absurdity of the conversation and because laughter was better than tears. "I can't claim to know. It should simply be a part of you, I suppose."

Rhona's borrowed room looked out over the courtyard and beyond to acres of hedge-lined farmland. Most of the estate could not be seen in the waning light and fog, but she appreciated its beauty. Wheels turned on gravel, drawing Rhona back to the window. A smaller coach than the one she arrived in, bearing the same crest on the door, rolled to a stop in front of the manor.

"He's invited a priest."

Emsley carried the cloak she held with her to the window. "Is the wedding to be today, my lady?"

"I don't believe so." Panic overwhelmed her racing heart. "Laird Crawford and I have barely spoken."

"Such a situation is not unusual."

"It's no longer usual, either." Rhona slipped her feet into a pair of house slippers, picked up a shawl from the bed, and walked to the door.

"It's not proper for you to leave the room this early before the meal. A maid will come—"

"Is this not to be my home?" Rhona waited for answer, and when Emsley provided none, Rhona left her maid staring after her.

"Father Allaway. Welcome."

"Good of ye to ask me here, Laird Crawford."

"You've heard too many confessions from me for formalities, Father. My father was Crawford to you. Please call me Braden."

"Only when we are alone in counsel, laird."

Crawford spoke aside to the butler and ushered Father Allaway into the study, where Charles and the others waited.

"Father Allaway, may I introduce the gentlemen responsible for escorting Miss Davidson."

Once pleasantries were exchanged, Father Allaway agilely lowered himself into an offered chair.

"Has it been so many years that yer now tae take a bride?"

"Some would say I waited too long."

Not long enough, thought Charles.

"Did I hear ye correctly, yer to wed

an English lady?"

Crawford shook his head. "My dearly departed English mother would have liked that, but no. Her mother was the daughter and only child of an English earl. Her father is a laird in the north." Crawford glanced at each man in turn. "There was a question of the lady's safety on the journey. These men will remain until after the wedding."

Father Allaway blinked twice. "English? The lot of ye?"

Crawford laughed. "Despite the influx of English crossing the border, and half-English like myself, Father Allaway still believes the English and Scottish are mortal enemies."

"Scotland has many friends in England, Father, including those in this room," Patrick said.

"Father, I've asked you to come to meet my bride, and if she chooses, to hear her confession."

"Of course! I'm thinking it won't take tae long, with her being only half-English." Father Allaway laughed without realizing that no one else in the room did the same.

"My lord." The butler stood in the doorway, stiff and without a blemish on his person or clothing. "Mr. Clayton has visitors."

"Of course. Please show them to the parlor." Crawford directed his attention to the men. "I apologize for not knowing you were expecting company. Will they require rooms?"

Devon stood. "They are members of our team and won't inconvenience you. If you'll excuse me, gentlemen."

Patrick lifted the glass of whisky to his lips and watched the men over the rim. Charles knew Patrick wouldn't ask about the men while in Crawford's presence, but from the look their superior sent both him and Tristan, explanations would be required later.

Rhona left her room with the intention of seeking an audience from Crawford, but she couldn't stomach it. She longed for a walk outdoors, but the darkness and weather did not permit it, nor did she wish to draw the men's attention. Instead, she wandered the halls, the soft soles of her shoes making not a sound on the carpets. She stopped in front of a painting by Berthe Morisot of a young mother gazing down at her baby. The mother watched over her child, content to spend hours memorizing the baby's features, sounds, and movements. Her mother's face replaced the mother's in the painting, and tears clouded Rhona's vision.

Since the night her father had told her that Braden Crawford was responsible for her mother's death, she never once imagined she'd be in this situation. Over the years, she'd learned to move on with her life, finding happiness in the company of her brothers and eventually, Charles. Despite her father's dislike for her, she'd known more joy and laughter than anger and heartache. Now, the emotions she once learned to accept surfaced, riotous in their desire to be remembered.

Rhona continued down the dimly lit hall until she had nowhere else to go except up or down on the servants' staircase. With great reluctance, she walked haltingly back to her room, hoping Emsley had left, but knowing she would have waited. In a strange home and given Rhona's behavior, she knew her maid would want to be certain her mistress was all right. She exhaled deeply and opened the door.

"You're still here." Rhona pulled her shawl from around her shoulders and laid it over the back of a plush chair before lowering herself onto the soft cushion.

"Of course, though I will leave if you desire it."

Rhona glanced at her maid. "I don't know how I will go through with this."

"Oh, you truly are scared." Emsley poured a cup of tea from the service a maid delivered while Rhona had wandered. "Drink this, you'll feel better. You must marry sometime.

He's a handsome man and rich, too. You'll never—"

"Please, not now." She drank her tea and set the cup aside. "Thank you, for . . . thank you. He is all of what you say and more." The words caused Rhona's stomach to clench.

"You'll not refuse him?"

Rhona laughed, but to her, the shallow vibration sounded like acceptance for what she what must do. "I will not refuse." She stood and moved behind the dressing screen. "I'd like to rest for a while. Would you please ask a maid to have our dinner sent up this evening?"

"Rhona—"

"Please, see that the maid is told."

Charles held back alone for as long as he could without drawing attention from Crawford or Patrick. He didn't doubt that Tristan and

Devon knew he waited for Rhona with the hope of speaking with her before they departed for the church. Unfortunately, everyone, with the exception of Crawford, waited outside. Rhona's maid appeared at the top of the staircase, and Charles lingered. Skirts of green silk swished behind Emsley.

"Patrick suspects what you're doing in here, but you know it won't happen, Charles." Tristan stood directly behind him and spoke in whispered tones.

Charles nodded. "This isn't right. None of this feels right."

Tristan set a hand on his shoulder. "Come, friend. The others have already left for the church."

Charles turned away from the pair descending the carpeted stairs and the man and servants waiting below.

Tristan led them outside, where a shock of cold air filled Charles's lungs. "It must be bad luck to marry this time of year."

Tristan turned away the servant who waited to accompany them to the church and addressed Charles. "We are free of curious ears and prying eyes. You have not been yourself. If it is the lady, then you must forget her."

"We were supposed to have more time."

Tristan nodded. "Devon sent his brothers on a mission of their own shortly after they arrived last night. I don't doubt they'll find whatever secrets have been kept about our roles on this assignment, but it will be too late by then."

Charles stared at the small stone chapel at the end of the frost-covered path. The chapel belonged to Crawford, and they'd been told that the priest who served in the parish visited the chapel daily. This arrangement explained the ease with which Crawford arranged an immediate ceremony. They continued to walk, the chapel edging closer and closer, a harsh reminder of Charles's present reality.

"Something else is bothering you, Charles. What is it?"

"Rhona's behavior. The night we arrived at her father's home, you saw the woman I once knew. Since we left, everything about her is somehow different. She didn't want this marriage."

"And yet, she's here."

Charles looked around. "Where's Patrick? He swore not to leave my side in the event I chose to interfere."

"He left this morning. An urgent message arrived."

"He offered no explanation?"

"Patrick rarely does."

"What did he say about Devon's brothers coming? I was certain he would say something but never asked me." Charles continued to watch the narrow road.

"Nor me."

A servant stood at the chapel doors and pulled one open upon their approach, but Charles stopped at the sound of wheels on gravel and turned to see a small carriage approaching. He stared and memorized every subtle change in her features. Her usual bright eyes were dark and fearful, and she moved like a woman dreading every step. The smile she wore contradicted what Charles knew to be an inner explosion of emotions. It was a look he knew too well. Her eyes met his briefly before Crawford escorted her up the steps and into the stone building.

Rhona's maid hurried to Charles's side and handed him a slip of paper. Before he could say anything, Emsley walked quickly to catch up to her mistress. The sound of a horse's heavy breathing against cold air drew their attention once more. Charles slipped the paper into his pocket.

Derek Clayton pulled the horse to a stop and slid from the saddle. He looked over their shoulders and pulled them aside. "Devon told us you believed Miss Davidson agreed to this marriage for reasons other than her father."

Charles nodded.

"You may have been correct. We

spoke with a magistrate in the next village over. There was some suspicion cast on Crawford when Miss Davidson's mother and uncle went missing."

Charles held his hand up when Devon came to stand at the door. "We don't have much time, Derek."

"Her mother and uncle were found dead not two days later. Davidson accused Crawford of their murder, but nothing was proven."

"She knows." Charles shook his head and called out for Devon to get back inside. He rushed across the snow and frost and entered the church, but they were too late.

"Tell him to let her go, Crawford."

"She's given them little choice, Blackwood."

Charles slowly edged around

Devon and two of Crawford's men, until he stood between Crawford and the man holding Rhona. He gave a brief indication to stop Tristan and Devon when they would have moved to stand beside him.

"She's still under our protection. Let her go." Charles spared a look at Rhona. He couldn't tell if it was fear or anger he saw. She didn't struggle, but her eyes darted as though searching for a way to loosen the man's grip on her arms.

Crawford held up a long, sharp blade. "She was set on driving this dagger into my heart."

Charles controlled each breath. His mind forced his body to remain calm rather than attack.

"She is to be my wife and no longer under your protection." Crawford stepped forward, closer to Rhona.

Charles reached her first. His own blade slid through the heavy fabric across the arm of Crawford's man. He released Rhona into Charles's arms, who flung her behind him, his own body acting as a shield. Charles pulled a pistol from his belt and pointed it directly at Crawford's chest.

"That was a foolish choice, Blackwood."

Tristan and Devon flanked Charles, holding their own guns on Crawford's men.

Devon leaned in and spoke aside to Charles. "I suppose you saw no other way to handle this."

"Don't overlook what a skirt and a pretty face can do to a man," Tristan remarked.

Charles ignored them both, though he appreciated their efforts to gain him both ground and time with their banter, but whatever happened here would not end in laughter.

"If a man wants another man's wife, he'll have to kill him first." Crawford stepped toward Charles until the barrel of the gun pressed against his chest.

Charles held the loaded gun steady, his eyes and hands unwavering. "Don't doubt it."

"I don't doubt you." Crawford turned his head to look at Rhona, who stood next to Derek and her maid. Rhona's maid clutched her arm, but it was the look in Rhona's eyes that surprised him. "She's promised to me, Blackwood."

"Promises can be broken." Charles lowered his voice so it wouldn't carry throughout the hall. "What will it take?"

Crawford spoke without

hesitation. "Marry her."

Nine

"No."

"What do you mean, 'no'?"

"The word explains itself, Crawford. What game are you playing?"

"No game." Crawford motioned for his men to lower their weapons.

The small chapel allowed for ease of overhearing what should not be heard. Charles imagined Rhona's silent rage. Crawford's behavior was as contradictory as Rhona's. The evening before he had behaved as a gentlemen and welcoming host. Charles believed him to be genuine, just as he believed the man before him was only another side to the same person. Despite every urge to dislike and distrust Crawford, he believed him.

Charles lowered the pistol and turned to address the others. "The laird and I need a few minutes alone."

Rhona moved forward, but Charles shook his head at her and inclined his head to Derek, who ignored Rhona's protests and ushered her from the room. The priest followed closely behind, and it wasn't until Devon and Tristan left that Crawford ordered his men from the chapel.

"Fear not, I would as soon let her slit my throat than harm her." Crawford offered the dagger to Charles, hilt first. "I could not risk anyone believing otherwise."

"I won't ask what fool of a man would consider giving her up, but I will ask what this is about. What happened before we entered the chapel?"

"As I told you, she was set on killing me." Crawford smiled. "I would tell you why, but I might guess that you know."

"About her mother and uncle?" Charles nodded. "We learned only moments ago. Would you care to tell me the truth?"

"Ah, you do not believe I killed her mother."

Charles tucked the pistol into his belt. "Rhona apparently does, but she was too young when her mother died. The only truth she would know is what her father would have told her." Charles paused. "How well did you know Lara Davidson?"

"I loved her, and I make no apologies for it."

"Did Davidson know of his wife's indiscretion?"

"He never gave her much thought. She bore him two sons, and he had no further use of her. That did not stop her from bearing him another child. It was because of Rhona that my Lara returned home. Her brother came to fetch her, and I never saw her again."

Charles paced the width of the aisle. "Why did you offer for Rhona, and why would Davidson agree if he believed you guilty of murder?"

"A man who is loyal to me is a servant in Davidson's household. When I learned of Calum's plans to find a husband for Rhona with the hope of easing his financial burdens, I sent a courier. I could not see Lara's daughter sold to pay for her father's mistakes."

Charles had learned of Davidson's

money troubles two years prior, but now it was imperative that they speak with Patrick. No matter how much information Devon's brothers manage to unearth, they could save precious time if Patrick revealed whatever secret he was keeping.

"You thought me a lecher?"

Charles fingers gripped the edge of a pew. "I did. My friend did not."

"Yes, Agent Clayton. Good sort, though I don't know much about him."

"He didn't know much about you either, yet he swore you were not the man I thought."

Crawford nodded. "Men rarely are, Blackwood. I have a score of years on you, yet I imagine you have seen more in your years than I have in my life. You are skilled, but your work has made you suspicious of everything."

"How much do know about us?"

"Enough to know that you are honorable and wealthy. You're a better man for her than I could ever be."

Crawford's words gave Charles pause. "You would not be quick to let her go without good reason."

Crawford pulled a small flask from his jacket pocket and took a deep swallow before offering it to Charles, who declined. "You're correct that only a fool would give her up, but I will do whatever I must to protect her. If that means marriage, then so be it."

"Don't play games, Crawford. Your English ancestry may keep you in favor with our government, but as I recall, you Scots prefer a more barbaric way of handling matters."

"Ways which you'll no doubt use if

necessary." Crawford motioned Charles to a pew and sat down in the next row. "Everything your research has told you about me, anything Rhona and her father have told you, is not entirely true. You would have done better to let her kill me."

Charles leaned back into the pew. "When did you know?"

"I knew what she believed me capable of doing and having done in the past. I saw it in her eyes when you first arrived. Hatred like that cannot be fabricated."

"Yet you were willing to marry her."

"Her father must sell her to the deepest pockets in order to keep his estate from ruin." Crawford leaned slightly. "I would not have held her to the arrangement for long."

"Then why?"

"If I tell you what I know, it won't be believed. I know the reputation of you and your friends, and I know you can learn the truth. Go back to the death of Rhona's mother, to the shameful deeds Rhona accuses me of doing." Crawford stood and moved around the pew to sit beside Charles. "Marry her, and I'll still give her father the dowry."

Charles didn't know if he wanted to shoot the man or laugh at the lunacy of this conversation. "My pockets run deeper than yours, Crawford."

"That I know, but I'll do it to keep her safe."

"From her father?"

Crawford nodded.

"I won't be marrying her, and neither will you. Whatever you believe you're protecting her from, she has the right to make her own choice."

"It doesn't work that way in our world, and you do best to remember that."

Charles stood and stepped into the aisle. "I know exactly how it works, and I promise you she'll be protected, but I won't force her into marriage."

Crawford stood nearly as tall as Tristan. "If you don't, then I will. She can't go back to her father."

"She won't be doing that either." Charles glanced toward the doorway, curious about how Tristan and Devon managed to keep Rhona from walking back in. "Was there any other agreement made regarding your marriage to Rhona?"

Crawford slowly nodded. "Your government had an interest in gaining favor with the Davidsons, but I don't know what that is. I don't care about their agenda, but I know they would have found a way to use me to get to her."

Charles swore.

"I thought only of her welfare. I would not have allowed them—"

"My quarrel isn't with you, Crawford." *Patrick on the other hand* . . . "Send a man to Davidson and tell him that you have broken your betrothal. I will supply the dowry."

"You'll marry her then?"

"No." Charles spun and walked briskly to the entrance of the church. The heavy doors fought against the ice forming around them. Tristan waited with the other men immediately outside. Devon stood near the carriage, which was where Charles knew he would find the women. He waited until Crawford's men and the priest returned to the warmth of the chapel before addressing Tristan. "Change of plans."

"It would appear so. You don't plan to marry her, Charles?"

"And follow your example?" Charles shook his head. "But I hope her father believes we're married long enough for us to solve an old case."

Tristan glanced at the carriage. "Rhona's mother."

Charles nodded. "Yes, but it won't be sanctioned."

"It doesn't have to be." Tristan walked to the carriage beside Charles.

Charles mounted his horse, and pulled the slip of paper from his pocket. He lips curved, and he looked over at the coach. Though he couldn't see Rhona, he smiled for her. The worst was not over, but his lady proved to be quite good at games of deceit.

The coach carried Rhona over hills not yet overwhelmed by snow. Her cheeks were still wet from the tears that fell when they crossed the border from Scotland. Her desire to see more of the world did not lessen the sadness of leaving home. Charles's land did not look too different from her Highlands, and yet it felt foreign. Snow-topped mountains guarded over the open valleys and lakes. Frost covered the earth as it covered her heart. Rhona watched the coach slowly drive past the small village of Keswick and wondered at the drastic change in her carefully-thought plans. Her chance to find justice for her mother's death was now lost. Crawford knew, and he let her go.

Her mind and heart did not agree on an explanation, and she feared they never would. Charles gave her the choice to escape marriage, but not about leaving Scotland. Whatever his plans, he had not sought her opinion or approval.

"My lady, we've arrived."

Beyond the trees, acres of land came into view through the coach window. Hills and meadows, and creatures hiding from the winter cold surrounded her when she stepped down. Charles held her hand for longer than was necessary, but she needed the extra support while her eyes followed the lines of stone until the top of the mansion met the gray sky. The stone steps were free of ice, giving her no further excuse to keep her hand in his. She slipped away and walked side by side with Emsley up the steps and into the house.

"She's angry." Tristan dismounted and handed his horse to one of Charles's stable boys.

"I'm familiar with the feeling." Charles thanked his driver and handed over his own horse. "Come, Ellis will remain out in this cold until we go in."

The butler and footman helped them out of their coats, and Charles ordered sandwiches to be brought in. He gave instructions for Rhona's care before joining his friends in the study.

"You always stock the best liquor." Familiar in his friend's home, Devon helped himself to the whisky. He held the glass bottle up, but only Tristan nodded.

"When will Derek and Zachary arrive?"

Devon handed a glass to Tristan, then settled into one of the plush chairs. "Before the week's end. They want to exhaust all the local sources up north. Now that we're alone, care to tell us what you discussed with Crawford?"

Charles contemplated the decanter of whisky before sitting down without a glass. "Tristan, as you surmised, there is more to the death of Rhona's mother than has been made public. Whatever business our people have with the Davidsons, particularly Alistair, is likely linked to Lara Davidson's murder."

Tristan leaned forward. "We can't

learn everything from here. We'll have to split up."

Charles stood and walked to his desk, opening the top drawer. "Devon, there is a man I'll ask you to see. His past includes a lifetime of nefarious deeds, but he also knows the men who commit far worse horrors. There's a chance he may have heard something about Lara's death." Charles pulled a bronze pendant from the drawer and passed it to Devon.

"What is that?" Tristan moved to Devon's side.

"The Blackwood crest. I may have been born British, but my family is as Scottish as Rhona's. My father once used the crest to communicate with this man. You'll have to return to Scotland, and be warned. Murdock Calhoun won't welcome you."

"And you want me to go?"

Charles nodded. "Tristan's title makes him far too British."

Devon laughed. "And Calhoun hates us all."

Charles was comforted by Devon's good humor. "I should be the one to go, but I cannot leave Rhona right now."

"No one expects you to." Tristan set his glass down on the desk. "I'll go to London. Whatever secrets our people are keeping, there are still good men in the agency."

"I will attempt to meet up with my brothers before they leave Scotland. If I don't, they'll await your instructions here."

"We need to know more about Wallace Davidson's connection with Rhona's betrothal to Crawford. It wasn't only convenience and money that caused the forging of that alliance."

Ellis stepped inside the study. "Excuse me, my lord, Mr. Ashford has arrived."

"Thank you. Show him in." Charles turned to the others. "This is a surprise. Did he not return to London on urgent business?"

Tristan nodded. "So he claimed, but he would not have had the time to make the journey and then return here so soon."

"You should delay leaving until morning."

Devon nodded and returned the crest to Charles.

"Wait, there's more." Charles pulled a folded slip of paper from his pocket and tossed it into the fire. "Wallace Davidson is very much alive." Charles smoothed the grin away before Patrick walked into the room.

"Welcome, Patrick. We weren't expecting you back this soon." Charles offered him a chair and a drink.

"I didn't plan to return. In fact, I never made it to London." Patrick thanked Charles and consumed half the liquid in his glass. "You do stock the best brandy. No, I did not make it far beyond your own borders before an agency courier delivered news of Alistair Davidson."

Charles glanced briefly at the others, no doubt wondering, as he did, if Patrick was here to share the information he'd kept hidden, or if he once again planned to use them as pawns. "Have they found him?"

Patrick nodded. "Hiding in a crofter's cottage a few miles from Crawford's estate. It appears our

original reports were correct—
Alistair planned to stop his sister's
wedding. Of course, Charles, you did
that for him."

Charles tapped his fingers lightly
on the surface of his desk, exhaled,
and walked around to sit in a chair
opposite Patrick. "Events happened
quickly. There was no time to send
word to you. Crawford surprised all
of us, me more than anyone."

"By offering Miss Davidson to
you."

Charles nodded.

"Yet, you declined to marry her."

Charles leaned casually back in the
chair, though his rigid body was in
need of action. Whatever Patrick
was not saying, Charles could
obfuscate as well, if not better, than
his supervisor. "I did. The choice of
marriage should belong to Rhona.
However, she chose to marry

Crawford in order to gain access to him."

"Why try with an audience? She must have known she would not have succeeded."

Patrick voiced the question Charles had asked himself since they left Crawford alone in the chapel. "Only the lady can answer that."

"And she is here?"

Charles nodded. "She's retired for the evening. I don't expect we'll see her again until morning. You are welcome to stay here for the night."

Patrick finished his brandy and stood while the others followed suit. "Thank you, but I must continue on to London. I only wished to deliver the news myself, along with instructions."

Tristan drew Patrick's attention. "A new assignment?"

Patrick hesitated, and Charles sensed that he didn't wish to reveal more than necessary. Charles thought the situation might be unusual, and far too secretive, even for their close network.

"Because Miss Davidson did not marry, there will be political fallout. The agency's priority is to learn all that we can from her brother in order to prevent the situation from worsening."

Charles slid his hands into his pockets, an action he rarely performed unless bored. At the moment, he didn't wish to do something with his hands he might regret. Striking a supervisory agent would be met with severe punishment. Charles opted to end the charade. "Fallout for whom? We've been fed pieces of information in short supply, unusual for us. I don't recall an assignment when we haven't either been told everything or given the time to root out the truth for ourselves."

Charles noticed both Tristan and Devon stiffen, but he knew they, too, wanted the clandestine situation to end. Tristan was the only one of them who had ever questioned Patrick or one of their assignments, and the action might have cost him his position had Tristan not been the agency's best. Tristan may be a duke, and Charles a lord, while Patrick was a mere mister, but within the agency's organization, titles meant little.

"The three of you have spent far too much time together." He glanced at each of them in turn. "Tristan was always the first one to question me if he thought I was less than honest,

Devon's strength is charm and subterfuge, but you, Charles . . . I wondered if your father's famous flair for diplomacy had been passed on. I'm pleased to see that it has." Patrick pulled an envelope from his jacket pocket and handed it to Charles. "There are secrets known to only a few until recently, and there are those who will do anything to keep those secrets safe. It has come to the attention of certain members of our government that at least one member of the Davidson family is privy to this information."

"And they don't know who?"

Patrick shook his head. "They suspect the lady's father, but they can't be certain she or her brothers don't know."

"But that isn't why they want Alistair."

Patrick smiled at Devon. "No, it's

not. Nor is it why they wished Crawford to marry Davidson's daughter. I believe the matters are entirely separate, but I speak the truth when I tell you I don't know everything." Patrick pointed to the envelope in Charles's hand. "What I do know is in there, but I suspect you've already begun your own investigation. Tread lightly, and don't tell me what you're doing."

Tristan stepped forward and Charles handed him the envelope. Tristan opened it and scanned the top pages. "I leave for London in the morning. Is there anyone I shouldn't approach?" Tristan cast his eyes toward Patrick.

"You have a gift for this work, Tristan, but it is your title that has opened doors for you, doors even I can't enter. Trust your instincts, and you'll know whom to contact." Patrick held up his hand and shook his head at them. "Ask me no more. This is one time when the agency's orders are coming from outside our circles. Do what you can, find the truth, and don't let anyone know what you're doing."

Without any more words spoken, Patrick exited the room. A few minutes later, Charles heard the heavy front door open and close.

Devon walked to the window and watched the hired coach slowly drive away. "Do we believe him?"

Tristan smirked. "He's a better liar than I thought. I can't claim not to admire him for it."

Charles pulled the crest back out of the drawer and handed it to Devon. He held the heavy disk, smoothing his thumb over the impressions on top.

"Will this Murdock fellow speak with me long enough to show him the crest?"

"You could be convincing as a Scotsman, at least long enough to get in the door." Charles pointed to the crest. "Show him that, and he'll talk. He has a debt to repay, and my father never collected." Charles offered no further explanation.

"It's early enough. The winds have eased, and if I leave now, I can buy passage on the next train north." Devon slid the crest into his breast pocket. "You never spoke of Murdock to either of us. May I assume that the agency doesn't know of him?"

"I doubt they do, which made him a convenient ally and source of information for my father. He had no direct dealings with the government of which I know, but he didn't like their involvement. My father used his position in the House of Lords only for personal gain. Kenton Blackwood would not have trusted any of them with his sources."

"I'll leave for London tonight as well. I feel an urgency to arrive before Patrick." Tristan faced Charles. "If we are to help her, she will have to tell you everything."

"A duel with Crawford would have been a more pleasant undertaking." Charles walked the men from the study to deserted foyer. "Never fear, Tristan. She wants to talk."

Charles located their coats and accoutrements. "Ellis would scold me soundly if he saw me looking after you. I'm rarely here these days. I'm not used to ringing for him."

"My lord!"

"Too late." Devon grinned.

"Ellis, our guests are leaving."

"I see that, my lord." Ellis finished helping Tristan on with his coat, brushed off his hat, and handed that over as well. Devon was fully clothed and softened his grin in deference to the butler. Ellis preceded them to the door and held it open to the early evening's waning light.

Charles stepped outside the door without a coat, much to Ellis's dismay. "Safe journeys."

"We'll return once we've learned what we can." Tristan glanced up at the second level of the massive home. "Good luck."

Ellis closed the front door and stared pointedly at Charles.

"Oh for heaven's . . . scold me if you will."

"Of course not, my lord. I simply

wish to inquire if the bells are working properly."

Charles exhaled softly. "I believe so."

"I could have the bells inspected. Perhaps the pulls are too short?"

"No, Ellis, the bells are working fine."

"Very good, my lord. Will there be anything else?"

"Nothing else until dinner."

Ellis bowed and retreated to the back of the house, where he would then descend the steps to the servants' working quarters.

Charles stood in the quiet entry hall, a fierce internal debate about whether to return to his study or attempt a conversation this evening with Rhona. Ellis returned before he managed a decision.

"My lord, Miss Davidson has requested a tray for dinner this evening."

"That is fine. Miss Davidson has traveled far and is tired."

"Very good, my lord."

Charles watched as the butler once more retreated to the nether regions of the mansion. The dining hall would be a cold and lonely room that night.

Ten

"You lasted longer than I expected. You were never one for idleness in the morning." Charles leaned against the doorframe of his study while his eyes slowly studied the delicate features and riding clothes. "Going somewhere?"

"I thought a walk."

"I don't know how you got past Ellis, but allow me." Charles pushed away and escorted her to the front door, opening it for mere seconds before closing it again.

A footman rushed into the foyer. "All is well, Tanner."

"Yes, my lord." The young footman bowed and hurried from the room.

"See there, you rendered the boy speechless." Charles held out his hands for her coat and hat. "You won't need those. Did you perchance look out the window *before* you decided to walk?"

Rhona pulled at her gloved fingers and nodded toward the door Charles had vacated. "Your study?" She didn't wait for an answer and stepped into the room. Rhona set her gloves down on the edge of his desk and allowed herself a minute to appreciate the beauty and functionality of the room. Her own tastes had never been overly feminine, and she enjoyed everything from the heavy plaid drapes and strong furnishings to the collection of both old and new books adorning the many shelves. Landscapes of England and Scotland graced the walls and another from a country she did not recognize.

"Where is this?"

Charles walked slowly to stand beside her, depositing her cloak and hat on a chair. Rhona noticed he looked at her, not the painting, when he answered. "Africa—a magnificent land. Do you know of it?"

"I've read of its beauty and danger and of the people." Rhona gingerly scrolled her fingers over one of the painted creatures. "You've been there?"

Charles nodded. "You should see it some day."

"Is it as beautiful as here? As Scotland?"

"No more or no less. It is merely different." Charles walked to the tea service brought in earlier. "Would you care for a cup?"

She smiled. "You remember how I

like it." She accepted the tea and the chair he offered. "I tell myself that I know you, but we are still strangers in some ways."

"Not in the ways that matter." Charles stoked the fire until sparks hit the stone. "It is time for us both to end any secrecy. You took a big step when you asked Emsley to give me that note."

Rhona's green eyes met and held his. She missed watching him and the way his eyes dimmed or shone, both reactions dependent upon his mood. "I did not believe I would leave the church—at least not alive or without restraints."

"Yet you believed murder was worth the risk?" Charles set aside the fire iron, lowered himself into the chair opposite her, and said nothing for almost two minutes.

"You do not believe I am foolish enough to think I could have gotten away with it."

Charles leaned forward. "It was an act?"

"Well, no, I did, and still do, want Crawford to suffer, but I was surrounded by his men."

Charles exhaled deeply. "Rhona, what exactly had you planned? Does it have something to do with Wallace?"

"I told you, I never wanted to marry Crawford. I was terrified and angry. My father threatened Wallace. I knew I could not risk my brother's life."

"Yet you went along with it."

"I had to be sure Wallace was out of Scotland. He was supposed to go to the continent, but I can't be sure. I needed time, and this farce gave me the time."

"Then why risk your life? Did you not consider what would happen if you had killed Crawford?"

Rhona sobered and set her tea aside. "I admit that I wished it. I saw an opportunity to gain justice for my mother's death. I almost didn't go through with it, nor am I certain I possess the courage to kill a man."

"You found the courage."

Rhona nodded and brushed at the tears sliding down her cheeks. "I stood beside him, and I couldn't . . . let him live when my mother was dead."

Charles embraced her hands. "Crawford did not kill your mother."

She raised moist eyes, her mouth open as if to protest. "That can't be. He was responsible for her death. I heard my father . . . oh my God."

"Listen to me, Rhona. It's not your

fault. You couldn't have known."

"I accepted what I heard. You're absolutely certain?"

Charles slowly nodded. "I didn't know until after I spoke with Crawford."

"And you believe him?"

"I do."

Rhona stood and began to pace. "Everything I believed about my mother's death was a lie? I'm not ready to accept that."

"Don't. We haven't confirmed anything. You don't have to accept my word or Crawford's. We're investigating your mother's case now—unofficially. We will learn the truth."

Rhona returned to the chair and faced Charles. "I want to accept your word without reservation."

"I will earn your trust again, Rhona, or die trying. I am the man you knew two years ago. I lied about my name and why I was there, but I never spoke falsely of my feelings."

Charles glanced at her. "I've wanted to ask. How did you know who I really was?"

"When I learned that you were coming back, my father took great pleasure in telling me who you really were. I had a few days to overcome my shock before you arrived." Rhona stared into his eyes. "I refused to satisfy my father by showing him that it mattered." Rhona leaned forward in the plush chair.

"What was your plan for Wallace?" Charles asked.

"He was not to send word until some time had passed, but I didn't know where I would be. I never expected to be here." She folded her hands in her lap.

Charles watched her fidget with a ring on her right hand. She had not worn a ring the last time he saw her.

"What is that?" He reached out and touched the smooth stone set in silver. She pulled her hand back in haste though appeared to regret the action.

"I'm sorry. It belonged to my mother. I thought to wear it for strength and to remind me why I was taking such a risk. What else did Crawford tell you?"

"To marry you."

Taken aback, Rhona withdrew further into the chair. "To what end?"

"To protect you. That is what he wished to do by taking you as his wife. He maintained that the only way to keep you safe was to release you from your father."

"My father has no control over me.

He threatened Wallace, or I never would have agreed to anything. I have a fortune, and I'm not so young that I cannot make my own decisions."

"You're certain Wallace will be safe?" Charles asked.

"I pray he will be. My father wouldn't tell me why he demanded the wedding. Do you know?"

Charles shook his head. "We have rumors, suspicions, but nothing confirmed. The reasons are likely political and financial."

"That makes sense. My father has always wanted more of everything. More power, more money, until he was consumed by both. He sacrificed everything and everyone for more. Unfortunately, he's not good with either."

"He was in financial trouble when

I last investigated him."

Rhona bobbed her head a few times and appeared to be collecting her thoughts. "I gave him money."

Charles scooted the heavy chair closer to Rhona's. "How much?"

"Five thousand pounds. It should have been more than enough, but his debts must be greater than I realized."

"Good God, Rhona. Where did you get that? We scoured your father's finances and found no mention of monies directed to you or your brothers."

"It's from my mother. She had an inheritance come down through her father, an English earl."

"When she married—"

"No." Rhona briskly shook her head. "My mother married before her father died. I don't know how it worked, but he could never touch my grandfather's money."

Charles stood and walked the length of his office a few times. "Does Alistair know about the inheritance?"

"Of course. I didn't gain control of it until I turned twenty-one, but I told Alistair."

Charles returned to his desk and pulled a small sheet of paper from the drawer. "How did your brother react?"

"He understood. Charles, what are you doing?" Rhona stood and walked toward him.

Charles wrote quickly, folded the paper, and sealed it. He then directed her to the door. Rhona stopped and firmly stood her ground. "What's going on?"

"I have to get a message delivered." Instead of walking out, Charles moved to the bell pull.

"Can you trust your butler?"

Charles smiled. "We have an understanding, or he allows me to think we do. He doesn't approve of your being here without a proper chaperone. I can ask someone from the village to come and stay if it would put your mind at ease."

"Emsley is not a proper one, but she'll have to do. I don't want a stranger watching over me." Rhona tilted her head in the way he always found endearing. "No one has ever confided in me or given me choices the way you have."

"I didn't give you a choice to come here."

"But I didn't have to marry." Rhona pressed, and though Charles didn't mind the direction the conversation was taking, they didn't have much time.

"You shouldn't have to marry a man you don't love."

"No woman should. I have heard of women embracing a freer way of life, making decisions of their own, and ignoring the wishes of their families."

Charles slowly nodded. "I am glad you're one of them."

Ellis entered on ceremony.

"We need a messenger, Ellis."

"One of the stable hands or your friend in town?"

"No need to be cryptic. Miss Davidson knows what's happening."

Ellis's brown eyes darted between them before settling on Rhona. "Very good, my lord."

"As to your question . . . from town. Can you get word to him?"

"It will be done immediately." Ellis accepted the sealed letter from

Charles and hurried from the room without pretense of backing up or bowing.

Charles turned back to Rhona. "Crawford wasn't chosen by accident. It's time to find out why." Charles walked to the door and opened it to the butler. "I know you're good, but it can't be done already."

"No, my lord, but a message was delivered here."

Charles reached out for the envelope. "In this ghastly weather? I didn't hear the door."

"The lad came to the back entrance."

"Lad? Where is he?"

"He is below."

"See that he is fed and warm, then have the coach brought around for him."

"My lord?"

"I don't care of his station. I will not send a child to find his way in this weather." Charles ripped open the envelope.

"Very good, my lord. The coach is being readied."

Charles looked up from the paper and smirked at Ellis. "I don't know why I bother giving orders."

"Yes, my lord." Ellis back out of the room and closed the door. Charles went back to reading the letter.

"Please, sit back down, Rhona."

"What's happened?"

"Please." Charles held her arm until she was sitting, then lowered himself into the chair beside her. "There is no easy way . . . this says that your brother, Alistair, has been killed."

"No."

"Rhona, listen."

She pulled her hands from his. "It can't be. He is traveling with friends. He is safe."

"It is said that he fell from his horse—"

"No one is better on a horse than Alistair." Rhona closed her eyes against the tears. "It's a mistake."

Charles reached across to her chair, lifted her into his arms, and set her on his lap. "I'm not a child," she said.

"I know." He wrapped his arms around her until she settled, her quiet sobs muffled by his shoulder.

Rhona lifted her head to look at him. "Alistair never fell off a horse in his life."

"I only know what the letter revealed—"

"No, you don't understand." Rhona wiped at her fallen tears, took a deep breath, and stood. "You know your own skill with horses, and I've seen it. There is no one I've ever known who can sit a horse better than you—except Alistair. He taught me and Wallace how to ride, and we're good."

Charles left the chair and placed his hands on her shoulders. "There's no chance?"

Rhona's laugh sounded like tears to him, but her eyes now held a determination he'd not seen in her before. "I would swear on my life that only an act of God or foul play could have thrown my brother from his mount." Rhona shook her head and walk toward the door. "I have to return home."

"No." Charles followed and reached out a hand to stop her. "You can't go home, not now."

"He was my brother!"

"And from what you've said, someone killed him. How do you know it's not the same people who murdered your mother?"

Charles feared Rhona's shallow breaths were the beginning to a fit of panic, but she soon controlled them.

"Wallace would have no way of hearing about this. He is the new heir, and I . . . he's the new heir."

"Rhona?"

"Nothing. Charles, please."

"I have to consider your safety first."

"You cannot keep me here."

"No, I can't." Charles reached past her to open the door. "If you must go, then I can't stop you, but I will have to go with you."

"Then come with me."

Charles followed her from the room and escorted her down the hall. Ellis stood nearby, but Charles indicated that they should be left alone. He kept a minimal staff since he was rarely in residence, but Charles still found the constant presence of others to be a nuisance.

"I believe you should stay."

"I have to find my brother. He could be in danger." Rhona stopped and faced him. "I assumed that if I only gave him enough time, that he would be safe from my father. I didn't once consider anyone else doing him harm. There have never been threats."

Charles gripped her shoulder. "No one has ever threatened your family? Sent letters, verbal threats?"

Rhona's body trembled beneath the weight of his hands. "Not to my knowledge. My father wasn't kind, and my mother was gone, but we were happy."

He brushed back a stray hair, and another fell over her eyes. Charles pulled her close to him and closed his eyes when she wrapped her arms around his waist.

"I have to fix this, Charles."

"I won't risk your life. Your family is dwindling, and all indications put you at the heart of it. You can't fix this alone."

Eleven

Soft white flakes melted on Rhona's skin while the wind threatened to rid her of the wool hat perched on her head. The woodland creatures rested, refusing to venture from their warm nests. She ignored the elements and breathed deeply of the cold air. As a child she had held certain beliefs, and though naïve, those beliefs fueled her and gave her the strength to live without her mother. Every truth she had believed was false because no matter what her mind told her, she trusted Charles. The realization that she could trust him more than her family frightened her.

All she ever longed for was freedom to live her life the way she chose. She had found peace with herself for many years, but she knew complete freedom was a dream so long as her mother's killer walked the earth.

Heavy fabric fell over her shoulders. She didn't have to turn to see who stood behind her.

"Your maid wanted to come out herself."

"She's never liked the cold."

"She's worried about you."

"I'll speak with her and calm her worries. Emsley is far more concerned about our future now that I am not marrying Crawford."

Charles stepped around her and blocked her view of the forest. She smiled and followed his body upward until her eyes met his.

"Your future is secure. I've seen to

that."

She studied him but couldn't see what he didn't want to tell her. "What have you done?"

"Your father expected a dowry. It was not right for Crawford to pay it."

Rhona silently talked through every possible situation that would allow her father to accept a dowry from a man other than her husband. "He won't accept it. I offered him money before you arrived. I tried everything to free myself of his plans, but he wouldn't take it."

"He already has. I had the bank draft sent before we left Scotland. A messenger delivered this a short while ago." Charles handed her the letter. "Read it if you wish."

Rhona pressed it back into his hands. "I don't. I've had enough of his lies, of feeling helpless. I've been wrong about many things, and I'm tired of being wrong."

She turned and looked back at the house. Rhona wasn't meant to remain in quiet parlor playing the dutiful wife. She may choose that life someday, but not yet.

"Help us find the truth and bring a killer to justice."

"You make it sound simple."

He closed the space between them and held her face in his hands. "It won't be easy. Stand beside me, work with me. I promise you justice."

Rhona's soft breaths quickened. "To make such a commitment would mean giving up my freedom. I'm not ready to do that."

"You make your own choices. Not me, not your father."

Charles saw her struggle with the rare opportunity he presented. She had never been given that freedom, and the society in which they lived still looked down upon that freedom.

"I have cared little for what's proper these many years, Rhona, but I would never do anything to dishonor you. Tristan's home is not too far, and I know his wife would welcome you. From there we can work to find your answers."

She surprised him. She always did. "Blackwood Crossing is closer to Scotland, and it is in Scotland where I believe we'll find the answers."

Charles grinned. "We have a lot of work to do."

A surge of excitement coursed through Rhona's every limb. Her heart pounded swiftly and she enjoyed a lightweight sensation coursing through her mind and body. When Charles had left her in Scotland two years ago, she dreamt of what adventures he might have taken. She longed to see wondrous places. Her heart and her home would forever be on Scottish soil, but she knew there was more to the world. She ached for it, and Charles was giving her the one thing she always desired.

She smiled at her maid, who did not understand her enthusiasm.

"Don't fret, Emsley."

"My lady—Rhona—why did you agree? We should be on our way home, to Davidson Castle."

Rhona clutched the pocket of her skirt. It held the letter her father had sent to Charles. She had read it only an hour prior and wept. "My father does not wish me to return."

"Why did you not say something?"

Emsley reached out to set her gloved hands on Rhona. "You should have married the Scotsman, my lady."

"Please, don't ask me to explain." Rhona looked out over the wintry landscape.

"It's madness to go to your brother. He's a prisoner, my lady. No good can come of this."

Rhona spared her maid a glance, sympathy for her ignorance escalating. She had not told Emsley of her plans with Wallace or for anything else. She claimed to trust the maid, her friend, but had not done so recently.

"Emsley, enough. If you are uneasy, I will secure passage and escort for you to return to my father's home or to London. If you stay with me, this is my path now."

"You ask me to stay with you, but

you won't tell me why you will follow this man?"

"There are few in this world I trust. I do hope you'll stay with me, but I cannot tell you more than what I already have. This man, Charles Blackwood, is a man I trust with my life. I will follow him if it means finding a way to the other side of my troubles."

Rhona waited for her friend to speak up and promise to stay with her, but Emsley said nothing more. She sat in a chair near the hearth and sewed. Not once more did she look at Rhona.

"Will you stay, Emsley?"

"It's not proper, my lady. You and I alone here in this house with a man not your husband, not your brother or father. He's a stranger, and the gossip will ruin your reputation." Emsley looked up from her thread and cloth. "But, I will not leave you."

"My reputation is not important. I have only to answer to myself and my God. What people choose to believe is not my concern." Rhona settled herself into the other chair by the hearth. The flames danced and warmed her blood. Still, Rhona preferred the cold. Shouts outside the mansion walls beckoned her back to the window.

"Can you see who it is, my lady?"

Rhona leaned as closely to the cold window as possible. "We're too high and the fog is thick. It's a lone rider."

Rhona turned from the window. "In this weather, he's mad. I'll go and—"

"You'll not!" Emsley dropped her sewing and stood. "You may not care about what is proper, but I insist you behave like a lady."

Amused, Rhona looked at her maid. "You speak like a governess scolding a nursery girl."

"You bring it out in me." Emsley sat back down and picked up a blouse in need of mending. "I'll say nothing more."

"You're normally quite fun and used to my odd behavior."

"At least you admit it's odd." Emsley glanced up.

Rhona's mother had raised her daughter to dine with queens and dance with princes. She was raised to be courted by wealth and title. A child of her family's station was destined for greatness. Rhona had enjoyed her mother's lessons and her talk of a grand future with a man of great importance. Then her mother died. Her governess ensured that Rhona never forgot her mother's lessons, but as years passed, their world began to stifle her.

Charles opened a new world for her, one that presented her with both freedom and danger. Her imagination bathed in the possibilities, and her spirit hoped for adversity and adventure. It may last a day, a month, or a year, but for however long, she would choose.

"You are not truly free, my lady. You are here by his grace. If you leave, where would you go? How would you care for yourself? You are not free."

Rhona's overwhelming joy tumbled down as rocks over a cliff. Not because Emsley was right, but because she must continue to lie to her friend. By her mother's wisdom and Charles's generosity, she was free.

Emsley shook her head at Rhona when she moved to answer the knock at the door. "Allow me to pretend you are still proper." Emsley opened the portal but moved quickly out the way. Ellis stood at the door.

"Lord Blackwood wishes your audience."

"Please tell him I'm coming."

Tristan and Charles looked up from the map laid out on Charles's desk.

"Miss Davidson, it's good to see you again." Tristan accepted her hand. "I apologize for my absence these past few days. Are you comfortable here?"

"Yes, thank you, Your Grace. I give you leave to call me Rhona."

"And please call me Tristan." He released her hand and Rhona walked directly to the desk to stand near

Charles, though her attention remained on Tristan while he spoke. "My wife, Alaina, would enjoy meeting you. Perhaps when we have accomplished all we need to, you'd consider a visit to Claiborne Manor."

"I'd be delighted. Your wife is an understanding woman to be away from you for so long."

Tristan laughed. "I retired once and will again after this assignment is complete. Alaina and I have a young son at home."

"You are a fortunate man, and Charles is fortunate to call you friend."

"When all of this is over, I hope you will also call me friend."

"All of this . . . it sounds like a much greater task the way you say it."

"It may be more complicated than we realized."

She enjoyed Charles's hand on the small of her back when he guided her around to the back of the desk. "Tristan was able to gather new information from a contact in London. We've mapped out what we know of your mother's travels the months before she died and Crawford's travels in the months after."

Rhona studied the pins and lines covering the desk-sized map. What she noticed most was that her mother had journeyed south far more than she remembered. "What are these darker lines?"

Charles said, "Those represent where your brother, Alistair, has been, at least from what we've been able to verify. It's not much, but it helps us to know whom he may have met."

Rhona looked up from the map.

"Alistair has been at university or abroad all these years. This information can't be correct."

"I'm sorry to say that he was seen in all of these locations." Tristan tapped the cities or towns on the map.

Rhona traced the dark lines with her finger. "What else?"

Charles handed her a sheath of papers. "Tristan brought these back. They're orders from someone within the agency addressed to Wallace."

Rhona glanced at the dates. "Impossible."

"Rhona—"

She turned on Devon. "No. I will tolerate suspicion on my father, and I will even keep an open mind about Alistair, but I won't believe Wallace is involved. He's far too young, and he's always been the kindest, gentlest—"

"Rhona." Charles gently turned her toward him. "We don't believe the orders either."

A delicate pink hue rose to Rhona's cheeks. "Oh. I apologize."

"Quite all right." Devon's grin appeared to put her at ease, but Charles continued to watch her. "We don't know how Wallace's name ended up on these orders, but there is someone inside who at least knows Alistair's true involvement."

Rhona set the papers down on the map and looked first at Tristan, then to Charles. "Do you believe my brother is guilty?" She saw his hesitation. "Please, it does matter what you think."

"It's too soon to know."

Rhona nodded. "I see. Where do we go from here?"

Tristan said, "Charles told me of

your arrangement. Are you certain this is what you want?"

"You disapprove?"

Charles grinned. "Someday Tristan will tell you the story of how he and Alaina met and wed."

"Charles is an honorable man, but I do hope you've considered the potential consequences."

"I've considered them, Tristan, but they aren't important."

Tristan smiled. "You'll do well in our company."

Rhona returned the smile but faltered as her eyes followed the dark line. "My brother came here?"

"No." Charles drew an invisible line across the land. "North of here, though I don't know if I believe the reports. It will be difficult to confirm now that he's—"

"Dead?" Rhona's lips tightened.

"Why don't you believe it?"

"The estate north of here is owned by Lord Kitchener. If the old man isn't complaining about poachers, he's arguing with merchants in town who won't deliver to his doorstep."

"You must be right." Charles and Tristan looked at her curiously. She said, "Alistair despised the company of anyone older than our father."

Charles asked, "If an old man, such as Lord Kitchener, proved useful to Alistair, would he then not make an exception?"

Rhona considered that but shook her head. "I don't believe so, but my brother has already proven to be someone other than who I believed."

"It's time we paid a visit to my neighbor." Charles smiled at her. "It would be my pleasure to have Tristan's cousin accompany us."

Rhona returned the smile.

"Cousin?" She looked at Tristan. "Do you have Scottish cousins, Your Grace?"

Tristan grinned. "Did I not mention the distant Davidson branch of the family tree?"

Charles leaned against Rhona, a gesture she remembered with fondness. "Are you nervous?"

"Not about meeting Lord Kitchener, but I do wonder if my brother was here, who else did he meet? You said the lord has no family."

"None that I've ever seen. He never married or fathered children, at least not legitimate. If there is family, they're not known to me, and Kitchener has been Blackwood's neighbor all my life."

"We'll soon know with certainty," Tristan said.

The coach rolled to a stop in front of the country house. Modest in size, the stone edifice appeared to have been built more than a century ago. Rhona looked more closely at the fine cracks in the stone. "Is he a lord of meager means?"

Charles stepped from the coach and assisted her down. "He receives a small yearly income, enough to keep up with the house and land, but I don't think he cares. I offered to purchase the estate three years ago and allow him to remain in the house, but he refused."

Tristan held out his arm for her. "Shall we, cousin?"

Rhona slipped her arm through Tristan's and walked up the stairs with the men. A butler waited with the door open.

"Will you require a stable for your horse while you're here, Lord Blackwood?"

"We don't intend to keep his lordship for long, Blakely."

The butler nodded and escorted the small group into a comfortable sitting room. A fire burned in the hearth, and lit lamps were set throughout the room. The additional light proved necessary. Heavy curtains were drawn across the windows, blanketing the room in darkness, save for the soft glow around the lamps and fire. Rhona removed her hand from Tristan's arm and pulled off her gloves in an effort to cool her skin.

Charles stood close. "Lord Kitchener doesn't like the sun."

Rhona thought of the cloud-filled sky on their way in. "Does the sun shine in England?"

Charles smiled and guided her farther into the room. "Lord Kitchener."

"Blackwood! Come, sit." Rhona expected their host to stand, but he remained seated in a chair too large for his body, a blanket covering his legs. "Forgive me, but my legs do not work as well as I would like." The lord instructed his butler to bring tea and motioned them all to sit.

Rhona waited for Charles to finish the introductions and smiled at Lord Kitchener's question about her presence. "My cousin was kind enough to bring me along for a visit."

"Is my neighbor a good host? You're welcome to stay here if he's not."

Rhona stifled the urge to fetch a glass of water when the lord pounded his chest against a succession of coughs. She suspected his bout of laughter brought on the fit. The butler walked in with a tea service, deposited it, and handed his lord a glass from the tray.

"That will be all for now, Blakely." Once the butler left, Kitchener motioned to the tray. "Forgive me again, but I'll be no help with that either. I don't like the servants fussing over me too much."

"I don't mind." Rhona smiled at him and poured tea into four china cups. She stood and offered a cup to their host.

"I don't like my name, never have. I want friends to call me Kit." Kitchener pointed at Charles. "This one won't do it."

Rhona felt a kinship with the lord and wished she had known him in his earlier days. "We will be friends then?"

"Any true friend of young Charles is a friend of mine."

Charles enjoyed the exchange between Rhona and the old lord. He had always liked Kitchener, and he had spent many hours with him as a child, when he was first told to call the old man "Kit" rather than "my lord." His own father had been a general of his household, knowing nothing of the love and kindness children needed. Proper address, manners, and titles were always required. Charles didn't regret his childhood, or the years after when his father began to groom him, but there was no love between father and son.

"I regret my friends and I are not here for a social visit. I want to ask if you've ever met an Alistair Davidson, or if he's been here."

Kitchener looked at Charles over the top of his tea cup. "He's kin to your lovely companion." He indicated Rhona.

Charles laughed. "There's nothing wrong with your eyes."

"Of course not! This one has the look of the young man, but her eyes are kinder and softer. Who is he to you?"

"He's my brother."

Kitchener bobbed his head and shrugged his shoulders. "I've seen the boy, but I don't know him."

"We were told he visited here many times."

"He has but not to see me." Kitchener held his chest again to control another fit of coughing. "Excuse me. This young Alistair is a friend to my nephew."

Charles allowed himself a moment

of surprise. "You have living family?"

Kitchener's face turned forlorn. "Regrettably, my brother's son outlived him. He's after the land and the money. Got himself into debt, but I won't pay."

Charles decided to speak with Kitchener later with another offer to buy the land. "Is your nephew in residence?"

"Alden was here a fortnight ago, but he never remains for long." Kitchener looked at Charles with the eyes of a man who had seen too much and lived too long. "What has my nephew done?"

"I don't have that answer yet."

"Charles Blackwood, I have known you the whole of your life. My ears still hear and my eyes still see. I know who you are, and I know what you do."

Charles exchanged a glance with

Tristan, who nodded once.

"Alistair Davidson was in the custody of my friends. It's important that we learn all we can about where he's been and whom he's met. Someone may be able to speak on his behalf."

"I don't know if you want to help him or crucify him, but Alden won't be much help." Kitchener motioned to a small desk standing against the wall. "There's a letter from my nephew somewhere on that mess. I don't understand it, but you might. I don't know where Alden lives, but you can find him through my solicitor."

Charles walked across the desk to find the letter, which was buried beneath another envelope from a firm whose name Charles recognized. "And who is your man?"

"Mr. Peter Dane."

The envelope showed the address of a London firm, and Charles knew all of the attorneys there. Peter Dane was not one of them.

"You've been a tremendous help, thank you. Is there anything I can do for you?"

"If Alden has found himself in trouble, I imagine we'll speak again soon." Kitchener pulled on the bell rope that hung from the wall beside his chair. "If he's done wrong, I won't speak for him."

Charles helped Rhona up, and the trio walked toward the door, where Kitchener's butler waited.

"Blackwood."

Charles turned, his hand still holding Rhona's arm. Kitchener stared but not at him.

"Alden once mentioned a girl with hair the color of Highland oak and eyes gray when the sky storms. I hope to see you again someday, Rhona Davidson."

Charles led Rhona from the room, and it wasn't until they were back in the coach and on their way, that Rhona asked him what Kitchener had meant. Charles glanced at Tristan, then out the window. He hesitated in answering, and it vexed him because he didn't have words to comfort her. He had promised himself there would be no more lies between them.

"Kitchener has a way of making words pretty, but he spoke of you."

"His nephew knows me?"

"Is your brother nice to look upon?"

If Rhona thought the question odd, she kept her thoughts to herself. "Both of my brothers are handsome. Why?"

"Alden may know you by sight, or he may have imagined you from your brother. There is no way to know until we find him. It does confirm that he is somehow involved." Charles pushed back the curtain over the window and left it open. He preferred to see where he was going. "If he has met you, but you don't know him, then his deception makes your brother more suspect."

"I feel as though I'm in the middle of a giant puzzle, and I don't know which piece to place first."

"That's the trick of puzzles," Tristan said. "Until two pieces fit together, you cannot know what image will begin to form."

"How do you know when you've found the right pieces?"

"When you can put them together and see the third, then the fourth, until all events fall into place."

"And this is what you do with your life?" Rhona met Charles's eyes.

"When threats are made on the lives of those who can't defend themselves, and when the safety and security of our country is at stake, someone must do what is necessary."

Twelve

"How is she?"

Charles softly closed the door to his study. His grip tightened around the handle. "As well as you'd expect." He pushed away from the door and walked to the window. The room was his favorite in the house, for the windows faced the valley and from here he could see the forests, lakes, and mountains. The village clustered along the lake shore while the house stood as a sentinel atop the hill.

Blackwood Crossing was not a stronghold built to secure the borders, but Charles always trusted that it was a symbol to the people of Keswick. It had survived two centuries of Blackwoods, and despite Charles's dislike for his own father, the former viscounts had always looked after the people.

Charles accepted a glass from Tristan and stared at the finger of whisky at the bottom. "God help me for thinking this way. With Alistair free, our chances of solving this case or the death of Rhona's mother have significantly increased." Charles turned from the window. "Devon, you didn't say how you came to be there."

"Our men were transporting Alistair north, and he was very much alive. I was near Kingussie when I spotted them."

Charles set down the untouched whisky. "Prisoners are to be transported to London."

"I told them as much, but they

were instructed to return him to the Northern Highlands."

"Davidson Castle. They were taking him home."

Devon nodded. "That is my guess."

"I do hate playing this game from the outside," Tristan said. "Patrick always follows protocol. Would you have countered his orders?"

"According to the agents, the orders came from Patrick."

Charles looked at his friends. "This may not mean what we all think it does."

Tristan said, "And likely isn't, but we must operate under the assumption that Patrick planned for Alistair's escape."

"You're serious?"

"Devon, I've worked more closely with Patrick than anyone else in the field, and if he taught me anything, it's to suspect everyone—even our own."

"Charles, who sent you the letter telling of Alistair's death?"

"It wasn't signed, but it bore the agency seal, and no one outside the agency has that kind of access. I need to tell Rhona her brother's alive but now missing."

"Alistair might come to her."

Charles swallowed once, emptying his glass. "We're not going to use her that way."

"She might be willing."

Charles turned on his friend. "Of course she would be, which is why it won't be mentioned. However, Alistair's escape does present us with an opportunity." Charles returned to his desk and the map. "If we can intercept him before the others, then we'll have a chance to question him on our terms."

Devon said, "The agency has men everywhere, many of whom we can't trust."

Charles grinned. There was no one in the British Isles better at subterfuge than Devon or better with disguises. Charles had managed to fool many in his career, but Devon was the only one who had managed to dupe them. "I'll keep watch at Kitchener's. Devon, you do whatever it is you do."

Tristan stepped forward. "I'll go and see Murdock Calhoun. He doesn't have to know I'm a duke."

Charles looked at Tristan. "He'll know you're titled. If ever there was a man our government could use, it is he. It doesn't matter now, but be warned that he won't be friendly."

Devon handed the disk emblazoned with the Blackwood crest to Tristan who said, "I'll be gone a sennight at least."

Devon reached across the desk and pointed to a small village on the map. "I planned to travel by horse from here before I was waylaid by news of Alistair. I found a man called Kevin Scott willing to supply me."

"Then I'll take the same route." Tristan secured the crest on his person and faced Charles. "Are you certain we aren't needed here?"

Charles discerned that Tristan was asking if Rhona needed them. "She needs us to find her brothers, and more importantly, she needs to know what happened to her mother."

Tristan nodded. "Then I'll take my leave and return in a week. Good luck to you both."

Devon said, "I'll need to visit the milliner."

Charles raised his brow. "Dare I ask why you need a lady's hat?"

Devon smiled. "Better not to know."

"Good luck to you then, friend."

Devon sobered. "We won't let you or Rhona down, Charles. I know this has become a matter of personal importance."

"It's as though we've journeyed back to the case involving Alaina. We watched how mad with worry and determination Tristan became. This should be simpler."

"You think so?"

Charles's eyes followed Devon from the room, wondering if his friend was right. He wouldn't delude himself to think he felt nothing for Rhona, but it was different for Tristan. He and Alaina had been meant for each other since the day they met, and neither ever gave up on that connection. Charles had placed duty above love when he left Rhona in Scotland. He wouldn't make that mistake again.

The sun descended behind the snow-topped mountains, coating the valley in moonlight. The fire spit and crackled behind Rhona, beckoning her to its warmth, but she remained by the window. From there she had watched Tristan leave, and then Devon a short time after. That was two hours ago, and yet Charles had not called for her except to have a maid ask if she would be dining downstairs. Rhona almost said no, but she no longer wished to hide in her room, waiting for something else to happen.

Rhona was used to feeling

ineffectual, and sitting alone in her room served nothing but her own worries. Charles gave her a unique chance to do something that mattered, and barely a day had passed before she reverted back to the fruitless existence in which she was raised.

She walked across the room to the bell pull but snapped her hand back. She'd spent every waking moment with Emsley for company. Rhona told herself that it was Emsley who deserved time with others. It was highly improper for her to dine without first changing, but tonight she didn't want to be proper. Charles told her that he had little regard for formalities when at home. She would follow his example.

A low-burning fire warmed the grand dining room, and the servants left the curtains drawn back, allowing slivers of moonlight in through the windows. The painting above the hearth appeared to have been commissioned for the house and the space. The picturesque scene, embodying the beauty of Charles's valley and Blackwood Crossing, brought a smile to Rhona's lips. For many years she had desired to travel beyond Scotland's borders, even if only to return to England, and now that she was gone, a part of her ached for home. At least here she enjoyed a sense of welcoming.

Rhona took advantage of her early arrival to walk the length and width of the room. Another painting hung above a long sideboard, a scene of animals from deepest, darkest Africa. She had read about the creatures from a book in Charles's library, but seeing their likeness was far more tantalizing to her imagination. Her mother used to tell her stories of their family history, of the battles they fought and the lives lost. For centuries, outsiders had tried to take Scottish soil from the Scots, and Rhona believed that the battles had been worth fighting. Her land was worth fighting for, as was her family.

Alistair's escape might mean his death, or it could be an opportunity for them to find him first. She was certain Charles had already considered that. When Charles informed her that Alistair was alive, a seed of hope had planted itself in her heart. She couldn't understand what benefit lying about her brother's death afforded anyone, unless it was meant to be a distraction. In which case they would stop looking for Alistair, but why when they would certainly learn the truth?

She had never questioned her brother's loyalty to family and country, but her sheltered life had not allowed much intrusion from the outside world. Charles's presence in her life had been a gale force, and she'd welcomed it without care for the tumult he brought with him. He was new and different. A man of the world interested in a young woman from the Northern Highlands—it was unfounded in her mind. Loving and losing Charles were the two most profound moments of her life since her mother's death.

"I often wonder what you're thinking."

Rhona smiled and slowly turned around. "I assure you my thoughts are not worth much."

"They're worth something to me." Charles pushed away from the door and walked toward her. The years slipped away, and Rhona remembered him as he was when they first met.

"I eagerly accepted your proposal to join your investigation, but I didn't consider how it might affect me."

"Have you reconsidered?"

Rhona shook her head. "No, but I want to be prepared for whatever I might learn. How do you do it?"

"It's not that simple."

"Please, I need to know."

Charles studied her carefully, searching for an inkling of fear, but he saw only conviction. He turned at the sound of footsteps in the hall. Ellis stood in the doorway, justifiably confused.

"My apologies, Ellis, we have

bypassed the parlor."

"Very good, my lord. Dinner is ready." The butler disappeared back through the doorway.

Charles pulled out a chair for Rhona. "When I'm in London, or on the rare occasion I venture to a party or entertain here, I assure you I am quite proper."

Once Rhona was seated, Charles sat in his place at the head of what he considered a monstrous table. The furnishings remained entirely as they were when his father lived. He did not agree with many of his father's actions, but they did share similar tastes in both décor and fine whisky.

"Let us enjoy the meal, and we will speak later."

"We are quite alone."

Charles smiled. "I assure you we're

not. My tales are not meant for sharing over a meal." The meal was served, and they ate in comfortable silence with the occasional comment regarding weather or Keswick. Rhona waited, but Charles sensed her impatience.

When the meal ended, Charles escorted her into the study. "I hope you don't mind, but it's my favorite room in the house."

She smiled. "Mine too, or from what I've seen."

"We can tour it now if you'd like."

"Your delay tactics won't work." Rhona regarded him carefully. "How do you live with the choices and the truths you discover?"

Uncomfortable, despite the comforts of his surroundings, Charles sat in one of two plush chairs situated before the stone hearth in his study. He thought speaking with

Rhona in work surroundings would make it easier on him, but he dreaded shocking her with the reality of his life. Her mother's death touched her emotionally, but she never saw what happened. She didn't witness blade or bullet slicing through Lara Davidson's body.

"It can be difficult. I don't want to say it can harden a person, but it does."

"You have proven to be honorable, not hardened."

Charles sensed in her a powerful courage, naïve though it may be. He decided to feed her determination. "Innocent people die even though we do everything in our ability to prevent it. Secrets are revealed, promises are broken, and we sacrifice everything."

"For the greater good?"

Always a man possessing great confidence, Charles wondered if she could truly accept what he'd done in the past, but not telling her would mean no future with her, and he was brave enough to admit that scared him.

He glanced up when she spoke again.

"Was there ever any other choice to make?"

This was the woman he once knew. The calm voice of reason. Even when he left her behind, she was angry, but she did not shout or curse him.

"I have regrets." He weighed his next words carefully. "But I would not have chosen differently."

Rhona drew on her lower lip, a nervous gesture. On her it was endearing.

"Doing the job isn't always enough, Rhona." Charles finished his whisky and set the glass aside. He leaned forward, his voice lowered, and his focus on Rhona. "What you have to understand is that what I do requires a certain distance between my emotions and the assignment. If I can't do that, I have to walk away or live with it, but I don't accept it. I don't forget what I've done or make apologies for it."

"That sounds like a cold way to live."

Charles nodded. "I don't want that for you."

"You said I could help, and I want to."

"I may regret opening up this part of my world to you." Charles stood and walked to his desk. "But I won't push you away. Let me show you something."

Rhona left the chair and stood on

the other side of the desk facing him.

"Tristan has gone to meet a man named Murdock Calhoun. I'm hopeful he'll have heard something about your mother's death." Charles pointed to another spot on the map. "Devon will meet up with his brothers here."

"What are they doing?"

Charles managed a smile. "Devon has his own way of unearthing secrets, and we like to give him a wide berth when possible. He'll return when he's learned something useful." Charles then pointed to their location at Blackwood Crossing. "We will remain here."

"How does that help? You would be out there with them if I wasn't here."

"True, but because Lord Kitchener's nephew is somehow connected with Alistair's actions, someone will need to remain close by. If your brother has managed to stay alive since his escape, then he'll need to hide."

"If Alistair has done all he's been accused of, then he's a fool, but he's not stupid. He won't return to a familiar place."

Charles nodded. "I agree, but Alden Kitchener may go to him, which is why you need to stay on my land."

"How am I to help if I'm sequestered here?"

Charles sensed her growing frustration. "I want you to be involved, but I also need to keep you safe. Everyone entangled in this may know who you are simply by looking at you. Kitchener saw it, and he's half blind, regardless of what he claims. I'll be nearby at all times. If you need me, ask Ellis to send a footman. He'll know how to find me."

"He'll know, but I won't?"

"If I told you, would you follow me?"

Rhona remained silent, which told Charles all he needed. He admired her spirit. "I'll leave in the morning immediately after breakfast."

"I'll endeavor to be useful here."

Breakfast over, Rhona returned to her room once Charles left the mansion the following morning. From her high window, she watched him ride out. The sun saw fit to shine, melting away what little snow remained on the long drive. Charles rode his steed easily over the stone and dirt and vanished beyond the trees.

"Are you truly unhappy?"

Rhona started and turned. "Must

you move about so quietly?"

"I didn't realize I was. You have a few items that need mending. There's little else for a lady's maid to do in a strange home."

"Hardly a thing to admit to your employer. Besides, you're also a companion." Rhona followed Emsley's movements, longing once more for solitude. "I'm going riding." Rhona walked across the room to the armoire and changing screen.

"You can't go riding alone, and you know I'm afraid of horses."

"Emsley, I ride often alone."

"When?"

Rhona cringed, grateful that the screen blocked her view of the scolding scowl she was certain Emsley wore. "When you thought I was napping."

"Rhona Davidson!"

"I don't nap, Emsley, I never have. I find it incredibly dull." Rhona struggled with her buttons but refused to ask for assistance. She had her riding habits designed to allow for ease of dressing, which was useful since she tended to ride when no one knew. Two of her habits allowed her to ride astride, which to her represented her first rebellion against what her father believed a lady should not do.

Rhona walked around the screen, expecting Emsley to block the bedroom door. Instead, the maid sat in one of the chairs by the hearth with her sewing set haphazardly on her lap.

"You're doing that in here?"

"You said you always preferred having me close by."

Rhona considered that. "Was I really so demanding?"

Emsley lowered the needle and thread. "You've always been kind to me and the other servants."

A tiny spark of guilt began to form, but Rhona quashed it. "I'll be careful."

Emsley nodded. "It's best that we're not at Davidson Castle. Your father would dismiss me if he knew how inappropriately I've allowed you to behave."

Rhona wasn't certain what happened, but for a moment she felt like the one being dismissed. She left the room and then realized her problem once she reached the front hall. Normally she would ask Emsley to speak with Ellis about preparing a horse for her. Rhona had seen the stables when they returned from Lord Kitchener's residence, but this wasn't her home, and she had no right to procure a horse on her own. Instead of walking the mansion like a fool, she went into Charles's study and found the bell pull. If the butler thought it odd that she was downstairs alone, he said nothing of it.

"I'd like to go riding, Ellis. Might you have the stables prepare a horse?"

He stared at her, but it lasted only a moment, so Rhona couldn't be certain. He offered his standard, "Very good, miss," bowed, and exited the room.

The cold air tickled at Rhona's neck, but she didn't mind. Her borrowed mount was a striking gray Thoroughbred. The stable boy who helped her voiced his uncertainty that a lady could ride such an animal, though he assured her the mare was the calmest and sweetest horse in their stables. Rhona insisted the mare was perfect, that she could ride, and she preferred to ride without company.

She smiled into the wind and stared across the hills and village to the expansive Keswick Lake below. Her time indoors had not been entirely wasted. Rhona had spent the hours apart from Charles and Emsley reading books and maps she borrowed from the impressive, yet functional, library. She filled her own library with the pretense that Wallace required a wide collection of books from which to read and study. Once her father realized that she used the library more than her brother, he forbade the addition of any more texts.

Rhona had longed to attend St. Andrews with her brothers or

University College in London in an effort not to embarrass her father in Scotland, but he refused. That didn't stop her from learning, and the result was a mind eager for knowledge. Rhona learned a good deal about Charles's home from the papers and texts in his study. She didn't believe he would mind. Unlike her father, Charles was a forward-thinker, willing to embrace new ideas. She hoped those ideas extended to her borrowing a horse and riding without an escort. Rhona promised Ellis that she would remain close to the house.

Charles didn't tell her where he would be that day but did say he would return before the evening meal. Rhona guided the mare across the damp fields to look upon a familiar view. Quietness surrounded Lord Kitchener's home, much as it had the day before. She approached the boundary Charles had pointed out and was surprised to see how close Kitchener's house stood to the edge of the property.

An approaching coach drew her attention to the drive, but it was the man descending from the vehicle who interested her. The wind's ferociousness increased, yet Rhona ignored it, held her hat in place, and continued to watch the man until he disappeared inside Kitchener's house. He stood tall, with hair the same red hue as her father's, and a bearing not unlike Alistair's. Rhona urged the horse towards a small copse of narrow pine trees. They offered minor protection from the elements but allowed her to view the comings and goings without being noticed.

Thirteen

"Did you enjoy your outing?" Charles stood in the doorway of his study, his arms crossed, and with what Rhona could only surmise as amusement in his bearing.

"Quite, thank you." Rhona removed her hat and cloak, handing both to Ellis, and thanked the man before he quietly disappeared to some corner of the mansion. "I didn't expect you for hours."

Charles smiled at her. "You sound like a wife."

Rhona's next remark lay silent on her tongue, and she opted for kinder words. "I didn't realize the time. I apologize if I worried you."

"Not at all. I saw you when I rode in and watched from the window." He pointed to a stationary telescope, a device she assured herself had not been there on previous visits to the room.

Charles offered her a drink, but she declined.

"Miss Hargrave asked for an audience while you were huddled behind the trees."

"Emsley? Is she well?" Rhona turned back toward the door, but Charles's assurance stopped her.

"She is well, I promise, but beside herself about what to do with you." Charles handed her the drink she had previously declined.

"It was not appropriate for her to discuss that with you. I'll speak with her, and she won't disturb you again."

"I was under the impression that you and she were friends."

Rhona nodded and drank from the glass, enjoying the warmth the smooth liquid provided. "We are friends, or as close of a friend as I've ever had. My father wasn't keen on visitors, and I knew only the women in our small village or my distant cousin whom I'd seen only once years before. Emsley is the first female whose presence was socially acceptable in my father's eyes."

"Yet, since your arrival, you've behaved differently with her."

Rhona set aside the glass and shook her head at Charles's offer to sit. He remained standing because she did.

"I owe her an apology."

"I didn't say that."

"You didn't have to, and were I honest with myself, I could admit how unapologetic I feel. Your home is the first place I've appreciated any true sense of freedom. I went riding today in part because I knew no one would stop me. I have no one here to instruct and demand, and I find it exhilarating." Rhona walked to the window and gazed through the telescope, still focused on the place where she'd hid only a short while ago.

"Your father was rarely in the country."

"No, but he had his spies." She spun around. "You treat me as an equal. Even your request for me to remain inside wasn't an order."

Charles looked at her curiously, and she dearly wished to know what thoughts his mind held.

"Rhona, you are my equal. Some might even say my superior in every way. I asked you to stay inside because I care about you and wish only to keep you safe."

The burning in Rhona's chest subsided as relief took over. "Thank you. I'll speak with Emsley now and return downstairs for dinner." Rhona moved to the door, but turned around, her hand on the doorframe. "May I ask why you returned early?"

Charles hesitated long enough for Rhona to suspect he may not answer.

"I hoped to tell you when I had irrefutable proof."

Rhona braced herself. "Proof about what?"

"I believe Alistair is in England."

Her blank expression conveyed the magnitude of her disbelief. "You said he was dead."

Charles ached from the pain he saw in her eyes, witnessed in her shaking body. He helped her sit in one of the plush chairs, but he rather doubted she felt his hands on her waist or heard his soft assurances. He promised to tell her everything and wished away the pain that accompanied her growing knowledge. Charles knew the surprises and sadness would get worse before the ultimate truths were finally revealed. She was possessed of the most contradictory emotions. Once the news penetrated her rational mind, anger and fortitude would take over.

"You never met my brothers. Not once in all the time we were together. How do you know it was Alistair?"

Charles smoothed a loose curl away from her eye. "I met your father. Do your brothers look like him? Do they possess his red hair and tall stature? You spoke of Alistair in detail when we first received word of his death. You weren't coherent, but you spoke of him quite fondly."

"Wallace and I look more like my mother, but Alistair . . . he is our father's son." She raised her damp eyes. "You could be mistaken, but you're not, are you?"

"Zachary, Devon's younger brother, is watching him."

"Forgive me. I'm not angry with you. I still believed him dead, but today I saw, or thought I saw, him entering Lord Kitchener's home."

Charles knelt so that he could look at her directly. "Are you all right?"

Rhona reached out and cupped his

face. "I will be. Right now I'm confused."

"Unfortunately, there's more." Charles gave her a slip of paper. "This telegram was delivered shortly after I arrived."

Rhona asked, "How did I miss all of this?"

"Unless you intend to turn your life over to clandestine operations, you needn't worry." Charles waited for her to read the three-line message from Tristan.

"He says Murdock Calhoun may have knowledge of my mother." Rhona looked up. "I don't know how. I've never heard mention of this man. Of course, there is a good deal too much I don't know about my mother or her past." Rhona returned the telegram to him. "He doesn't say when he'll arrive."

Charles walked to the fireplace, where the flames turned the telegram to ash. "We don't send our travel plans over wires. There's far too great a risk of interception."

Rhona said, "I don't understand why you have to be in this alone. Would it not be more efficient to work with New Scotland Yard, or perhaps there are other agents willing to help?"

Charles smiled. "Scotland Yard and every police force from here to your northern borders know of our existence in that they believe we exist." Charles sat up while he continued. "It was once easier to go unnoticed before the advent of the telegram and railroads. Some of our agents have had the misfortune of losing their subjects because word reached them before the agents could. Our anonymity is essential to our success. Sharing cases openly with any other investigative agencies would be detrimental. Our greatest strength is in information gathering. To rely on the research of others might mean we miss an essential component."

Rhona's eyes conveyed an equal amount of confusion and irritation.

"I realize this is not what you want to hear, but please understand that our methods do work. We cannot formally ask for outside assistance."

"Formally?"

"We have our sources, most of whom prefer to remain unnamed."

"Is that what Devon is doing?" Rhona asked.

"Yes, and we won't hear from him until he returns. His disguises must remain as unknown as our sources."

Charles stood when Rhona did. He

waited for her to speak words of understanding and acceptance, but she didn't.

"I must go to Emsley. I owe her an apology and explanation." Charles recognized Rhona's pause as her way of deciding whether or not she wanted to say something more. "I don't have your patience, Charles, but I have no other choice but to submit to your methods. I need to know what happened to my mother and what's happening to my family. I'll do whatever it takes."

"I feel it would be best if I leave you to your independence."

Rhona shook her head. "Emsley, I don't wish for you to leave."

"I'm not your sister. I'm your maid. I speak to you at times as an equal, but I am not. I realize that I have not been good for you. You are a true lady by birth and right, and I am a commoner."

"Emsley, no." The conversation had slipped away from Rhona's control the moment she uttered the words, "I'm not leaving Blackwood Crossing.'"

"I've not behaved well, but I cannot go on pretending to be who you believe I am."

"Are you not a lady? Did your mother not raise you properly? Did you not have a governess to see that you were schooled as a lady should be?"

"All of that and more," Rhona said. "If you truly wish to leave, I won't prevent it. I will see that your way is paid and provide a good sum until you secure another post. I ask only that you wait until I may find a new companion, perhaps from the village. I cannot remain here without one."

"I do want to stay with you, but I fear I am not who you need."

"I have discovered a freedom in this place, a freedom I only lived in dreams. Do not ask me to go backward." Rhona would let her go if her friend fought her on this new path she'd embarked upon.

"Then I will remain as your lady's maid and companion, to serve you as I was hired to do."

Emsley gathered Rhona's cloak and the riding habit she wore earlier, asked if there was anything else Rhona needed, and then quietly left the room, just as a maid would do.

Charles departed the house the following morning, once again

without offering to share details.
Rhona paced back and forth in front
of the bedroom window, surprised
when she saw him depart in his
crested coach rather than on
horseback. She changed into a riding
habit and struggled with the laces on
her boots.

Rhona borrowed the mare and
rode away from the mansion,
directing the animal to the estate
border. The man who entered Lord
Kitchener's residence did not leave
during her watch, and she
desperately wished to see him and to
confirm with her own eyes that it
was Alistair. It was foolish to think
he would still be there or appear
while she looked on, but it wasn't
Lord Kitchener's mysterious guest
who happened upon her in the trees.

"Charles warned me I might find

you here."

Rhona's body turned quickly, her balance on the mare in jeopardy. A familiar face, yet one she did not know. "You're one of Mr. Clayton's brothers."

"Zachary. The sun is not your friend in this winter cold."

"It is far warmer than my Highland winters." Rhona shifted in the saddle while her eyes examined her surroundings. "How did you happen upon me without sound?"

"Practice." Zachary looked at everything except her, as though he waited for something to happen or someone to appear. "I will ride with you back to the house."

Rhona pulled up on the reins. "Am I in danger on Charles's land?"

"No, my lady."

"Please, it's Rhona. If I am safe here, then I prefer to continue my ride. Charles showed me a map of his land, and it appeared quite extensive."

"You'll stay within his borders?"

Zachary was not as skilled as Charles when masking his thoughts. He looked skeptical, but Rhona wasn't going to give him a reason to doubt her.

"I promise."

Zachary nodded but did not move away from the copse of trees until Rhona had reached the south end of the mansion. She knew because she turned around twice to see if he watched. He then appeared to vanish.

Rhona kept her promise and rode the boundaries of Charles's land, to the best of her remembrance, without crossing into neighboring estates. Lord Kitchener lived to the north. To the west lay a small lake and to the south lay forests. To the east, Rhona knew sat a manor house with five hundred acres. Charles had told her that no one currently owned the land. The lord who owned it previously had passed earlier in the year, and they had been unable to locate a rightful heir. If, by the end of this year, an heir was not found, the lord's will decreed that the land be set aside in a preservation trust.

The manor could not be seen from any vantage along Charles's border, but Rhona's curiosity grew when two riders passed through the trees one hundred yards in front of her. She remembered her promise to Devon's brother.

Rhona hid the best she could behind the horse, but her riding boots were not suited for walking in the snow. When the men were out of sight, Rhona waited until she heard only her horse and the wind. She guided the mare slowly through the trees, cringing every time the mare's hoof stepped upon a dry twig, but no one heard them. When she was only one hundred yards until she would cross off Charles's land, she saw the house, and it wasn't what she expected.

Though in dire need of upkeep, the mansion covered almost as much ground as Blackwood Crossing. Barren trees lined the long road, which extended from the front of the house, followed a circle, and then wound a path to the main road somewhere beyond her current view. Rhona glimpsed the two riders disappearing into what appeared to be the stables, but they never came back out. With her body now chilled through, Rhona chided herself for venturing so far. She would return now and tell Charles what she'd seen. Rhona turned the mare and slowly walked back into the trees.

"Ye'll miss all the fun if ye leave."

Rhona shuddered at the cold from the tips of her fingers to the blood around her heart. The man before her was not one of the riders she had seen. This man hadn't bathed in far too long, his front black teeth numbered only a few, and his hair matted against his head beneath a ragged hat. By contrast, his mount was of fine quality, much like the Thoroughbred mare she rode.

"Leave us, Thomas."

Rhona stiffened, for this voice was the opposite of the filthy man who smirked and rode away. She refused to turn her horse around when instructed. The man behind her laughed and guided his horse around her instead. Rhona first saw the head of a magnificent steed, then hands gloved in black leather, boots tall and shined. She did not believe it possible for her heart to freeze, but the cold pain in her chest could be nothing else.

"You should have kept your distance, Rhona."

"I mourned you, Alistair, and then I learn you're alive and that you've escaped. I didn't want to believe it was you I saw enter Lord Kitchener's." Rhona watched her older brother's expressive eyes, a mirror image of their father's. "What happened to you? I thought you were on the continent, celebrating your completion at Oxford."

"There's a great deal you don't know, and I had hoped to keep it that way. How is it you're here and not at home?"

Rhona assumed their father would have notified Alistair when he first made the decision to marry her off. "I was to be married to Laird Crawford."

"Yes, but not yet. Father said that would not happen until I returned home. We were to attend the wedding as a family."

"You and Father made many plans without me." Rhona started at a clanging coming from the house. "Why are you here?"

"When I returned to Scotland, I learned of Wallace's disappearance. I've searched for him, but I've been unsuccessful."

"Why does the British government believe you guilty of treason?"

"You shouldn't believe everything the British tell you, Rhona."

"I don't know what to believe anymore or who to trust."

"I don't know why you were told I died, but I had to escape. It was the only way to prove my innocence. I must first find Wallace. I learned that our brother may have a connection with a Lord Kitchener, and I wanted to be close by in the event he showed himself here."

Alistair obviously didn't suspect that Rhona knew his story was a lie. She wanted Charles to know the situation before making any decisions. She must convince her brother to let Charles and his friends help. If her brother was not guilty of the crimes the British claimed, then he should accept assistance. "I have friends who are, as we speak, searching for Wallace and for answers about mother's death. They can help. Please, come back with me."

"Why mother's death?"

"I can explain everything. Come, we're not far."

Alistair nodded. "Very well. I left a pouch of papers and documents I've gathered since my arrival. We'll retrieve them and go to your friend."

Rhona hesitated and with good reason. "I prefer to wait here."

"That's not wise." Alistair nodded toward the house. "My companions are good at finding people, which is why I hired them, but I don't trust them, especially since one of them saw you out here."

"It's quite all right. They wouldn't dare come onto Blackwood property." Rhona turned her horse and started back toward the trees.

"Rhona."

She shifted in the saddle, only to

stare into the barrel of a pistol.

Rhona debated whether the mare could outrun a bullet. Her dagger, tucked safely away in her room, was of no use. Alistair allowed her to lead the horse, but he followed behind. Rhona may have done some foolish things in her life, but tempting death would not be one of them.

Once dismounted, she preceded Alistair into the house. Candles glowed along one wall. Dust discolored the white sheets covering the furniture, and every corner was hidden beneath cobwebs and filth. "You've been staying here?"

"I know, it's deplorable, but I didn't want anyone to know my location." Alistair turned to face her. "How did you learn of my presence?"

Rhona shook her head. "I didn't, not for certain. I saw you visit Lord

Kitchener." Rhona stumbled over a mussed rug in the hallway.

"Careful. Here, take my arm."

Rhona pulled away. "Now you're concerned? Turn the pistol around on yourself, and I might believe you."

Alistair stopped and looked down at her. "You used to be more respectful."

"You used to be my brother."

Fourteen

Rhona slowly wakened, a rank stench permeating her senses. Cold, damp stone pressed against her back, but when she tried to move away, the coarse rope securing her wrists prevented movement.

"Alistair?"

Still clothed and in possession of her boots, Rhona called out for her brother again, but only silence responded. "How could I have been so careless?" Rhona decided that arguing with herself would only cause a headache. "Alistair! I know you're here!"

"Why do ye insist on speaking like an Englishwoman when it's only us?"

Rhona focused her eyes on the lantern swinging from Alistair's hand. Her vision adjusted to the new light and she turned her gaze to her brother. Dressed in robes, he looked like a monk and no longer sounded like the Oxford-educated man he was.

"What have you done, and why are dressed like a holy man?"

"Me dear sister, ye should have remained home and out of me affairs."

Rhona pulled away from the wall as much as the rope would allow. The dampness from the stone began to seep into her clothes. "I don't understand any of this. You've become a crazed man."

"Ye'll know soon. Untie her."

Rhona hadn't realized someone else walked in with her brother, but it was her brother's unfortunate-looking protector who untethered her hands. His hand circled her arm, and she immediately pulled back. His fingers left behind an intense pain. "They will look for me, and they will find me."

"Yes, yer friend, Charles. Blackwood owns the massive estate bordering Lord Kitchener's. Is that where ye were when ye saw me?" Alistair shook his head, making a tsking sound as he stepped closer. "That's highly improper. Ye should have more respect for yer family."

Rhona remained silent, the drip of water echoing through hallow halls, the only sound until her brother laughed.

"He'll nae find ye. Bring her, Thomas."

Rhona fought against the rough

grasp, her boots meting out their own punishment on Thomas's shin.

"Bloody 'ell."

"Can ye not handle one woman?" Alistair took hold of Rhona's arm and dismissed the other man. "See that everything is prepared." Thomas limped from the room.

"Ye were always an embarrassment. Ye wished to behave as a man, ride like a man, think like a man. Why could ye nae simply be a lady?" Rhona tripped as Alistair dragged her through a stone hallway.

She pulled up, forcing Alistair to stop. "You were always kind to me and Wallace. You looked after us and stood by me against Father. Was any of it real?" Rhona tightened her jaw and blinked rapidly, refusing to let her brother see any sign of tears— any sign of weakness.

"It was real, but I couldna take yer side forever. Ye should've done as ye were told."

Alistair pulled on her arm, compelling her feet to catch up to the rest of her body.

"Where are we?"

"And ye ask questions like a man."

"This charade has gone too far."

He stopped and caused Rhona to trip and fall against him.

"Ye think this is a charade?"

She shrugged. "I can hope."

Alistair tugged on her arm, and once more she could choose to follow him or fall down. Rhona chose to remain upright and comply, that is until she saw the other men in robes. The stench of death lingered in the air, a pungency she had not known since she witnessed her father's men burn a dead horse whose leg had broken on a hunt.

Rhona whispered to her brother with the hope that the others could not hear. "I would like to leave now. I won't ask for an escort or even my horse. I'm quite fond of walking."

"Quiet!" Alistair pulled her closer. He smelled of strange oils and spices. "Yer fate is in me hands. If a painful death is not what ye seek, ye'll do as I say."

"How long has she been gone?" Charles lifted his tall, lean frame into the saddle and accepted the Thoroughbred from the stable boy. Ellis stood nearby, and for the first time in Charles's memory, the butler looked distraught.

"Three hours, my lord. I watched her as you instructed, then a small fire started in the kitchen stove, and I lost sight of her."

"I should have followed her, Charles."

"No, Zachary. She is my responsibility, and I know how stifled she's felt, but I don't believe she would deliberately allow anyone to worry. In which direction did you last see her ride?"

Zachary said, "Toward the south of the mansion. Most of your land spreads south and west, and the estate east is abandoned. I didn't think she would find trouble."

"Trouble may manage to find her." Charles urged his horse into a run, hooves kicking up wet grass and moving smoothly over the frost-shrouded land. Charles reined in his horse at the edge of the trees separating his land from the former Lord Gaspar's.

"Rhona, ye want to live?"

Rhona wasn't certain if her brother realized how ridiculous the question was. She nodded.

"Then ye'll remain quiet and do as yer told."

"You treat me as a child. If I am not to leave this chamber, and if these men are to be the last people I see on this earth, at least tell me why."

"Quiet."

Rhona watched in surprise as a man appeared from the darkness, hurried to the center of the room, and scraped something off the stone pillars. The other robed men disappeared into three separate tunnels. "What's happening?"

"Someone is here." Alistair cursed and swung her around to face him. "Ye'll come with us."

Rhona vehemently declined.

"I'm not asking ye."

"I told you they would search until I was found." Rhona grasped her brother's arms. "Come back with me. Whatever this is, they can help."

"Ye have to come, and we have tae go now!"

Rhona pulled away. "They won't stop searching. If you will not do the right thing, at least live until I can find a way to save you from yourself."

Alistair stared at her in surprise with eyes that looked more like the brother she knew from her childhood. She could not contemplate what events led him here, but something in his eyes conveyed fear and uncertainty. "Go, Alistair. They will find you soon enough."

Rhona worried that he would

argue, but instead he pulled the hood over his dark red hair and escaped through one of the tunnels. Rhona took a moment to inspect her surroundings. She heard movement above and her name called out.

"Well, this could have been worse." Rhona lifted the single lantern left hanging from the wall and walked toward the tunnel from which the man had come who warned the others.

"Charles?" Rhona now stood in a kitchen after navigating a length of tunnels and stairs below the house. Footfalls became louder and she called out for Charles once more before hurrying across the room, opening the door, and falling backwards. The lantern toppled from her hand and broke, the light extinguished.

"Rhona!"

"Hmmm?" Rhona gingerly lifted her arm to brace the back of her head, even as Charles rushed to lift her. "Slowly, please."

"I'll ask what happened once you're safe."

"I'm safe now, but there is much to tell you, not that I understand any of it." Rhona peeked at him and waved away his confusion. "We'll talk, but first I'd like a bath. I saw you cringe when you got close."

Charles managed a smile. "A gentleman wouldn't remark."

"Thank you, but I know how putrid I smell."

Charles removed his heavy coat and slid it over Rhona's shoulders. "The mare is still outside, but you'll ride with me."

"There's no need to be noble. I stink."

He grinned at her, and she loved him for it. "I only care that you're all right, and I have no intention of letting you ride in your condition."

Rhona sank into the oversized porcelain bathtub and completely submerged herself beneath the hot, scented water. She lifted her head to take in a breath and sank down once more. When she emerged the second time, the fragrant lavender oil overpowered the stench she carried from the tunnels. Rhona lifted the bar of soap and a sponge from the tray Emsley set beside the tub and began to rub the sweet-scented lavender over her body.

Emsley had offered to wash her hair, and Rhona now wished she hadn't dismissed the offer. Her desire to be alone outweighed her desire to hurry along the bath, but she managed to cleanse her long locks before the water cooled. It was with reluctance that she stepped from the bath, though she welcomed the comfort of the towel Emsley had left on a stool beside the fire, along with her robe.

Rhona used a smaller towel to dry her hair using the warmth of the hearth to speed the process. A brush helped removed the tangles from her hair, but her curls returned after each stroke. Her eyelids lowered, and she imagined herself slipping away. Darkness had fallen and it wasn't until Emsley returned to announce dinner that Rhona realized how late it had grown.

"I'm sorry, but I had your riding habit burned. One of the footman said he could clean the boots properly." Emsley shuffled about tidying the room and setting out an evening dress—one of Rhona's favorites. A deep-green velvet gown that had once belonged to her mother. Rhona refused to part with it, despite its going out of style. Her mother had worn it once to a ball the night after Rhona's fifth birthday. To Rhona, Lara Davidson had been the image of a Scottish queen, and she cherished the memories the dress conjured.

"Emsley, I owe you another apology, and I fear it will not be the last."

"It is not my place to instruct you. You are your own mistress now."

Rhona set aside the brush and towel and walked across the room to the dressing screen. "I'm incorrigible and stubborn, and you were right. Charles was right,

Zachary was right, even Ellis was right to look at me as though I was daft when I requested the horse first be brought around."

"Is freedom everything you hoped it to be?"

Rhona peeked around the screen and smiled. "I'm forgiven?"

"Of course, my lady." Emsley handed her the undergarments. "Is it?"

Rhona sensed that Emsley's question hinted at envy, but that would hardly make sense. Emsley's station may not have been lofty, but she had the freedom to venture into the world, without the confines of class and family to hold her back.

"It is exhilarating."

"You were in grave danger, my lady."

"No, not in any true danger."

Rhona worried over the ease with which she told the lie. She'd explained to Charles about seeing her brother, but she still had details to discuss with him. Rhona stepped out from behind the screen, where Emsley assisted with the small buttons on the back of her dress.

"You're lovely, and might I say, glowing."

Rhona laughed. "I scrubbed my skin enough, I'm not surprised."

"I think the fresh air and exercise were good for you." Emsley handed Rhona a heavy shawl of black wool.

"Thank you. Please take the evening off. I'll remain downstairs after dinner."

"It's not my job to take an evening off. I can't imagine such a thing." Emsley paused and then said, "I've heard it told that speaking of experiences can help calm a person."

Rhona wondered at the trepidation she sensed in the maid's voice. "I believe that's true, and I thank you. Charles will ask me so many questions, I won't possibly have the energy to tell it more than once."

"Of course, my lady. I will be here when you return to the room."

"I hope you'll enjoy the evening at least a little. Charles's home is more comfortable and not less formal I should think, except for Ellis. He's positively Victorian."

"He runs a strict home, but he's been kind. Forgive my question, but will we be at Blackwood Crossing much longer?"

Rhona studied her companion. "Are you unhappy here?"

"No, of course not. I miss Scotland, I suppose."

"I thought you would enjoy returning home to England. When we are finished here, perhaps we can visit London." Rhona smiled at the contorted expression Emsley wore.

"That would be lovely, my lady."

Emsley had returned her smile, but Rhona didn't believe she meant it. She waited until Emsley left the room and then found Charles downstairs in his study.

"Ah, forgive my deplorable manners. I often forget I'm an English gentleman, and one who should have waited in the hall or the parlor." Charles welcomed her into the study. He wasn't alone. "You've met Zachary and you know Devon. He returned an hour ago."

Rhona nodded to each of them. "Gentlemen." She had hoped for time alone with Charles. Speaking of her brother the way she must, Rhona preferred not to have an audience.

Charles said, "Shall we adjourn to the parlor for drinks before dinner?"

Grateful, Rhona accepted Charles's arm and escort. Dinner was an enjoyable and relaxing affair, free of conversations about their work. Zachary asked her about the Northern Highlands, and Devon regaled them with humorous anecdotes from his travels. Rhona decided she had never spent a more enjoyable evening with a group of gentlemen. The meal concluded and Devon and Zachary excused themselves for a game of cards. Charles remained behind and helped Rhona from her chair.

"Now we'll have privacy for that discussion."

He followed her back into his study and offered her a drink, then smiled.

"Would you rather have tea?"

"I would like to keep my mind clear."

Charles walked to the bell pull, and when Ellis arrived, asked that tea be brought up. "I can ease into the discussion."

Rhona shook her head. "There's no need for painting flowers where there should be thorns. I fear my brother is doing something horribly wrong."

Rhona studied Charles's eyes and features for a sign of what he might be thinking. The retelling of the day's events didn't take long, but then Charles began to ask questions. With half a pot of tea gone, Rhona braced for the next question.

"If this is too much for you right now, we can continue later."

"I'm fine, truly. Ask what you must."

"How were they dressed?" Charles asked with a casual glance and a swirl of the whisky he had yet to drink.

"Why is that important?"

"You don't remember?"

"Of course I do. They dressed like priests in robes."

"What color were the robes?"

"Black or a dark blue, perhaps . . ." Rhona tilted her head, looking across at him. "Why?"

"Please try to remember. The color is important."

She closed her eyes and replayed those moments. Her brother dragged her down the dark tunnels, a pungent smell, something rotten filled her sense. Water dripped all around her but never fell on her body or clothes. Her feet tripped more than once over loose stones, but her brother continued to pull her behind him. A flash of light blinded her eyes seconds before they reached the large chamber. Five men stood in a circle, silent, with hoods raised over their heads. A short stone platform raised in the center. The sixth man walked into the chamber and whispered to another. They stood beside each other wearing . . . Rhona opened her eyes. "Dark blue robes, but . . . my brother's robe was a dull red. I remember thinking it odd when I first saw the others." Rhona looked at Charles. "Is that what you need?"

Charles nodded. "Tristan, Devon, and I have been at this many years, and we've never seen what you did today. They are called the Order of Thoth."

Rhona set the tea cup down. "From Egyptian mythology?"

"What do you know of Thoth?"

"Nothing really. I know that Thoth was the deity of scribes, but Alistair is not a writer nor has he spent time with books outside of university." Rhona stood as though indecisive, and then sat back down. "Please tell me what this means."

"We've never been able to confirm the group's existence, but there have been enough details and rumors to warrant learning what we could." Charles leaned forward in his chair. "They use the name of Thoth, believing that he can imbue his devout followers with wisdom, which will lead to wealth and power. This group has misconstrued the original purpose of Thoth. In truth, they are nothing more than devious men bent on rising to the height of power, accumulating wealth and knowledge."

Rhona considered the improbability that her brother would ever be involved in such an organization. Yet, everything she believed she knew about her family had slowly unraveled from the day she had left home.

Fifteen

"Why would my brother wear red and the others blue?"

"That I don't know, nor do I know anything else about this group, but suspicion has fallen on them for murders in the past. No one has been able to confirm or deny their existence . . . until now." Charles considered the woman sitting across from him. He had expected her to argue for her brother, to condemn what she believed to be lies. Yet, he began to see in her a wary acceptance. "You don't have doubts?"

"I do, but I've watched you and listened to you and your friends when you discuss facts and theories. You follow what you learn until you learn something new, regardless of personal attachment. Above all, I want to know who killed my mother. If that means following a path I don't believe, then I will follow it. Besides, my brother damaged any belief or trust I ever had in him when he held a gun on me."

Charles always knew her to be determined and strong-willed, but he realized now that he had failed to give her enough credit for a sharp mind. He felt proud and amazed at his good blessing for having her in his life, even if he didn't know how long she would be with him. The thought of her ever leaving disturbed him in a way he wasn't willing to voice.

"We aren't always unattached from our assignments. When Tristan met Alaina, and we realized how close they'd become, our involvement became one of a personal nature. Neither Devon nor I fully understood how it affected Tristan, but we saw what was between them and what he was willing to do for her."

"He broke the rules."

Charles nodded. "And we were willing participants. None of us would hesitate to do it again. Sometimes personal attachments can impede a case, but more often it propels us in directions we might otherwise have missed."

"Why did you agree to be my escort?"

Charles wouldn't lie to himself and claim that the unfolding of events was not to his liking, but those emotions he'd worked to suppress during the journey to Rhona's wedding slowly rose once again to the surface of his heart and thoughts.

He risked confusing her at a time when she would need all of her strength to find her mother's killer, especially if the killer turned out to be someone she loved. In the end, she may choose to return home to the Northern Highlands, and he could not bear to experience what she had when he had left.

"I was called upon, with Tristan and Devon, to do so." The answer lacked every raw emotion Charles struggled to contain.

"No other reason?"

The smile formed slowly while he memorized the way her mostly red hair shimmered under candlelight. Her gray eyes sparkled, revealing the eagerness he sensed in her. "Do you remember the night we sneaked away after the staff had retired? The stars and moon lit our way to the bridge that crossed over the stream."

Rhona nodded and smiled in remembrance. "It was a cool night, but I don't remember being cold."

"Do you remember what I told you that night?"

"The words haunt my dreams."

Charles knelt before her and slid his hand up her arm, gliding over the silky fabric. "It's as true now as it was then."

"Charles, when this is over . . ."

He waited, hoping. The soft knock at the door halted further conversation. Charles stood and called out, "Enter."

"Apologies, Charles, but we need to talk."

Charles motioned Devon and

Zachary into the study.

Devon bowed his head to Rhona. "I am truly sorry to interrupt."

"Please, I've monopolized him. In fact . . ." Rhona looked to Charles. "Have you told them?"

Her smile always warmed the cold edges of his soul. "Not everything, but now will do." Charles regretted the interruption, but there would be time for him and Rhona later. It may even be enough time to convince her that home was no longer Davidson Castle. "They do know about Wallace."

Rhona blushed. "When my father threatened to use Wallace against me, I reacted. I only needed enough time for him to get away."

"We did manage to locate where he was a few days ago, but he's no longer there."

Rhona nearly leapt up from the

chair. "Where?"

"London."

"But he was to leave the island."

Devon said, "We don't know why he was there, only that he was in a hotel until yesterday."

"Then perhaps he left for the continent as I asked him," Rhona said with conviction. "As for Alistair, if there is any chance of saving him, I must try."

Charles motioned to the unoccupied settee. "This is where we explain the rest of what's happened." Charles retold Devon and Zachary what Rhona had relayed to him while she filled in any small detail he forgot.

Devon linked his fingers and bent forward. "We will do all we can to keep your brother from harm, but when we find him, he must cooperate. The Order of Thoth has supposedly existed for more than a century, and if your brother has had any part in their rumored activities, we won't be able to save him from his fate."

"I know you will do what you must, but promise me I can speak with Alistair first. Out of a sister's desperation, I told him to run. If he hurts anyone or himself, I will be responsible."

Charles shook his head and gripped her hands. "You are not accountable for your brother's actions. I do promise you can speak with Alistair *if* he doesn't force us into a confrontation."

Rhona nodded in agreement, yet Charles wished he could offer her absolutes. He yearned only for her happiness, but he feared sorrow would meet her first.

"Alistair may now have returned to Scotland. How do we find him?"

"Tristan will have news about your mother when he returns. Until then, Devon and his brothers will help us locate Alistair and Wallace. It's possible they've joined together."

Rhona shook her head. "They weren't enemies, but they were never close. Wallace is a kindhearted young man. I may have misjudged Alistair, but I refuse to believe that Wallace is not the brother I know."

"Wallace never argued with Alistair or your father about inheriting?"

"Never. As you know, my father was rarely home, and Alistair wasn't either. I even paid to secure Wallace's first year at Oxford."

Charles stared at her. "An unusual arrangement."

"My father had his heir and didn't bother with Wallace after he sent him to Eton. I didn't know at the time that my father was in dire financial circumstances. Wallace deserved university and all the chances my father might have given Alistair."

"You're absolutely right. How did your father manage to keep the estate, the servants, the horses, all of it?" Charles stood, his thoughts animated. "It wasn't only the appearance of wealth. When I was there two years ago, your father was possessed of true wealth, but we know his ancestral money was already gone." Charles walked to his desk and rifled through the papers on it. "He had no occupation and no family with funds enough to help support his lifestyle. The British government sent me there to investigate his possible involvement in treason, but once the case was closed by the main office, I didn't look any further."

Charles found what he wanted beneath a sheaf of financial documents and bank papers. "According to our sources at The Bank of Scotland, your father accepted and withdrew large transactions over a five-year period. We believed early on that these were a loan or investment."

"People borrow money, Charles. That alone doesn't implicate my father."

"No, not alone it doesn't, but there is never record of any money going back into the accounts after those five years."

Rhona stood and moved to stand in front of the desk, her eyes focused on his. "When was the last transaction?"

"Three months before you were sent to Crawford."

Rhona watched the flames spark and dance. Ash and smoke rose and drifted into the brick chimney, escaping into the night air. She sensed Charles's presence nearby, knowing he waited, but what was she to say? With every kernel of truth, she discovered something about her family she didn't want to know. Her father's betrayal stung less than she anticipated, and she discovered within herself a lack of empathy for what may come to him. What chipped away at her defenses were her father's promises and lies and his betrayal to the family.

Finally, she left her place beside the fire and returned to the chair across from Charles. She noticed his body relax when she sat down but wondered at the tenseness in his eyes.

"Will you leave with Devon to search for Alistair?"

"We will have greater success if we both search, but I don't intend on leaving you here alone."

"Then let me come with you."

"I have disregarded propriety by bringing you into my home. We behave as though it is not wrong, but we both know that if people learned you were here, your reputation would be in shatters."

"I told you before, I don't answer to gossips. Does it bother you?"

"No. If the decision rested solely on me, I would never wish you to leave."

Rhona experienced the oddest

warming sensation surround her heart. "Then I will go with you."

"It's complicated. Here at least you have your maid. Out there, it would be we alone, sometimes with the others, but primarily alone."

"I told you, I don't care about gossip."

"It's not gossip. Damn, woman, it is me I worry about."

Rhona stiffened and drew back, not from fear, but surprise. She understood, and the independent corner of her mind desired to know what might happen if they were ever truly alone again. Two years ago, they'd managed to steal kisses under star-filled skies, or on rainy afternoons when her companion slipped away to give them a few minutes alone. Those kisses led to a night Rhona had carried in her thoughts and dreams ever since. Her family was near to falling apart, but in this moment, Rhona's desire for one man began to shake her resolve.

"You're right, Charles. I should not have made the suggestion."

Rhona may have imagined the disappointment, or flash of regret in his green eyes, but she prayed not. They were both playing the noble one, sacrificing what they most wanted for the truth. Her mother had talked often of love and promised Rhona that one day when she was a woman, she would meet a man to cherish, a man who would make her believe in a forever love.

She remembered asking her mother if that is what Lara felt when she married. Her mother never answered, saying only that she knew the strength of that kind of love. She made Rhona promise to never sacrifice love for duty, but that is what Rhona was willing to do when she went to Crawford. She would have sacrificed her life and any chance of love. She would have been wrong.

"Rhona, are you all right?"

She shifted her thoughts back to Charles. "Yes. How am I to help if I cannot go with you?" Rhona watched Charles carefully as he seemed to battle an internal struggle.

"Will you trust me again?"

She nodded, struck with an absolute truth. "I trust you more than anyone."

Charles exhaled deeply, and Rhona could only think it was the answer he sought. "I will leave tomorrow with Devon. Zachary will stay here and see to your safety."

"Charles—"

"On this I will not waiver. If I am away from you, I must know you are looked after, or I will do nothing but worry."

Rhona chose not to argue. "Where will you be? How will I reach you?"

"I promise you will always know where I am."

Rhona smiled but did not feel any joy. She and Charles spoke to one another as though they'd been together for years. She could not imagine feeling this safe with anyone else. "I need to help."

"Be patient."

She told him she would be patient for however long was necessary, but Rhona knew herself too well. Patience and kindness were her mother's greatest virtues. Rhona had always tried to be kind like her mother, but patience eluded her. She would do this for him, for Charles, but she wanted a promise in return.

"When you find the people who killed my mother, I need to be there."

His leg brushed against the fine leather of his saddle when he mounted the black Thoroughbred. His grip on the reins was natural and easy, allowing the great animal to move at his own pace over the frosted ground. The railroad required a hefty sum to attach a stock car that would allow the horses to travel with them. Charles and Devon planned to journey by train to meet Tristan in Scotland, but they would need horses at multiple stops. Charles was not confident they would always be able to find reliable mounts.

With the extra horse for Tristan trailing behind, Charles rode alongside Devon over dirt and ice until they reached the cottage of Murdock Calhoun. Tristan greeted them outside.

"I expected you tomorrow."

Devon said, "Our travels were unimpeded by weather or man. We were fortunate."

Tristan helped them settle the horses into the small stable, empty save for one lone Highland pony. "Charles, did you realize how ancient Calhoun was when you sent me here?"

Charles smiled. "I expected he would be, but his mind?"

"Clearer than yours." Tristan stepped in beside Charles. "Did you have difficulty leaving her in England?"

Charles recalled the morning he left Blackwood Crossing. He and Devon had left as the sun rose over the hills, when the rays first glistened on Lake Keswick and shrouded the village in light, if not warmth. Rhona had not come down to see him off, a choice for which he did not blame her. He did see her standing at her bedroom window, clad in a white linen robe, her copper-red hair tumbling around her shoulders. She stood there, even after she knew he stared.

He should have said good-bye as a man would to his wife, but instead, he studied every detail he could see from that distance, memorizing her. She was not his wife, a truth he began to hate. His thoughts returned to Tristan's question, but he asked one of his own instead.

"When you must leave Alaina now,

is it more difficult than before you were married?" Tristan and Devon stopped before they reached the cottage door.

"It was always difficult. I am here when I wish to be with her, and it has always been that way. I know she will be home when I return, and that eases the disappointment I feel when we're separated. The temporary retirement I enjoyed made me realize I prefer to be with her and Christian." Tristan said, "It is different for you, Charles. You knew Rhona long before now, and if I recall, there has not been another woman or a dalliance since that last mission."

Devon said, "A man gives up other women if his heart is linked with only one." He grinned. "But not until."

Charles slowly nodded, and in an effort to redirect the conversation, smiled at his friend. "Then you have nothing to fear, Devon. Your debauching days will not end."

Devon laughed. "One can only hope, friend. Come, let us learn what Tristan found so interesting."

Tristan stopped them, his fingers circling the iron handle. "Charles, Murdock remembers your father, and there are things he is willing to tell only you. I did learn enough for me to believe that he knows something of Lara Davidson's death, but he alluded that he may also know something about Rhona's brothers. Some of it will be difficult for Rhona to hear."

Charles stiffened, but nodded. "Don't worry. I will listen to all he has to say."

"Miss Davidson. Mr. Clayton."

Rhona looked up from the journal, where she was taking notes. Refusing to waste time while Charles and the others were away, she asked Zachary to go over the information they had thus far.

"Ellis? Is something wrong?" Zachary asked.

"No, sir, but there is a gentleman here to see Lord Blackwood. I informed him that his lordship was not here, but he demands to speak with someone."

Rhona turned the papers over and stood. "Who is it?"

"Chief Constable, Sir John Dunne."

Rhona turned to Zachary. "Do you know him?"

Zachary nodded. "We met once

when I first came to Blackwood Crossing to work with Charles and my brother on assignment." Zachary looked at the butler. "Send him in."

Ellis nodded. "Tea, my lady?" he asked, but Zachary shook his head at Rhona. She said, "He won't be here long."

Rhona wasn't entirely certain what Zachary planned, but if Charles trusted him, then she would as well.

He turned to her. "Dunne will ask you questions. It's in his nature, and he's shrewd. Don't speak of your relationship with Charles or tell him why you're here. You are Charles's cousin."

"Is this necessary?"

"Yes, please sit as though we're simply having a proper conversation." Zachary urged her around the desk and into one of the plush chairs. She felt like a puppet about to be placed on display and wondered why Zachary showed such concern over the constable's presence.

A gray-haired man with white beard and rigid bearing walked into the study. Though time had caused his body to fill out, he was still a man possessing good posture and physical prowess. Rhona studied the constable from the polish on his boots to the discerning gaze he cast over the room before settling on each of them. Rhona stood but allowed Zachary to introduce them.

"Charles's cousin, you say?" Sir John studied her, and it took great effort not to squirm. He said, "I wasn't aware that Blackwood had family left in England."

"Not England, sir, but the Highlands o' Scotland." Rhona

slipped into her gentle brogue and flashed the constable a smile.

"Ah, yes. I recall Blackwood mentioning his ancestral family may still live there. Curious that you've never graced our fair region with your beautiful presence before, my lady."

"Nobody regrets that more than I." Rhona settled back into the chair. "'Tis lovely here."

Rhona relaxed when Sir John finally smiled, as though he accepted her.

"No place lovelier, my lady." Dunne turned to Zachary. "Mr. Clayton, it has been too long. The butler tells me that Blackwood is unavailable."

"Regrettably, yes. I arrived only this morning to discover his absence."

"You'll remain here until he

returns?"

Zachary nodded. "I've come from London. Charles sent word that he and my brother have been delayed. Hunting in the north country."

Rhona watched in curious fascination as the benign conversation between the two men continued, curious how they all lied with such convincing ease.

"Is the matter pressing?" Zachary asked.

Sir John shook his head. "I've come to Keswick because of reports about suspicious activity on the abandoned estate to the east. Has either of you seen anyone who shouldn't be here?"

"No, as I said, I only arrived this morning," Zachary said.

"Neither have I." Rhona stood, deciding she'd enjoyed the

constable's company long enough. She avoided Zachary's gaze and addressed the other man. "If there is nothing else . . ."

Rhona continued to smile, but she was no longer confident in their ruse.

"I thank you for your time, my lady. Mr. Clayton, please keep a sharp eye and send word around if you notice anything amiss."

"Of course, Sir John. I'll see you out."

Rhona closed her eyes and slowly exhaled. A more terrifying man she'd never encountered. She understood now Zachary's concern and why he called Dunne shrewd. No man, excepting Charles, had studied her with such care. What she didn't understand was why it mattered if the constable knew who she was or why she was here.

Zachary gave the impression that he shared Charles's distrust of local police. She put the question to him when he returned to the study.

"I'm sorry, but that man cannot know who you are."

"Yes, but why?"

"Because the men he is looking for are no doubt those you encountered with your brother. To reveal yourself would be to jeopardize the official portion of our mission."

Frustrated, Rhona returned to the desk and her papers. "What good has all of this done?" She lifted and dropped the top sheets. "We've gathered thoughts and memories. You've all spoken with men and women, who may or may not have known my mother. Charles and the others have gone to speak with an old man who rarely leaves his home and yet somehow knows my mother. How do you wait and do nothing?"

Zachary stood across from her. "It is not nothing. Your mother's death occurred more than a decade ago. Old crimes are difficult enough to solve, but when someone has gone to great trouble to hide their misdeeds, uncovering the truth takes time."

"You sound like Charles." Rhona sat down in the large chair and leaned forward on the desk, grateful Emsley wasn't around to scold her about posture. "I feel useless here, and every hour is a repeat of the hour before."

"Charles's journey north will not be futile. Trust in him."

"There is nothing more we can learn here." Charles swung himself up onto the Thoroughbred's back. The door of the cottage closed, with Murdock Calhoun on the other side. Charles hated that the man once revered his father, but the ailing Scotsman still enjoyed an unfailing memory, and it had proven valuable.

"This will devastate her."

"I know, Tristan, but I promised her there would be no more secrets." Charles gripped leather to leather. Smoke from the chimney blew north with the winds, and snow had turned to rain. "The roads will be too dangerous for travel tonight. We can get on the train in the morning."

Tristan said, "I have been staying at an inn nearby that will suffice."

They traveled the narrow road leading from Calhoun's to the main road, where Tristan informed them the inn was half a mile in the opposite direction from the train.

With it serving as the closest accommodation and their need to be out of the inclement weather, the detour wasn't a concern.

The inn soon revealed itself, but it was the small group of riders advancing toward them that drew Charles's attention. They slowed their horses and moved off the roadway to allow the others easier passage. Charles watched the man in front, unable to pinpoint the time in his memory when he'd seen him before.

Tristan inched closer. "The fore rider bears a remarkable likeness to our lady, Rhona."

Charles ignored the wind and wet rain and focused on the unruly dark hair, the same red as Rhona's. His bearing was regal and eyes, bright and defiant. "We may have trouble."

Rather than remain as they were,

Charles, Tristan, and Devon spanned the narrow road. If the men wanted to pass, they would have to go around or go through them.

"Are you Blackwood?"

Charles studied the younger man. "You have the advantage, sir. We've not met." The men were close enough now. Despite the wind, their words did not have far to travel.

"You know me well enough, you English bastard. Where's my sister?"

"Wallace Davidson."

"Ay. Where is she?"

"She's safe."

"My father said you took her. You had no right."

Charles caught the movements of the men on either side and behind Wallace. Each set their hands near their waist and hips, no doubt ready to draw pistols.

"Your father sold her to another man. I simply bought her freedom. The choice to come or go is hers alone."

Wallace shook his head furiously. "I have not heard from her since I left home. She would not abandon me." Charles watched him spread open his outer coat, now plastered against his body from the steady fall of rain.

"How did you find us?"

Wallace's hard stare bore the same emotion he'd seen on more than one occasion—from Rhona. "My brother sent his men to find me and tell me what you'd done."

Charles swore lightly and inched his fingers closer to his pistol. His glance darted between the riders. He wondered if all of them were Order of Thoth. "I assure you, Rhona is safe. We return to England in the morning. Your sister's worry for you will drive her mad. If you don't mind traveling in our company, you may come with us."

Wallace said, "I don't understand you"

The horses danced beneath them. They sensed their riders' tense bodies and protested the long exposure to the elements.

"Explanations are better left to your sister. Come with us now, Wallace."

Charles must have failed to keep the urgency from his voice because one of Wallace's companions drew his gun. The rider's aim was off, and his body collapsed onto the horse from the force of Tristan's bullet. Wallace's horse reared, and the young man ushered his horse to the side of the road. After a few seconds, the rider fell to the ground in a heap on the muddy road. Charles aimed again and shot the man directly in front of him, only wounding him. What ensued was a bloody massacre, camouflaged by gunfire and smoke.

Sixteen

Charles slumped in the chair, his hands rubbing back and forth over each other, smearing blood from the cut he had yet to bandage. His finely-tailored black jacket lay on the floor where he had discarded it. Covered in the blood of another, the jacket would never be worn again. Tristan's chest slowly rose and fell on the inn's large bed. The stark white bandage contrasted with the blood stain in its center. They would have to wait at least a day before they could move him.

"Here, you don't want that infected." Devon knelt on the floor in front of Charles and looked up at him. "Do I need to knock you out?"

Charles laughed, but he wasn't sure it was his own voice. "Get it done."

Devon poured the liquid over the cut, or deep gash, if Charles was being honest with himself. "Waste of good whisky." His teeth ground and jaw clenched, but his hand remained steady as Devon plied the wound with needle and thread. Three small stitches were all that was necessary, but it might have been a dozen for all the movement Charles had in his hand.

"Can you move it at all?" Devon asked.

Charles flexed his fingers and touched his palm. "Yes, but I wish I hadn't." He held the hand to his chest. "I'll live. So will he, thank God."

Devon cleaned up the floor and

disposed of the used needle and bandages. "You saved his life, Charles."

Charles stood. "No, I'm the reason he's in that bed."

"He would not have acted differently."

Charles stared at his sleeping friend, then walked to the open window, where cool air entered to help dissipate the stink of blood. The pile of bloody cloths used to staunch Tristan's wound lay on the floor near the hearth. Once boiling water, now cool, served to wash the blood from Devon's hands. Charles looked down at the blood, drying on his fingers.

Wallace stood by the window, staring at Charles. "My brother sent his men for this purpose?"

Charles glanced back at Tristan. "It's possible."

"Do you promise that my sister is safe?"

"I do." He leaned gingerly against the wall. "She refused to believe you had any part in your brother's actions."

"Her trust is not misplaced. I would never betray Rhona."

Charles set his hand on Wallace's shoulder. "I believe you."

"I have a favor to seek of you, Blackwood."

"Anything."

"If anything happens to me, take the stallion to Rhona."

Charles leaned against the wall. "Will it mean something to her?"

Wallace nodded. "Promise?"

Charles wanted to tell the young man that nothing would happen to him, but that was a promise he couldn't make. "I do."

Devon motioned Charles over and

spoke in hushed tones. "If Alistair sent men to find his brother, only to have him search for us, then Alistair already knows too much. Someone we spoke with betrayed us."

Charles nodded, his eyes focused now on the darkness outside the inn. "I have to get back to Rhona."

Both men watched as Wallace crossed the room and left them alone.

"Zachary won't let any harm come to her."

"I know, and I trust your brother with my own life, but Alistair knows where she is. Zachary won't be enough to stop them. If Alistair proves to be anything like his men . . ." Charles listened, but heard only the soft fall of snow and the wind that carried it. He closed the window and shutters.

"Alaina."

Charles walked to the bed and stared down at his oldest friend. "Even in fitful sleep he thinks of her."

"Alaina has been through much worse, and Tristan will recover."

Charles turned to Devon. "You'll take him home?"

Devon nodded. "I promise. Wallace?"

"He'll come with me."

The early morning light helped disguise their departure. Once the train crossed over into England, Charles breathed a little easier, knowing he would soon be back with Rhona. She would have her brother again, and he prayed that would bring her some solace in light of Alistair's most recent betrayal.

He watched the passing landscape as the train slowed. "We're not far."

"Do you want me to find Wallace?"

"No. He and Rhona will find strength from one another. Until then, he deserves time to process what's happened." Charles made his way to the dining car, but the young man was not there drinking as Charles might have done at that age. He walked the length of the train until the only place he hadn't searched was the last sleeping berth. The door slid open easily, and Charles stepped inside. Thick curtains blocked out any natural light. He reached for a window to pull back the cloth. His eyes adjusted, and there perched awkwardly on the bench, appearing to sleep, was Wallace. His once white shirt bled red from the knife sticking out of his chest.

Charles lowered the lids over the

younger man's eyes and stared down at the features similar to Rhona's. His aspirations to leave behind the life of an agent were the dreams of a foolish man, and yet he'd never despised his work or desired to withdraw more than he did now.

He searched around Wallace's clothes for any personal belongings. Charles pulled an envelope from the young man's coat pocket and a dagger from his boot.

Rhona lifted her skirt to prevent her feet from tripping over the edges as she and Zachary descended the stairs below the abandoned house. The familiar rankness almost convinced her to retreat back to the comforts of her bedroom at Blackwood Crossing, but she'd come too far to turn away now.

She promised Zachary she would behave, so when she decided to investigate, her protector was not easily convinced to go with her. Rhona had to further promise that she would do whatever he said. She willingly agreed since her desire to return to the tunnels outweighed her sense of independence.

Armed with a dagger in her belt and a pistol she didn't know how to use, Rhona continued down into the tunnels, following on Zachary's footsteps. She used the wall once to brace herself when her foot slipped on something wet, but then she quickly pulled back, took a deep breath, and continued on. Zachary held a finger to his lips, and she nodded to indicate she would be silent.

The vacant chamber felt more

imposing this time without the distraction of her brother and the other men. Once Zachary motioned that all was clear, Rhona walked the length and width of the stone-encased room but found nothing to suggest what Alistair and his Order might have been doing there.

"What did they have on the stone?"

Rhona shook her head. "I couldn't see it. They scraped something from the surface and placed it in a bag. That's all I saw."

The low platform in the center lay empty, the surface smooth except for three long corrugations running the length of the flat stone. Rhona ran her gloved finger along the edges of the groove closest to her. A dry blackish-gray powder clung to the top of her finger, but the dim light of her lantern didn't provide enough illumination for her to see what it was.

"Here, Zachary."

He closed the distance in three strides and lifted some of the powder with his finger. Bringing it close to his face, he carefully inhaled the scent.

"What is it?"

Zachary rubbed the powder off his fingers and pulled Rhona away from the stone. "Finely ground ash."

"A tree?"

"Not the tree. Come."

"We've not learned anything new."

Zachary pushed her toward the stairs. "Yes, we have. Let . . ."

A shock of cold air lifted hair from around Rhona's neck as Zachary stopped speaking. She turned toward the tunnel behind her and pulled up the hood of her cloak. Her feet moved slowly backward, her eyes never wavering from the entrance to the tunnel. The same tunnel through which Alistair had departed when she told him to run. Zachary kept himself positioned between her and the room.

Inhaling a deep breath and offering up a silent prayer and plea, Rhona extinguished the lantern and moved carefully toward the steps, feeling her way along the wall. She pressed herself against the stone and climbed four steps when she saw the light floating nearer. Zachary pressed her closer to the wall, preventing her from seeing anything until the men moved to the altar.

Chains clanked on the stone surface when one man pulled them from a hollow below the pillar. Another lifted a dagger from inside his robe and set it next to the chains. The third laid down a small pouch but left it closed. Rhona's eyes adjusted to the darkness and she steadied her breathing, but her heart pounded and she lifted her hand to cover her mouth. Zachary apparently didn't trust her to keep quiet because he raised his own hand and placed it over her mouth. The men remained silent until the tallest of them lifted three candles from the hollow. One by one, the man lit each candle with the flames from his torch, melting the tops until wax fell in a circle.

Rhona closed her eyes against the onset of tears, though she didn't know how the tears had formed. She wasn't frightened. Zachary turned her until he stared directly into her eyes and removed his hand from her mouth. She nodded and carefully stepped up, the soft leather of her boot silent on the stone. The men began speaking, and she stopped moving. Zachary pressed her forward, but she shook her head.

The language was somehow familiar. Scottis, as spoken by her grandfather, but she did not understand most of the words. The language had changed. Rhona listened to the voices and had no doubt that one of the men was English. She memorized as much of the talk as she could, then once more backed up the stone steps, one at a time. At the top, the door was closed, though Rhona was certain they had left it opened. Using his body, Zachary pushed against the door, and Rhona cringed at the sound of metal scraping wood.

She held her breath, but no one came, so they opened the door enough to squeeze through it. The sudden cry from her own lips was unexpected, the searing pain from loose iron slicing through her skin. Her cry had not gone unnoticed.

"Run," Zachary whispered harshly and pulled her along by the hand.

The fine fabric of her sleeve did little to stop the blood seeping from the cut on her arm. The shouts grew louder as they ran through the house. She slipped on the dusty floor, but a second later, she pulled up. When a heavy wood door slammed in the nether regions of the house, Zachary let go of her hand and told her to keep running for the horses and not to stop until she reached the mansion.

Her chest heaved against the bodice of her dress. She lifted her skirts and ran to the trees where she'd hidden the mare. It took her three times with great effort to mount the animal, her arm burning. Torches emerged from the house, but she was already on the horse. Guided by moonlight, Rhona raced through the trees and did not slow down until she reached the front steps of Charles's home. She thanked the mare before her eyes rolled back, and blackness welcomed her as her limp body slid from the animal's back.

Seventeen

"You cannot stay in here, my lord."

Emsley?

"I'm not leaving Miss Hargrave."

Charles.

"I must bathe her. It's simply not proper!"

Good grief, Emsley. He's not a lecher.

"I will avert my eyes, but that is the most I will offer."

They can't hear me. I can't hear myself.

Rhona wavered between light and dark as the blackness slipped away, but with clarity came pain. With great effort, she opened her eyes, only enough to see that she wasn't dreaming. Charles sat at the foot of the bed, his back to her. Rhona welcomed the heat from a warm and damp cloth moving first up one leg and then down the other.

"Charles?" Her voiced sounded strange, but he heard her.

"Rhona."

"My lord!" Rhona would have smiled at Emsley's dismay but ignored the maid when she covered her legs with the sheet.

"You worried me." Charles pressed his hand gently against her forehead and smoothed away the hair that had covered one of her eyes. "Here, drink this slowly." He held a glass to her lips, and her mouth eagerly accepted the cool water.

"How are you here? How long have I been asleep?"

"I arrived last evening, but I was told you've been this way for nearly three days and nights."

Rhona shifted her head to look out the window, but she was met with darkness. "It's still dark."

"This is the fourth night. Zachary didn't sleep for two days, and Emsley hasn't left your side."

"Zachary! He told me to run, but he wasn't behind me."

"He's all right and refused to leave your side until I returned."

Rhona's body may have ached, but her memory remained clear. She lifted her arm to test its strength, but the pain gripped her, and she welcomed it. "I wasn't certain I still had it. When the mare stopped, I could no longer feel my arm."

"You lost a good deal of blood. The mare caused quite a disturbance when you fell. Ellis managed to stop the bleeding, and Zachary carried you up here. He blames himself."

Rhona tried to move her head again, but the effort cost her. "He's not to blame for anything. I only wish it wasn't a waste." Breathing became difficult, and she struggled to rise.

"It wasn't." Charles pressed his hand gently against her good side. "You shouldn't move."

"I feel stiff and uncomfortable. Please, help me sit up." Rhona gave over control of her body to him. Once she was upright, with pillows supporting her back, she called Emsley over. The maid dropped clothes into a pot of steaming water and moved quickly to the bedside.

"Thank you, Emsley. I'm sorry if you worried."

"You're well and alive, my lady. Mr. Clayton said you were not in any real danger. I have not been able to get more than a little soup in you. Perhaps some tea and a large bowl of broth the cook has been keeping warm?"

Rhona nodded, and noticed the glance the maid sent Charles. His eyes were focused on her, but Rhona imagined he wouldn't care either way. Emsley hesitated in her departure but eventually left them alone.

"She doesn't approve of your or my behavior."

Charles smiled at her. "I'm fond of your behavior."

"Even the side of me prone to foolhardy ideas?"

"Not foolhardy." Charles's moss-green eyes expressed interest. "What do you remember?"

"Everything, I think. It was a harmless outing until the men arrived. I didn't expect them to return, not after they were chased off by the constable and his men."

"Zachary saved your life. It wasn't foolhardy, but neither was it harmless. The doctor told me that any more blood loss and you might not have recovered. You're still pale. Are you certain you're all right?"

"A little tired and hungry."

Charles surprised her when he leaned forward and kissed her forehead. "Your maid should be up soon with the soup and tea, but then you must rest."

Rhona reached out with her good arm and clasped his arm with her hand. "Wait, I need to tell you what I saw, or more, what I heard."

"It can wait."

Rhona shook her head. "I'd rather talk. I promise to rest once I've eaten."

Charles stared at her for a minute, causing her previously clear mind to become muddled. He settled next to her and intertwined his fingers with hers. It was an embrace she welcomed and gave herself a few seconds to enjoy the warmth and comfort of his strength. She told him of her brief examination of the chamber room before the men arrived, but it was the conversation that most interested her.

"I can repeat what I heard, but I only understood a few words."

"Devon has made a study of languages and may know."

"It's Scottis but centuries old."

"If he doesn't recognize it, then we'll find someone who does, but I'll wager on Devon first."

"Charles, there was something else there. Zachary said it was ash. I know what that must mean, but I had hoped . . . it was human?"

"Most likely. In less civilized times, the Order of Thoth was rumored to perform sacrifices, but no real evidence was ever found—until now."

"The ash could have been old."

Charles smiled in an effort to comfort her and erase the images of her brother killing and burning a man. Perhaps she was right and the ashes were left over from years ago, but Charles harbored doubt.

Rhona's next words were interrupted by a fit of coughs. Charles helped her with the glass of water, which she welcomed. Once her thirst was sated and her coughing under control, she asked, "How did you come to be here so quickly? And where are Devon and Tristan?"

Charles had faced bullets, swords, knives, and a disapproving father. He'd risked his life and fortune more than once, each time coming through a better and richer man. His life had always been about risk and adventure, but there was only one thing in his life that gave him cause for regret. He'd once broken a woman's heart, and he was about to do it again to the same woman. Charles would rather face another bullet than face Rhona's tears.

"Tristan was wounded, and Devon saw to it that he returned home safely. I expect him here in a day or two."

"How was Tristan hurt? Will he be—"

"Shhh, he's all right. A bullet won't keep him in bed for long."

"A bullet!" Rhona attempted to

rise, but Charles pressed her back into the pillows, careful to avoid her injured arm. "What happened?"

"Your brother found us."

"Alistair?"

Charles shook his head. "Alistair's men found Wallace and led him to believe that I'd taken you."

"Wallace searched you out?"

"Yes, but he didn't realize what was happening until Alistair's men drew their weapons." Charles stood and paced the length of the bed, then sat back down on the edge, close to Rhona. He lifted her hand into his and pressed them against his chest.

"Tristan wasn't the only . . ." He lowered his head.

"Did something happen to my brother?"

He lifted his head and looked at her. The blue-gray eyes he loved sparkled with unshed tears. Charles nodded. "He was stabbed on the train. Wallace was returning with us." Rhona tightened her grip on his hand.

"But how? Who was it?"

"I found him after . . . there was no one else. The train stopped and passengers disembarked. If the man was on board, he was gone by the time we started looking."

"Where is his body?"

"In the village mortuary. I'll take you to see him whenever you're ready." Charles handed her the envelope he'd found on Wallace. "I haven't read it. He also wanted me to bring you his horse. He's in the stable."

Rhona looked upward, tears streaming down her cheeks. "Mador is my horse. I wanted Wallace to have the best, even if he was running away." She pounded her fist on the bed. "He should have kept running."

"He loved you."

Rhona released Charles's hand, but it was her soft smile and understanding eyes that amazed him. "I'd like a little time alone now."

Charles hesitated and felt a tear on his own cheek when she lifted her hand to caress his face. "Please, just a little time."

He closed his eyes and nodded, kissed the palm of her hand, and left her side.

"Charles?"

He turned.

"I'm sorry for what my family has done." She turned her face into the pillows. Charles waited and watched, but when he heard the first cry, he left the room. In the hallway, he sank to the floor and listened while her tears fell and her sobs tore into his soul.

The fire still crackled and morning light peeked through the slight opening in the heavy drapes. Charles opened one eye and then the other, certain he didn't enjoy the daylight intruding upon his pitiful slumber. A groan escaped his lips when he moved his tired body from the uncomfortable position. His office chair did not a bed make, though he'd slept in worse conditions. By the time Rhona's tears subsided, and he no longer heard her cries, the night was late and his mind awake. He had retreated to his study, the one place in his home where he'd always found solace.

"You're still with us. Good. You look awful."

Charles focused on the voice, seeking the culprit. His gaze passed over the empty glass and half-filled decanter of whisky.

"I said you look awful."

"I heard you." Charles righted himself and stood. He stretched his limbs and carried the offensive liquid back to the liquor cabinet. "Tristan is well?"

Devon nodded. "I almost wasn't when Alaina saw his condition, but he settled her down well enough. They're special."

"They are. What they've found is rare." Charles lowered the bell pull.

"I took the liberty of ordering up tea and something to eat, but may I suggest a bath first?"

Charles glared at his friend, then looked down at his person. "Tea first, bath second."

Ellis entered the study, pausing

when he saw Charles's condition. A footman followed close behind with tea and scones. The servant poured two cups and lifted the silver lid from the tray. Charles glanced at the butler. "You've seen me far worse, Ellis. Has Miss Davidson awakened?"

"She called for her maid a short while ago, my lord." Ellis waited for the footman to leave and added, "Is the lady well, my lord?"

"No, Ellis, but she will be. Will you please see that a bath is prepared?"

"Of course, my lord."

"Thank you."

Charles lifted one of the scones from the tray and drank half a cup of tea before sitting down. His mind began to feel normal and his immediate hunger sated. Charles looked at Devon. "You didn't remain south for long."

"I didn't wish to intrude on them. Tristan told me to stay and then he would be well enough to leave in two days."

"You didn't believe him?"

Devon laughed. "I did, but one hard look from Alaina and I switched sides. Tristan is on his own until he fully recovers." He sobered. "Did you tell her?"

Charles wished he didn't know what Devon meant. "Last night."

"How is she?"

"She'll heal in time."

"You're not at fault for Alistair's choices."

"I know that, but Wallace was her brother. It will destroy her to lose another, no matter his crimes."

"Alistair will kill you if the choice is you or freedom."

Charles absently finished his scone

and tea. He wished for something stronger but required a clear mind. After over-imbibing last night, he planned to avoid the bottle for a few days. "When did you arrive?"

"As it happens, quarter of an hour before you woke."

"Ellis settled you into your usual quarters again?"

"Good man, your butler. I've had to fire another one before I left home last." Devon looked up at him, wearing a grin. "I don't suppose Ellis has a brother."

"He's a singular one and loyal." Charles walked to the door and turned. "I won't be long. We can have breakfast and discuss what comes next."

"Will Rhona be joining us?"

Charles hoped she would, but it would take time. Her mind wasn't the only part of her body in need of healing. "There was an accident."

Devon leapt from the chair. "Was she injured?"

Charles nodded. "Her arm was sliced open, and she lost a good deal of blood. I owe your brother everything. He kept her alive until the doctor arrived and stayed awake for more than two days looking after her. He'll be glad to see you."

Charles left the study and made his way upstairs to his suite of rooms. He discarded his clothes on the floor, silently apologizing to Ellis for the mess. Steam rose from the large bathtub in his dressing room, and he sank into the hot water. His aching body protested but soon relaxed in the soothing concoction of oils Ellis had poured into the bath.

An hour later, Charles made his way back downstairs, but not before stopping at Rhona's door. Silence answered his knock. He pressed his palm against the door before continuing down to breakfast. He stopped at the entrance to the dining room, though it wasn't Devon's cheerful grin that prompted his own smile.

"She claimed not to be hungry, but I decided to prepare her a plate."

"Thank you, Devon." Charles tried not to appear too eager as he walked across the room. "I didn't imagine I'd see you again so soon." He indicated her arm. "Does it still pain you?"

Rhona nodded. "The pain is maddening, but I refuse to take any more of the doctor's medicine. It muddles my thoughts. I hope conversation will help to alleviate the worst of the pain."

Charles bent forward and lowered his voice. "Rhona—"

"I don't wish to cry today. There is nothing to forgive, but if you need it, you have it. My heart is not filled with anger toward you."

Devon set the plate of food in front of Rhona. She lifted her fork only to set it back down.

Charles spread jam over a slice of bread and set it on the plate. "I realize you may not be hungry, but you must eat something. It will take time for your strength to return. We'll all breakfast, and then we'll talk."

Breakfast turned into a quiet affair, though Rhona attempted to give as much to the conversation as Devon and Charles. She mourned and would continue to mourn for days and weeks to come, but her search for the truth was not over.

When Devon asked if she'd seen more of England than tunnels and bedrooms, she knew it was banter meant to alleviate her sadness. In truth, Charles's corner of England possessed great beauty, and she found herself surprised that she'd thought little of Scotland these last few days.

The meal concluded, and Charles helped her pull out the chair. She asked, "Will you be leaving again?"

"Not today. The doctor will return this afternoon to examine your arm, and only then will we make our next plans."

"We can speak now?"

Charles nodded. "Would you like Devon to join us? He may be able to identify what you heard."

"What's that?" Devon asked.

"There's much we haven't spoken of, but if Rhona is amenable, I'd like for you to join us."

Rhona nodded. "Please, Devon. I prefer to say it only once." She accepted Charles's arm and walked with the men from the dining room. A disruptive pounding and yelling at the front door halted the trio. Ellis managed to reach the door before either Devon or Tristan. Rhona wished he hadn't.

"Ye vile whoremonger!" Calum Davidson shoved his way past the butler. "Ye take me daughter and kill me son. I'll have ye out!"

"Da, no!" Rhona tried to step forward, but Charles pushed her behind him.

"Davidson, your malice is justified, but I will not have you disrupt everyone under this roof. Come."

Charles indicated the way to his study.

"Should I prepare a room for the gentleman, my lord?"

Rhona looked up at Charles, and no doubt, he saw his own worry mirrored in her eyes.

"Not yet, Ellis. The gentleman is Rhona's father, and I don't know how long he'll be with us."

Rhona reluctantly followed Charles into his study, her day worsening by the minute. She knew her father well and feared that he would not see reason. He may even blame her for causing Wallace's death. If she had married Crawford, these unfortunate events would not have unfolded.

Charles's warm breath caressed her skin. "You're safe here."

Rhona nodded, comforted by his

words, but her trepidation did not dissipate. Her father stared at her as she walked into the room. His gaze traveled over her, stopping briefly on her arm. She pulled into herself, uncomfortable with his inspection and the loathing she saw in his eyes. Rhona stopped, refusing to enter the room farther.

Charles gently squeezed her hand and walked past to offer her father a drink. "It's early, but you may want this." Charles held out the glass, but Calum vehemently refused.

"I'll not drink, eat, or sleep under yer roof, Blackwood."

"Very well." Charles set the glass aside and offered him a chair. Rhona watched and waited for her father to decide whether he would stay and talk or fight. He remained standing.

"I'm here for me daughter."

Rhona stiffened. "I'll not go."

Devon and Charles both stood between her and what they all perceived as a threat.

Charles said, "Laird Davidson, perhaps we should speak in private."

"Na!" Calum shook his fists at Charles. "Ye'll nae keep her now, and I'll nae talk about it with a lecherous Englishman."

"Da, no." Rhona gave up her silence and stepped forward. Charles inched closer, in his own way telling her not to go too far. "I have been safe here."

"Ye've lived here while he was killing yer brother."

"That was Alistair, not Charles, who killed my brother."

Calum lowered his fists. "I'll nae believe these lies."

"Not lies, Father. If you will stay and listen to what has transpired, you will—"

"Ye believe yer brother guilty of the crimes they lay against him?"

"I've seen what Alistair has become. Charles hoped to save him, but he's caused Wallace's death. Alistair escaped capture once. They will not allow it to happen again."

Calum's face paled. "Capture?" He turned on Charles. "Ye imprisoned me son?"

Rhona pleaded. "Please, allow them to explain."

Calum finally settled into one of the chairs. Rhona sat in the chair farthest from her father with Charles close to her. Devon remained standing beside Rhona's chair, as though he and Charles still believed her in danger.

Much of what Charles told her father she already knew. She watched as he processed the details about their orders to escort her to Crawford and the incident where she attempted to kill her betrothed. Her father's surprise indicated that Crawford had remained silent. She met her father's gaze, but he quickly looked away. Charles surprised her by leaving out some of what had transpired, including why he and the others had returned to Scotland, Alistair's appearance in England, and Rhona's injured arm.

"Ye'll come home, Rhona."

"I'm sorry, Father. I will not return where I'm not wanted."

"That's over now."

"No. Don't you realize you lost me when you forced me from my home to marry a man I didn't want? You threatened my brother's life if I did not obey. Your actions led us here. When I left, I swore I would never return."

Her father rose. "Ye'll nae defy me."

"I will, and I am not sorry for that."

"Ye'll nae be welcome back when ye carry his bastard and he throws ye out."

Rhona closed her eyes and forced her mind to focus on anything but the pain of her father's words. "So be it."

Charles stood and placed a comforting hand on Rhona's shoulder. She welcomed it despite her father's wrath. Calum stepped toward her, but Devon and Charles blocked him from both sides.

Charles faced him. "One question, Davidson. How did you come to arrive with such speed? You would have had to leave before my message about Wallace reached you."

"Ye'll regret this, Rhona." Without

another word, Calum left. Rhona cringed when the front door slammed loud enough to echo through the lower rooms.

"I will have no regrets," she whispered.

Charles's hand dropped from Rhona's shoulder when she stood and faced him. "Why did you ask my father how he came to be here?"

"I ask a lot of questions. I don't always mean something by them."

Charles watched her eyes study him as though her mind alone could dissect his thoughts. His relationship with his own father was perhaps one of the greatest disappointments of his life. Kenton Blackwood loved wealth, and his only friends were men who could increase that wealth. He amassed numerous estates during his lifetime but failed to be at home for even one of his son's birthdays. He never forgot a business meeting or forgave a debt, but he forgot to show up for Christmas and never forgave Charles for choosing to serve his country, despite his father's wishes for him to be a lord and only a lord.

Rhona's courage impressed him more than his own. Charles spent many of his formative years creating scandals and doing his best to forget he was a Blackwood. Charles didn't miss a father he barely knew.

Charles saw that Rhona no longer stared at him but at the empty doorway, where the man who should have loved her shattered her last hope to return home. It wasn't the time to reassure her that she would always have a home at Blackwood Crossing. Her wounded heart needed healing, and for the first time since he promised never to lie to her again, he considered withholding the truth—for a time.

"Charles?"

He turned his attention to Devon who nodded toward the doorway where Zachary now stood.

"Zachary, thank you for joining us. Devon, we have need of your vast knowledge, or so I hope." He motioned him over and urged the others to take their seats. "Have you continued your study of languages?"

Devon nodded. "Any language in particular?"

"Rhona heard something. I left this part out of the conversation with Davidson. Rhona went exploring—"

"What Charles means to say is that in a moment of foolishness, I convinced Zachary to come with me to the abandoned house."

Devon leaned forward eagerly. "Is that where the arm was injured?"

Rhona nodded. "Three men returned, none my brother, but they spoke in an old Scots language I couldn't translate, not entirely. I recognized two words, but Charles thought perhaps you may know."

Devon spoke up. "Repeat what you heard."

Rhona spoke clearly, surprising Charles. He rarely heard her speak her own language, and though this one was not familiar to her, the sounds flowed with ease from her lips.

When she finished, she asked Devon, "Do you know it?"

"I believe so. One more time, please."

Charles listened intently, and when Rhona finished the second time, he looked at Devon who had moved to the desk for a writing instrument. When he completed the translation, he handed the paper to Charles. "The words aren't all Scottis as you believed. Some are Norn."

"No one speaks that anymore," Zachary said.

"Some still do in the Northern Isles of Scotland."

Charles looked at Rhona. "The men you heard, were they Scottish?"

"Most of them, though I'm certain one was English."

He looked up from the translation. "Are you certain this is correct, Devon?"

"I'm not as familiar with Norn, but yes, I'm fairly certain. It makes no sense."

"Not in context, but it's familiar." Charles studied the paper. "Does this remind you of anything?"

Devon nodded. "Our first mission in Scotland, we met a man whom we thought uncouth and disregarded him."

"That's not the only time. When I was . . ." Charles looked at Rhona and quietly apologized for her hearing only. "When I was in Scotland two years ago, I came across something similar, written much like that translation."

"Was someone in my family involved even then?"

Charles shook his head. "I found no evidence of conspiracy on behalf of your father or brothers. Until now, they eluded us all, but I did see it in your library."

Rhona nodded. "Alistair's desk was in the library. My father preferred the study."

"It was in the library, and it makes sense that it belonged to Alistair."

Devon said, "Yes, but we don't know what it means."

"No, but it is likely connected to the Order. Unless we can make sense of it, this is of little use to us."

Zachary asked Charles for the translation. "I'll spend some time with this. I'm rather fond of puzzles."

"Pardon me, my lord."

Charles stood and turned. "Yes, Ellis?"

"Mr. Ashwood has arrived. Pardon, but were we expecting him, my lord?"

Charles smiled. "No. Please send him in." Charles glanced at the others. "Rhona, I'm not certain you should be here for this conversation."

"You'll discuss my brother?"

Charles nodded.

"Then I have a right to stay."

"Patrick will say more if you're not here. He won't take kindly to your brother's death for fear it will drive Alistair deeper into hiding."

Charles knew he placed her in an unfair position.

"I've earned the right to stay, but if you feel it best—"

Rhona was saved from having to leave when Patrick entered the room. Charles motioned for her to retake her seat. Patrick's stance was rigid and his face bore an expression Charles hoped to never see on the man.

"How did this happen, Charles?"

"Patrick, welcome. You know Miss Davidson."

"Miss Davidson, I apologize for my rudeness. Perhaps we can speak alone, Charles. Devon, Zachary, I'd like you here, too."

Charles set a hand on Rhona's shoulder and offered Patrick his chair. "Unfortunately, Miss Davidson recently succumbed to a serious injury, and I prefer she stay here until the doctor arrives."

Patrick gazed at Rhona. "Nothing too serious, I hope."

"It will heal, sir, thank you."

"I fear, my lady, that we will discuss a subject that may cause you considerable pain."

Charles interjected. "She knows everything now." Charles's concern wasn't for Patrick or the agency. He had always considered Patrick among the trusted, but on this particular assignment, he was uncertain where Patrick's loyalties were.

Patrick said, "You were officially ordered off this mission. Any personal investigation was to be kept quiet. Now an agent is seriously wounded and a man murdered on the train while in your custody."

"You knew I wouldn't walk away, and Wallace was not in custody. He was returning with us to see his sister."

"You still don't believe he was involved? When, then, did he disappear?"

"That was my doing."

Patrick's focus turned to Rhona. "Please, explain."

"It has no bearing on any of this." Charles lowered himself to fill the space beside Rhona.

Patrick's jaw twitched. "Do you at least know who killed him?"

Charles smoothed Rhona's hand flat when he felt her tremble. "Our only suspect is Alistair." Charles studied Patrick carefully. "How did you learn of Tristan? Are you watching us?"

Patrick glanced once at Rhona, and Charles suspected it was becoming difficult for him to hold his temper in her presence.

"I have my orders, just as you do."

Devon bolted upright and faced Patrick. "Your orders? Is this what years of loyal service have earned us?"

Charles urged Devon back, for he did not want a physical altercation to take place in front of Rhona. Devon may have a reputation for charm, but his temper and skills in a ring surpassed anyone's Charles had ever met. He'd seen Devon question authority, just as they all had at some point, but never openly or with such rancor. Patrick held steady, but physically he would be no match for

Devon. Charles stepped between them.

"I share Devon's sentiments, but this is neither the time nor place. Are we to be cut loose?"

Patrick shook his head. "The agency doesn't willingly lose their best men, retirement or not. You are being watched in the event Alistair Davidson attempts to contact you. I, along with the agency, hold you all in the greatest respect and trust."

To Charles, Patrick's words and manners were those of a man posturing and telling them what he thought they wished to hear. Charles would play whatever game necessary. "Then allow us to do our job. This is about more than Davidson's supposed treason."

"You don't believe him a traitor?"

Charles glanced behind him at Rhona. "I can't prove or disprove his intentions. He would not have come after us if he didn't have something to hide."

"I'm pleased you see reason." Patrick shifted so he could look around them. "Miss Davidson, I am sorry for the loss of your brother. It was not the outcome we desired."

Rhona only nodded, and Charles was grateful for her silence. Until he could determine if Patrick was loyal to them, the less interaction Rhona had with him the better.

"Come, Patrick. Devon and I have a few more words to say." Charles waited for Patrick and Devon to precede him from the study. He placed a hand gently on Rhona's shoulder as he passed and hoped she understood.

Eighteen

The doctor secured Rhona's arm with a fresh bandage and handed a bottle of medicine to Charles. "This will help her sleep."

Charles doubted Rhona would drink it, as she'd already refused to finish the first bottle the doctor provided, but he nodded and thanked the man. He rang for Ellis to escort the doctor out, then settled down in the chair next to Rhona's bed.

"He's left now. I'd like to leave the bed."

Charles set the bottle on the small table to her right.

"I won't be drinking that."

"I know, but I couldn't let him know that. However, I can ask you to rest. You'll heal more quickly."

"Charles, how am I to help from here?"

"You're not, but you do make a captive audience from beneath those covers."

Rhona sat forward. "You learned more about my mother?"

Charles nodded. "Calhoun has proved that he is still wiser and sharper than most men half his age. It won't all be easy to hear."

"I want to know."

Charles leaned into the chair and watched every blink of her eyes and every twitch of her fingers. The doctor told them she was not to experience any stress until she healed, but Rhona had already borne more than any woman ought to.

"Calhoun had heard of your family, more specifically your mother. He doesn't leave his village these days, but back then, he traveled throughout Scotland and once knew many families. He learned of a scandal involving his friend and an Englishman named Crawford."

Rhona tensed. "Braden."

"Yes. Braden, the man you knew as your betrothed. Calhoun was well acquainted with the Crawfords and eventually learned a secret. Braden had a child. Calhoun met the child's mother only once, when she was heavily burdened, and described her in great detail. Her name was Lara."

Rhona shook her head and pushed aside the bedcovers.

"Rhona, wait."

"No. You're saying that my former betrothed was in love with my mother. It's not possible. My mother would never have committed adultery." Rhona scooted from the bed and lifted her robe from its hook in the wardrobe. Charles watched her failed attempts to cover herself, and ignoring her protests, helped slide the robe over one arm and rest over the other. His hand brushed her neck, and he felt something wet. He turned her and lifted her chin.

"There's more to say, but are you certain you wish to hear it?"

She breathed deeply and slowly nodded. "Do you believe what this man told you?"

"I do."

"Crawford loved my mother."

"It's possible. Calhoun said that Braden mourned for months after your mother left because he received word that their child died after taking only one breath." Charles helped her into one of the chairs by the hearth and then occupied the other. "A letter arrived from your father, demanding that Lara return home. She had no choice but to do as he asked or risk losing you and your brothers. In a drunken stupor, Crawford later told Calhoun what happened."

"My father knew? All this time he knew she was with another man. Did he know the child wasn't his?"

"Only your father can answer that. Murdock claims that no one else knew about Braden's indiscretions." Charles reached for her hand. "Crawford told me that it was he who contacted your father and offered for you, and I believe he made the offer to protect you."

"But I would have been married to the man who . . ."

"I don't believe he meant for it to

be a true marriage."

"Why did he fear for my life to an extent that he would be willing to make such a commitment?"

"I'll know soon."

"You're going to see him? I'm going with you."

"It's not safe. Whatever Alistair is involved with is not related to your mother's death, of that I'm certain. You are his sister, but you are still a threat to him and his Order."

"Then I am safer with you."

"Only a few know you are here, but if we are seen traveling together alone as man and woman, your reputation would be shattered, all prospects gone."

"Don't leave me out of this."

He studied her. "As my wife, your reputation would remain intact."

Rhona stepped back and almost

fell into the chair, but Charles caught her.

"You're proposing?"

"I would have done it sooner and under far more pleasant circumstances, but you should marry because it is what you wish to do, not for duty or necessity. I've kept you hidden to help spare potential ruin and fear I have given you less freedom than a husband would have."

Rhona steadied herself and looked up at Charles. "When I first arrived, I didn't know who you really were. I had trouble separating Charles Pearce, the only man to know me, body and heart, from the agent who came to escort me to my wedding. I loved Charles Pearce. He was a simple man who gave me hope, but you were another. When I accepted your proposal to come here to

England and stay with you, I believed the only thing I knew about you was your name—Blackwood. Yet, I've come to realize that the man you pretended to be was you all along."

Rhona held onto his hand and smiled up at him. She loved the man before, and she loved him still. The proposal was hardly something of romance novels, but it was honest. "Why did you not ask sooner?"

He looked taken aback. "Your father, Crawford, both were forcing you into a marriage you didn't want, or at least only long enough to—"

"Kill him?" She smiled at the subtle joke. Though it held some truth, she owed Braden Crawford an apology. "Your noble intentions were more dangerous to my reputation than an unwanted marriage would have been to my heart."

"You don't have to say yes, Rhona. When Tristan married Alaina, I was pleased for him, but I didn't understand why she said yes. I knew he loved her, but she was quiet about her feelings. I soon realized they shared a mutual love, but they married for the sake of her honor. My intentions are selfish, not noble."

His green eyes conveyed uncertainties, unusual to see in the most confident man she'd ever known. "If I don't say yes, will you disallow me to go with you?" Rhona thought she saw disappointment in his gaze but said nothing.

"No, the choice is yours. You will always have me, Rhona, no matter what you decide."

She let go of his hand and gingerly lifted her arm from the bandage.

Ignoring the pain from the wound, Rhona reached out and took both his hands. "When you left two years ago, I swore never to trust another man, and if I did, it wouldn't matter because I would never love another. I will marry you, Charles. And I don't expect you to give up who you are."

He squeezed her hands. "This is my last assignment."

Rhona was stunned but couldn't deny her overwhelming relief. "How long do we wait?"

Charles smiled. "Who said we'll wait?"

Nineteen

"Congratulations!" Devon embraced Charles and kissed Rhona. Zachary shook Charles's hand and he, too, kissed Rhona's cheek.

"We're in need of something to celebrate," Devon said. "Tristan will not want to miss this."

Charles glanced at Rhona. "I prefer not to wait, but Tristan should be a part of this."

Rhona agreed wholeheartedly. "Regardless of the circumstances that brought us back together, I'm grateful to be here with Charles and with you both. Devon, I know you continue to help out of loyalty to Charles, and I love you for that.

Zachary, I can never repay what you've done for me. I am here now because of who you are, who all of you are."

Ellis supervised a footman who carried in a tray of champagne, and Devon helped the butler, much to the older man's dismay, pass the glasses all around. Charles pulled Rhona close to his side. His eyes met and held hers. His tender smile broke down her barriers, and for a brief time, she forgot the horrors and secrets that had brought them together.

When the hour grew late and Rhona was left alone with Charles, she walked to the window and gazed out at the heavy flakes, which began to fall against the late-afternoon sky.

"It was kind of them to leave us." Rhona glanced to the door. "I am surprised Emsley hasn't appeared. She's been distant these past few days. I fear I've been a terrible friend to her."

Charles moved to stand beside her. "How did you meet her?"

"She came to be my maid and companion shortly after you left two years ago. Emsley told me of her life in London, and though it wasn't far from home, I still desired to see it and to travel. Her stories only amplified that desire. The only time I ever left Scottish soil, you had to save me and take me back."

Charles leaned in close. "I'll share with you a secret that may curb your longings."

She waited.

"London is a glorious city, a place of culture and sophistication."

She waited again for the part that would "curb her longings," as he put it. "Do you visit often?"

"Only when it's required."

"Why is that?"

"Well, my dear, there's a rather putrid smell about the place."

Rhona laughed. "Putrid?"

"How many cities have you seen?"

Rhona shrugged. "Since I left home, only those from the train window."

"Consider yourself fortunate. It is in the countryside where you may breathe of fresh air and wander across fields without the cacophony of gossip, wails, vendors yelling, factory whistles blowing, and the general din of city noise."

Rhona turned around and found herself inches from his arms. "Is there any place you enjoy?"

"Home is where I'm at peace, though your Highlands are a place of great comfort to me. I have a home in Scotland."

Rhona was well and truly surprised. "Why have you never said so?"

"I've been there only once, a long time ago. It is farther north than your home—in Caithness. There's not much nearby, but it's in good repair, according to the old man who has watched over it since before my birth."

"Then why hold onto it?"

"I don't have the right to let it go. My great-grandfather built it, and it belongs to the Blackwood line, which will someday be more than only me."

Rhona enjoyed the rush of pleasure his words gave her. "You want children?"

He nodded. "I wasn't always sure I'd be a good father, and I still have my doubts. My own was absent most of my life, and when he wasn't, he tried to mold me into a version of himself. I want better for a child of my own."

"You'll be a remarkable father." She lowered her head, hiding the doubts she knew he would see in her eyes.

"Do you not want children?"

"Of course, I was only thinking of my own family. They're lost to me now, and I admit, I miss them terribly."

"Do you regret your choice to come here?"

"No, never that." Rhona moved past him and walked the length of the room, her fingers brushing across the spines of books and shelves. She ended at his desk. Papers were neatly stacked, and the map with markings from their last journey north brought her back to a painful reality.

"I need to see him, Charles. Laird . . . Braden."

Charles pointed to her arm. "The doctor wouldn't approve. How does it feel?"

"It hurts, but not nearly as much as not having answers."

"The circumstances are different with each case. The truth does not always want to reveal itself, and learning what we have about your mother has brought us closer to a motive, and the motive always leads us to the person responsible."

Rhona considered that but did not like where her thoughts turned. "If my mother had relations with Braden, and if he truly loved her, it is only my father who could wish her punished. When the news of my mother's death was delivered, I was with my father. He wept and mourned for days after. He was never the same man, never loved again."

"Grief manifests itself differently in all of us. Did he mourn her because he loved her or because he was responsible? We can't know without asking."

"You wish to ask my father if he killed his wife?" Rhona paced the carpet behind the desk. "I don't know if that is a truth I want revealed."

"We can stop now and be done with all of it." Charles walked to her side and held her still. His large hand covered the strip of bandage over her shoulder.

"We can't. You see, I'm selfish, too. I cannot come this far and give up, and I cannot be happy creating a life of my own until I know what happened to hers." Rhona felt the moisture build in her eyes. It blurred her vision, and she blinked the tears away, allowing them to glide down her cheeks. "Promise me we won't stop."

Charles reached up and wiped away the tears. She stared into his eyes as he ministered to her. "I promise we'll never stop."

It was time to tell Ellis everything, though Charles suspected the butler already knew more than they realized. It would not be the first time he brought the longtime servant on the inside of his missions. The first time Charles came home with a deep cut in his shoulder and a bullet wound to his side, the secret was revealed. Charles wished to take

Rhona to Claiborne Manor since Tristan would not be able to travel. Regardless of their current troubles, Rhona deserved a happy day and a true wedding, surrounded by people who cared about her. It would be small, and her family absent, but she still deserved a special occasion.

"You wished to see me, my lord."

Charles glanced up from his desk. "Yes, Ellis. Please, come in and close the door."

"We'll be leaving for one week, traveling to Claiborne Manor for a wedding." Charles stood and smiled. "My wedding."

"Very good, my lord. It has most certainly been long enough."

Charles sent Ellis a scolding look, but it did nothing to the butler.

"My current assignment is more personal than any other, and it involves Miss Davidson's family. I don't wish to leave while so much is still unresolved, but neither do I wish to delay the wedding."

"Your lordship could marry here. We would enjoy celebrating a wedding."

Charles nodded. "It is also my preference to wed at Blackwood Crossing, but it would be wrong not to include Tristan and Alaina, and they are unable to travel right now." Charles told Ellis the shortened version of recent events, including Tristan's wounds. "When we return, we will immediately leave for Scotland. I don't know how long we'll be away, but I would like one of the grooms to ride along the eastern borders twice a day. If he sees anyone or anything out of the ordinary, you must send word to both me and to the constable."

"Has Chief Dunne been informed of the situation?"

"Only what was necessary. The men who have been spotted at the abandoned estate may be quite dangerous."

"Is this how Miss Davidson came to be injured, my lord?"

Charles nodded. "Her safety is my primary concern, but I also promised to help her. I'll need your help to keep that promise."

"You can count on me."

"I know, and I'm grateful."

The loud chime of the bell at the front door brought both men to attention.

"We're not expecting anyone."

"Very good, my lord." Ellis departed the room, but moments later, he reappeared at the study threshold. "Mr. Ashford, my lord."

Charles turned over the top pages of his stacks and folded the map. "Wait a few minutes and show him in, and then send a groom for Devon and Zachary. They went riding."

Ellis nodded and backed from the room. True to Charles's request, ten minutes passed before Patrick was shown into the study.

"Thank you, Ellis. That will be all."

Now alone with Patrick, Charles offered him a drink, which he declined. "I didn't expect you again."

"Nor did I plan to return. I was half a day from Edinburgh where I was to meet with my supervisor. They want a detailed accounting of what happened to Wallace Davidson, and they are quite interested as to why you're still investigating."

"I don't need their permission. When Tristan and I came out of retirement, it was as a favor and with the understanding that we are free to leave again, whenever we choose. Has that time come?"

Charles thought he saw panic in Patrick's eyes, an unusual emotion for a man he believed bereft of feeling.

Patrick shook his head. "I'll take that drink now." Patrick accepted the fortifying liquid. He stood in the center of the room, silent. Charles waited. "We can't afford to lose you, not now. Davidson's death is a great loss. We are now, more than ever, certain he had information of other persons of interest and that he may have been involved with the Order of Thoth. I recall you came across evidence of the order on an earlier mission."

Charles wondered how much Patrick already knew. There had

been no evidence of Wallace's involvement, and everything about his behavior suggested the order too constrictive for him. If both he and Alistair were involved, then Rhona was in more danger than they realized. The Order was believed to be a family affair, though it was possible Rhona's father was never involved. Once inducted, leaving the Order was not an option.

"I recall the evidence. It was one of my first missions to Scotland."

"Do you remember anything useful?"

"The language was obscure, and we weren't certain what it was at the time."

"Pity, but you can understand the agency's concern with the loss of someone potentially valuable to our causes."

Patrick attempted to play a mind

game in which he no longer possessed a talent.

"I did what I must, and I would not hesitate to do it again."

"Very well, Agent Blackwood. Perhaps Miss Davidson would speak with me. She may know something about her brother's activities without realizing it."

Charles had no intention of allowing Patrick to question Rhona, especially not about her brothers. "I'm afraid she is unavailable and will be for a fortnight."

"Has she gone home?"

"Her father did visit," Charles said in a measured attempt to avoid the truth. "He was quite adamant about her leaving with him."

"And you wouldn't allow it?"

"It wasn't my choice to make. Rhona has a mind of her own, and she does not fear the repercussions."

"I will admit my surprise when I learned she was under your roof without a proper chaperone. Her betrothal and the subsequent cancellation of her wedding were not entirely private."

Charles stood. "Who spoke of it?"

"We don't know, but the wedding would have formed an alliance our government wanted. They see no value in her unless she is able to join her family with Crawford's."

Charles studied Patrick and realized it was possible the other man didn't know the truth about Rhona and Braden's relationship. "It will never happen. I preferred not to tell anyone until the deed was done, but Rhona and I are to be married. We leave in the morning."

Though the change was subtle, Patrick's eyes widened and his face tightened. "You're risking a great political alliance."

Charles took Patrick's glass from his hand and set it aside. He walked to the bell pull and rang for Ellis, ignoring Patrick's questioning looks. The butler arrived within a minute. "Ellis, Mr. Ashford is leaving."

"We're not through here."

"Do you still need our help? Are Devon, Tristan, and I still of some value to you and the agency?"

Patrick nodded.

"Good, then we are finished here. No one bothers Rhona. She is under my protection and will soon be my wife. It's not about politics or what the government wants or needs for that matter. If they require a pawn, they must look elsewhere."

"It's not that simple."

"It will have to be. You could tell

me everything, and I mean everything, or you can leave now. Tell whoever is giving you your orders that we will see this through. If anyone else in Rhona's family was involved with Alistair's suspected treason, you will be notified."

"You've long passed insubordination."

"When have you ever known him to care about that?" Devon stood in the doorway, arms crossed and body relaxed. "It seems I've missed too much." Devon walked in and stood beside Charles. "In all our years working together, you've never questioned our methods or choices. What makes this time different? Who is really giving your orders?"

Charles waited for Patrick's response and saw that Devon touched on something their supervisor was reluctant to reveal.

"Who is not important?" Patrick stepped closer to them and lowered his voice since Ellis remained by the door. "They needed the alliance, Charles. Without it, powerful men will lose too much, and they will blame her and you."

"Has someone threatened her?"

"Not directly, but they're becoming desperate."

"No more evasions, Patrick. Why does it have to be her, and what do these men stand to gain?"

Charles saw Patrick's hesitation and swore he would not allow him to leave without first telling them the truth.

"A good deal of land and appointments to political and government positions. There is an enormous amount of money that has already passed hands, and these men did not get all they paid for."

Devon said, "It wasn't only her father who sold Rhona to Crawford, was it?"

"No." Patrick looked at Charles. "I promise I was not aware of all the circumstances prior to the wedding."

"And once you learned?"

"I had hoped you would see reason and send her home. Calum Davidson is desperate because he took money from powerful men, and he has no way to repay it."

Charles was missing something. "Why is Rhona's marriage important?"

"Crawford owns great land holdings in both Scotland and England. Part of the arrangement Davidson made with Crawford was for a majority of the land in England, more than three thousand acres. The acreage touches the coastline, but it has never been developed for shipping and industry."

"Industry and ships? This is why Rhona was bartered like a ware at the market?" Charles raised his fist, but Devon held him back and pushed him away.

Devon asked Patrick, "How much money was paid to Davidson?"

"A great fortune. When the marriage did not take place, Crawford offered to pay the monetary dowry, in addition to what you already paid, Charles. However, he refused to give the land."

"He was not supposed to pay anything." Charles waited a minute to calm himself before speaking again. "What are these men threatening? They must know they cannot force Rhona to marry Crawford."

"They do know that, but they have threatened her father."

"By threatening Rhona's life," Devon said.

Patrick nodded.

Charles regretted the loss of someone he once called friend, for no friend would betray him this way. "How long have you know?"

"Since my last visit."

"Davidson has made it quite clear that he cares nothing for his daughter. Threatening her life wouldn't force him to do anything." Charles decided to gamble. "Is it the Order who is pressuring him?"

Patrick shifted and his eyes twitched enough for Charles to recognize surprise.

"Tell me. When you sent me to investigate Davidson two years, did you know about his involvement?" Charles waited.

"We had our suspicions, but you uncovered nothing."

"Nothing would imply that everything I brought back with me from Davidson Castle, and subsequently delivered to you, was of no value. Why then send me there?"

Patrick crossed his hands and shrugged. "You're not always privy to everything. There have been times when we sent you blind on a mission. Why does it matter now?"

Charles slammed his fist down, rattling the few items on his desk. "Because I never would have left her alone up there! Do you know what could have happened to her if the Order had decided to use her sooner?"

"It had to be this way."

Charles looked to the doorway,

where Ellis watched in awe and waited as instructed. "Mr. Ashford is leaving now and will no longer be admitted to this house while Miss Davidson is in residence."

"Very good, my lord." Ellis waited by the open door. Patrick stared at him, but Charles refused to back down. Patrick pulled a folded paper from his jacket pocket and set it on the edge of Charles's desk. Without another word, Patrick left the room.

Once alone, Charles turned to Devon. "The wedding will have to wait."

"Tristan will understand if you don't wait and wed here."

Frustrated, Charles picked the paper left by Patrick. "Rhona deserves better than a rushed ceremony." He read the brief paragraph and walked to the fire, dropping the message into the flames. "We must leave for Scotland tomorrow."

Devon stepped toward Charles. "What did it say?"

"The location of where Alistair Davidson is expected to be in three days' time."

"Patrick does know."

Charles nodded. "He may have known before we were given this assignment, yet he's careful to ensure no one else knows that." Charles turned away from the fire. "There's only one reason why Patrick would want everyone to believe he's at odds with us, even to the point where he might lose our trust."

"He suspects someone around us."

Charles concurred, then called out for Ellis. The butler stepped into the open doorway. "Please ask Miss Davidson to come back downstairs.

Alone."

"Very good, my lord."

Devon asked, "Do you have someone in mind?"

"Everyone is suspect, and yet there are only two people who have recently come here and I know for certain it's not Rhona. Miss Hargrave, her maid, has been with her for more than two years now. Rhona trusts her."

A figure filled the doorway, surprising both men. "I let myself in, Charles. I hope Ellis won't mind too much."

"You're daft." Devon hurried over to Tristan's side. "Alaina would never let you leave in your condition, not without her."

"Which is why I'm here, too." Alaina stepped into the room behind her husband. "Christian awoke, and I fear he's not pleased about it."

Charles stepped toward his friends and reached out for the boy. "We'll change his mind." Charles tossed the toddler into the air once, then twice. Christian laughed and then settled comfortably into Charles's arms. "This is a wonderful surprise."

"We should have sent word before our arrival, but I suspected you would have tried to stop me."

Charles nodded. "We would have. That's not a grazed wound you suffered."

"He insisted." Alaina looked at Charles. "I do apologize for the intrusion. I brought along my personal maid, Karen. She's helping with Christian until he's old enough for a proper governess."

"You must never apologize to me, my dear. I still hold hope in my heart that you'll leave Tristan and move north." Charles paused.

"Scoundrel."

"Reformed scoundrel," Devon said.

"Oh?" Tristan and Alaina both looked directly at him.

"We were leaving tomorrow for Claiborne Manor. I didn't want either of you to miss the wedding, but something has come up."

Alaina offered a wide smile to Charles. "Tristan told me about Rhona.

"Yes, and I'm glad to hear you've found some sense, old friend," Tristan said.

"My lord?" Ellis appeared under the threshold with Rhona.

"We've company." Charles covered the distance between him and Rhona, placing her arm through his.

"It was not our intention to disrupt your household, good man." Tristan smiled at the butler.

"Of course, Your Grace. We are always honored to welcome you." Ellis looked at Charles. "I will see to his room at once, my lord."

Charles smiled at the group when the butler left the room. "His household, Tristan?"

"Isn't it?"

Charles laughed. "I suppose it is. Alaina, my dear, it is my pleasure to welcome you and your son into my home and to introduce you to Rhona."

Twenty

The smaller woman's embrace caused Rhona a moment of awkwardness, for it had been the first time a woman outside her family had shown her a true act of friendship. Rhona smiled down at Alaina for she stood at least three inches taller. "He's right, I prefer you use my given name."

"And I insist you do the same with me."

Rhona nodded. "Of course." She looked around at the small gathering. "I hadn't realized you were coming here. We were to leave in the morning—"

"Rhona, we must speak about

that." A pain shot through Rhona's neck when she snapped her head up to look at Charles. His eyes intimated that she should not worry, but his stance was stiff.

"Not to worry, darling." Charles held her hand and addressed the others. "You must all forgive me, but I need to speak with Rhona privately. Ellis will settle you in. Tristan, your usual suite."

Tristan nodded. "Come, my dear." He guided Alaina and Christian from the room, and Devon followed closely behind.

Charles closed the door and walked Rhona to the chaise by the window.

"Ellis said you wanted to see me. He's a man of little emotion, but I suspected it was not to be a pleasant meeting."

"I am sorry. Unfortunately, my plans have been waylaid. We can marry tonight, but we must leave in the morning for Scotland."

Rhona exhaled slowly. "To see Craw—Braden?"

"To find Alistair. I wish you would remain here where you'll be safe, but I made a promise and intend to keep it."

Rhona folded her hands in her lap, her eyes studying Charles. "I don't understand. You've found my brother?"

"I believe we know where he'll be, and it's important we find him."

Rhona stood and paced the section of rug in front of the window, then sat back down. Tears welled in her eyes, and she hated herself for asking her worst fear. She did not want to lose another brother, no matter his crimes. "What will happen to him?"

"I don't know. I have reason to believe we won't be the only ones searching. I've already wronged you for a dozen lifetimes, and I will not do so again. I will do all in my power to keep him alive, but we must speak with him. The threat against the British government is not over, and I cannot walk away from my duty, not if I believe there is a way to end this without bloodshed."

"I can't lose another brother. I've tried and tried to move past Wallace's death, but I know it will never be all right that he's gone." Rhona allowed Charles to pull her close to his body and envelop her in his arms. She sought comfort in his presence and listened to the steady beat of his heart.

Charles held her head close to his

chest, and she closed her eyes, speaking softly, "We can leave tonight." She pulled back and wiped the few tears from her eyes. "We can get to Alistair first."

Charles shook his head. "Leaving tonight will not help. The last train will have left by the time we reach the station, and horses and coach will take far too long."

Rhona raised her eyes to look into his. The green depths promised her more than she felt she deserved. "I'm sorry. I should have told you many times before that I love you and never stopped loving you. There is nothing on this earth I desire more than to be your wife, but I cannot do it right now with a happy heart. Please, we must get to my brother."

Rhona's breath halted as Charles leaned in and gently pressed his lips to hers. Every emotion she believed to be buried two years ago rose once again.

"Tell Emsley. You'll need to finish packing, and we'll leave in two hours."

Rhona remained silent for fear that Charles might change his mind.

"Go. I'll arrange everything."

She nodded and hurried from the room. Rhona rushed down the hallway and up the stairs, ignoring the glances of the butler and an upstairs maid. Pushing into the room, she glanced around, looking for Emsley.

"Emsley, are you here?"

The other woman walked in from the dressing room. "What's happened, my lady?"

"We're leaving tonight for Scotland." Rhona hurried to the wardrobe and removed two of her simplest dresses and a riding habit.

"My lady, please wait." Emsley gathered the clothes from her arms and nodded toward the window. "It grows dark early, and the snow has started again."

"I know, but there are reasons why we must leave now. Please, help me pack. Only the small trunk."

"Your dresses will wrinkle."

Frustrated, Rhona set a pair of fine leather boots in her trunk. "I don't care about wrinkles. We'll fold them carefully and perhaps they will not require pressing."

"You know I only want to see you happily married, but I don't understand."

Rhona straightened her back. "I appreciate that."

"It's not my place to say this, but are you certain you wouldn't be happier returning home?"

Rhona stiffened and set her favorite shawl in the trunk. "You're right, it's not your place to say such a thing. You've been a friend to me, and you don't have to like my choices, but if you wish to remain my companion, then you must accept them."

Emsley nodded. "Very well, my lady. I will remain silent."

Rhona watched the maid fold and pack items into the trunk without voicing another opinion. Guilt was not an emotion Rhona enjoyed carrying with her, but she wondered if she'd been too harsh on her friend. Not a friend, but a maid, as her father used to remind her.

"Emsley, I must apologize."

"It's all right, my lady." Emsley closed the lid on the small trunk. "You'll have all you'll need for a short journey. I could not fit any of your formal gowns."

"I don't believe I'll need them."

"Will there be anything else, my lady?"

"You'll be ready in an hour?"

Emsley folded her hands and looked directly at Rhona. "If it pleases you, I would like to take my leave from your service."

"Emsley, please." Rhona suffered the impact of her cross words. "I cannot stop you, but I do wish you would stay."

"I am sorry, my lady, but I feel it best that I leave. I do not wish to leave you unchaperoned, but I was told another lady arrived tonight. I could leave in the morning."

Rhona reached out for Emsley's hand. "I've made you so cross with me, and I truly don't deserve you. Is there nothing I can do to change your mind?"

Emsley appeared as though she may in fact rethink leaving, but Rhona's disappointment in the maid and herself increased. "We should return to Davidson Castle, my lady."

Rhona dropped the maid's hands and stepped back. "Why are you concerned with where I go and with whom? I've told you what my father said. I am no longer welcome in his home."

"He'll change his mind, I know it."

"I don't see how you could when I know him best, and I know he does not rethink a decision once it has been made." Rhona contemplated her options, but the course had already been set. "You may leave in the morning. I will see to it that you have your salary and a reference before I leave tonight." Rhona exited the room and with a bruised spirit went in search of Charles.

"We're coming with you." Devon stood in the doorway with Zachary.

"You know I always welcome your company, but this is personal." Charles slid the last sheaf of papers into a satchel. "Tristan has said the same, but if either of you wish to—"

"Bloody nightmare out there." Derek swept into the room still clad in his coat and hat. Ellis appeared behind with a disapproving look focused on the new arrival.

Charles smiled, but only in his attempt not to laugh. "It's all right, Ellis."

Derek swung around. "Oh, forgive me, Ellis." Derek removed his own coat and handed it with his hat and gloves to the butler.

"Very good, sir." Ellis held the wet

items away from his body and walked away.

"Forgot how much he hates when I don't ring the bell."

"I believe the act would cause him more shock than the wet trail you left in the hall." Charles shook Derek's hand after he had embraced his brothers. "A drink?"

Derek nodded. "Thank you."

Devon turned to his brother. "Zachary planned to follow your trail tomorrow and bring you back. You've been gone longer than expected."

Derek swallowed half the contents of the glass. "I sent a wire, but the man at the telegraph office in Aberfeldy was more interested in the bottle than his job." Derek looked at the full satchel on the desk and glanced between Charles and his brothers. "What have I missed?"

Charles set the rest of his papers in a drawer. "Devon can fill you in. What was in Aberfeldy?"

Devon said, "That will be difficult since I'm going with you."

"As am I," Tristan said.

Charles looked at his friends for a moment. "The only people more stubborn than Blackwoods are Claytons and Sheffields."

Derek walked to the window and pulled aside the curtain. "It's dark now and the weather is dreadful. You don't think to leave tonight?"

Charles nodded. "Timing could be essential. We have to leave for Scotland if we are to find Rhona's brother before our agency men do."

Devon interrupted long enough to tell his brother the abridged version of events.

Derek said, "My timing couldn't be

better." He set his glass on a silver tray and folded his arms. "To answer your question, Charles, Aberfeldy is where a kindly and hospitable widow sent me. How I found her is a longer story, but she was quite helpful. The local parish keeps meticulous birth and marriage records. The widow was once married to the groundskeeper at the church and spent most of her life in the parish. Claimed to know everyone who was ever born or wed during that time."

Charles leaned back against his desk. "You have quite a flair for rhetoric, Derek."

Derek waved that aside. "It is well worth the wait, my friend." He handed a folded sheet of parchment to Charles.

"This is from an official record

book," Charles said.

"They won't miss it. If you'll look toward the bottom, you'll find an interesting entry."

Charles scanned each line from the bottom up and his breath hitched. "Did you ask anyone about this?"

Derek nodded. "I asked the widow. She remembered the birth, but more importantly, she remembered there was no wedding. Now, look at this one."

Devon asked, "Did anyone see you take these?"

"You insult me, brother."

Charles read the second record, and after doing so, acknowledged an overwhelming need to burn the papers. Instead, he passed them along to Tristan.

"Two children born to Braden Crawford. Mother is listed as Lara Crawford. Children are Glenna and

Margaret." Tristan looked up. "Do you know the date of Rhona's birth?"

Charles nodded. "She was five years old. Derek, what else did the widow tell you?"

"That the children were born and left the parish in the course of one week. She never heard of them again. Crawford is the only one who can tell you the truth."

"And I cannot tell Rhona she had sisters, not without validating these records." Charles bowed his head, images of Rhona's anguish flashing through his mind when he tells her what they've discovered.

"Will you delay?" Devon asked.

"Delay what?" Rhona hesitated at the door, tears in her eyes. Charles pushed away from the desk and went to her.

"What's happened?"

"Nothing that can't wait a few minutes. Is everyone here going with us?"

"They don't believe telling them *no* is a valid reason."

"I don't mind, truly. Must we delay our departure?"

Charles exhaled and considered the options. A wiser man would not let her go with him. A smart man would wait. Charles optioned for the third choice. "No, we won't delay, but there are complications."

"All we've met with are complications. I don't care."

Charles glanced back at the small group. "We'll leave within the hour."

Tristan and Devon understood and filed out of the room with Devon's brothers.

"Derek has returned?"

"Yes, and he's brought news. It's cold out, but would you mind a walk?"

Rhona smiled at him. "I would like that."

Wrapped in wool and fur, Rhona stepped outside the front doors, welcoming the fresh air and burst of cold. The snowflakes fluttered now, falling to earth one at a time, each leaving a unique mark on the land. They flattened beneath her feet as she left her own mark on Charles's land. He remained silent, and the whisper of wind and branches filled the void.

"You say nothing, Charles, but I'm not fragile."

Charles pulled her close to him and covered the hand that rested on his arm. "Forgive me, but I will always wish to keep you safe. We continue to uncover only sadness and more questions."

"Which is it this time?"

"Both, I'm afraid." Charles watched the sun begin to fade behind the barren and snow-covered hills. "When I tell you what Derek has found, you'll have to make a choice to first find Alistair or the truth about your mother."

Rhona stopped, and her grip on his arm halted his walk. "They are not one and the same?"

"I don't know if they're connected, but I don't believe they are. Your family holds more than one secret, Rhona, neither of which will give you peace."

"What did Derek find?"

Charles handed her the records. He watched her confusion as she read line by line, and he saw the change when she realized the significance of what she held.

"I have sisters?" Her head whipped

up. "Can this be false?"

"Derek believes it is true. He met with a widow who was in the parish when they were born."

"It's true, then. Braden Crawford loved my mother. He was their father." Rhona closed her eyes and crumbled the papers in her fists. "He signed the register."

"We won't know any truth until we ask him." Charles enveloped her in his arms and rested his cheek on the top of her head. She'd left the house without a hat, and her cold hair felt silky against his skin. "What were you crying when you came downstairs?"

"Emsley is leaving me."

Charles lifted her chin. "What happened?"

"I don't know, but it was sudden. Emsley has always done her best to remind me I'm a lady and should behave like one. She's quite proper, and I know I've been difficult. She wasn't only my maid. I may have been wrong to treat her informally as I have."

"Where will she go?"

"I don't know. Emsley is not one to fear change, but I do worry for her."

Charles lifted Rhona's hand to his lips for a gentle kiss. "I'll see to it she has enough until she's settled with a new employer. Ellis will have instructions for her transportation. Does she plan to return to London?"

"I would presume so. She came to us from her family's home in the city."

"Then we'll have to trust that she will be safe. Would you like to stay and see her off?"

"Do you wish to be rid of me?"

Charles smiled. "Never." He

rubbed Rhona's shoulders when he felt her body shiver. "Have you packed?"

Rhona nodded. "Charles?"

He waited while she struggled with her words, and they were not what he expected.

"Alistair must come first."

Zachary burst into his brother's room during the early hours of morning.

"I've got it!"

Devon grumbled and shifted, his mind more alert than his body. "What the bloody hell are you doing in here at this hour?"

"The translation."

Devon sat up in bed, the cover slipping from his chest. "You know what it says?"

"They're going to Dunkeld, and we

may already be too late. We have to tell the others."

Twenty-One

The cathedral at Dunkeld stood as a barren corpse waiting for the unholy to enter. Not a light flickered or a candle burned in the windows. The darkness increased Rhona's trepidation about entering, but she refused to be left behind with Alaina and the baby. Tristan's wife argued, but for the sake of Christian, she agreed to return to Claiborne Manor when they left for Scotland. Rhona might have exhibited guilt for the trouble they caused the men, but her thoughts and fears rested on what they might find here.

"Should there not be a sign they are here?"

Charles sat beside her in the coach, across from Devon and Tristan.

"Alaina was disappointed to miss this."

Rhona glanced at Tristan. "Has she ever done something like this before?"

The men smiled, and Charles leaned in. "You'll enjoy Alaina's company, my dear, and her stories."

"Quiet." Devon lowered the curtain over the coach window, allowing only a sliver of sight. "It's time."

Charles sobered, and Rhona wondered if she'd been wrong to insist she come along. If she put any of them in danger . . . "Charles, you were right. I should remain here."

Charles glanced at her and then out the window.

"I'll stay with her," Tristan said, and exchanged a studied look with

Charles. Rhona imagined a good deal of meaning was behind the interchange.

Charles squeezed her hand and exited the coach with Devon. The air inside grew colder and it was more apparent now with Charles gone. "Tristan, would Alaina mind terribly if I borrowed your heat?"

Tristan transferred to the opposite seat and scooted next to Rhona. "Alaina would ask any one of them for the same favor were I not there."

"It was foolish of me to insist I be here, but I worry about Alistair."

"Do you worry for him, or that it will be Charles who is faced with killing him?"

Surprised, Rhona looked up at him. "You don't waste words."

"Charles is like a brother, and I know him better than anyone. He'll keep his promise, but not if it means risking someone else's life."

Rhona pulled the curtain aside and watched the dim light move past each door and window of the cathedral until it vanished. She wanted to go in, but if he wished to stop her . . . "Tristan, what was that noise?"

"Stay here or it will be my head Charles removes."

"Rhona?"

"She's in the coach. I told the driver to keep watch." Tristan hunched low to the ground beside Charles. "Where's Devon?"

Charles indicated the other side of the courtyard. "He's searching for a way in without drawing notice. She promised to stay in the coach?"

Tristan looked at him. "We heard a

gunshot, Charles. There wasn't time for promises. Who fired?"

"It wasn't us. We heard it, but Devon was closer, which is why I'm still out here. How's the wound?"

"Healing. She won't come looking, will she?"

"When you first met Alaina, would you have thought she'd brandish a gun and kill a man to save you?" Charles crouched lower. "Do you see that?"

Tristan nodded. "I see the lantern, but no sign of Devon."

A single gunshot echoed off the stone, and the clouds parted to reveal a gray moon. Charles pulled his pistol from the leather shoulder holster. "I need to go in."

"And I'm coming with you."

Charles shook his head. "You can't carry him out if he's hurt." He didn't give Tristan a chance to contradict. Charles moved along the pillars and arches, his boots quiet on the wet snow. He pressed his body against the wall outside the entrance to the church, looked once more at his surroundings, pushed open the door, and slipped inside.

More than fifteen minutes had passed since Tristan left her alone in the coach, and Rhona imagined horrors happening inside, the worst being that all three men lay dead or unconscious. Rhona didn't know what she could accomplish on her own and chided herself. A shadow crossed in front of the cathedral between the shadows and trees. She pressed herself further into the carriage seat, holding the curtain open only enough to watch the shadowy figure.

The lanky man stopped under one of the high arches, one hand on the stone. His face came into Rhona's view and her stomach knotted. Alistair turned and disappeared into the courtyard. Her heart raced, and her breathing increased until she heard only the worried thoughts in her own mind. She remained still until another echo of gunfire reached her ears. Closer now, but from where, she could not tell.

Rhona called out to the driver but received no response. Opening the door, she stepped out, keeping her body close to the carriage, but she well-nigh stumbled upon the body of the driver in her effort to circle around the conveyance. She stifled the worst of her cry with her gloved hand and sank to the ground. Blood spread over the driver's otherwise lily-white shirt.

Gravel crunched unmistakably beneath heavy footsteps. Rhona pressed herself against the tall wheel and peered through the spokes, but the mist rolled in and obscured her view of her surroundings. She no longer saw the cathedral, though she knew it stood strong and spacious only a short distance away. The footfalls were closer now, and Rhona searched for a way to leave. She did not believe herself lucky enough for the approaching man to be a friend.

"Ye should nae have come."

Rhona inched her body around, looked up in despair, and leveraged her body up with the wheel. "Why have you done this?"

"I have nae choice, Rhona."

"You do, Alistair! We all do." She stared at brother, too angry for tears. "You killed Wallace!"

Alistair looked surprised. "What do ye know of it?"

"Enough to know that the Order of Thoth is not meant for you. Why, Alistair? You were to inherit, become laird, and raise a family. I don't understand why."

Alistair lowered the pistol to his side, and Rhona still clung to the hope of escape. For all her desire to find her brother, she did not wish to be alone with him any longer than necessary. He lived and that is what mattered.

"Rhona, there are truths about our family ye don't ken."

"Then tell me. Wallace died because of your foolishness. He was a good boy with a full life waiting for him. Please don't follow him to the grave."

"There is nae other way left for

me."

Rhona tempered any fear and stepped toward her brother. "Yes, there is, and that is why we've come. There are men searching for you, government men and police. They believe you know secrets about treasonous acts and that you are part of this Order. They've told me the Order has killed men and women for power and money. Tell me you were never a part of any of it."

Alistair's eyes held a glint of arrogance. Rhona no longer recognized him.

"Why did you join them?"

"It's a family curse."

"What do you mean?"

"Ye dinna know about Father?" Alistair grabbed her arm. "It dinna begin with us."

Rhona couldn't think about the implications of what Alistair was telling her. "Please, brother, it's not too late for you. Help me."

Alistair looked past her toward the cathedral, but mist still shrouded the building. "How many came with ye?"

"Why?"

"Ye don't trust me?"

Rhona brushed away her brother's hand on her arm. "After what you've done? Never again."

He reached for her arm once more, this time giving her no choice but to remain in his grasp. "Ye dinna have to trust me, but ye do have tae do what I say."

His speed forced her to use his body and strength to get her across the wet grass. Light rain began to sprinkle down upon them, but Alistair was undaunted and continued to move at a quick pace. He let her go at the first arch to the courtyard, long enough to pull the knife from his boot and sheath it in his belt. Rhona's heartbeat quickened.

With pistol in hand, Alistair grabbed her arm once more and kept her close as they entered the courtyard. Rhona looked frantically around for any sign of Charles and the others, but all was still. The mist remained outside of the cathedral, allowing them to move about with ease. Alistair's calm demeanor contradicted her raging worry. Rhona's unease chose an inopportune time to be heard. She pulled slightly on her arm to test the strength of his grip. He wasn't letting her go.

"Perhaps they've gone inside the parish."

Alistair nodded, but his focus appeared to be on the entry door.

"We should go separately and perhaps one of us will find them."

"I'm nae daft, Rhona." Alistair pulled her along, walking through the courtyard past the few gravestones, and without a care, he pushed open the front door. Rhona panicked and tugged on her arm but did not gain her release.

"We don't know what's inside, Alistair."

"The Order is inside." He pulled on her again. Rhona raised her leg and pulled out the knife from her own boot, the one Charles placed in the leather before leaving the coach. She raised the knife and sliced the top of Alistair's arm. Her brother stared in disbelief.

"What have ye done!"

"You would hurt them."

"I'm bound tae the Order, as are

ye."

Rhona vehemently denied any connection. "You chose to join them, not me."

"Father made the choice for ye."

Her chest constricted and pain overwhelmed her.

Alistair raised his pistol and pointed it at her heart. "Ye dinna deserve Father." His body convulsed and he lurched back into an arch, pressed against something Rhona could not see, for she looked away. When he slumped to the ground, his fingers still gripped the gun. Tristan stood before her, a bloody knife in his hand.

Her eyes lowered again to her lifeless brother. Rhona turned away, praying for the tears to come, but her eyes remained dry. She felt a hand on her arm and faced Tristan. He held a finger to his own lips and held her hand as he guided her into the cathedral. Once in a small room, he closed the door and wiped the knife across the sleeve of his shirt. Rhona lifted her hand, now smeared with her brother's blood.

"Rhona, listen to me. Charles is with Devon in the catacombs."

She peered up at him. "Dunkeld has no catacombs. Where is Charles?"

Tristan shook her and lifted her chin, but Rhona's mind drifted back to her brother. "I lost another one. Where is Charles?"

"Rhona, you must stay here. I have to help Charles."

"Is he alive?"

"He's alive." Tristan pressed a hand to his side, and Rhona saw blood through his shirt. It was enough to bring her thoughts around to the immediate present.

"Your wound has opened."

Tristan waved off her worry. "It's minor, and it's not all mine. I know Charles promised that no harm would come to Alistair."

"Alistair did this to himself." The void within Rhona's soul expanded. "That man tonight was not the brother I knew." She raised her damp eyes to look at Tristan. "Please, I cannot lose Charles."

"You won't. Stay here and lower the bar on that door when I leave." Tristan handed her a clean dagger and exited the room. Rhona searched her body and realized the knife she used to score Alistair's arm was gone. She held the dagger in her fist and stepped farther into the room.

One of the long tapestries gracing the walls rustled from behind. She spun, chiding herself when she heard nothing besides her own breathing. Rhona pulled back the heavy material and peered into the dark opening. An arm snaked around the corner and pulled her close to a strong body. Her knife clanked against the stone floor. She clawed at the hand covering her mouth, but her fingers came away wet and sticky. The man dragged her back into the room.

"You'll not scream or you'll meet the sharp end of my dagger."

Rhona pulled away, but the man held her close, squeezing until she complied. He uncovered her mouth but did not release her arm. She glared up at the man, struck by the familiarity of his face. "No, it cannot be."

"You remember me."

Rhona nodded once, her worst fears confirmed. She had fought desperately to cling to the hope that her father was not involved. "You were careful not to look at me that day at Davidson Castle."

Charles adjusted his coat beneath Devon's head and pressed down against his friend's chest. The bullet had caught them both by surprise, but it found a path back to Devon once it hit the stone wall. Charles blocked out the sound of Devon's heavy breathing and listened to the moans traveling through the tunnels. He knew they weren't far from the stairwell that would take them to the courtyard. Four robed bodies lay less than five yards from them, and Charles knew at least one more was injured. Movement in the shadows drew his attention, and it was with great relief that he saw Tristan emerged.

"What are you doing here? Where's Rhona?"

"Bloody hell, Charles." Tristan knelt beside them. "She's safe for now, locked in a room. What happened?"

Charles nodded toward the bodies. "A bullet ricocheted. There are three more, one of them wounded. You're bleeding."

"Most of it isn't my blood." Tristan cut a thick strip of cloth from one of the robes and returned to Devon's side.

"There was another one outside?"

Charles saw his hesitation and asked again.

"Alistair is dead. Rhona was there."

"Damn him." Charles removed his hands to allow Tristan access to Devon's wound.

"The worst of it has stopped, but he's unconscious. Can you carry him out with your side injured?"

Tristan nodded. "I'll manage."

"I have to go after them."

"It's not worth it. We came here for Alistair. The agency can send men to chase the bloody beggars."

Charles tucked his pistol between his back and the waist of his pants and wiped Devon's blood from his hands. "One of them is Calum Davidson." He witnessed Tristan's surprise before he turned away, skirted around the dead bodies, and followed the dark tunnel into hell.

Twenty-Two

Lives lost long ago lay in stone tombs, and water dripped down the walls, falling between cracks on the tunnel floor. Charles lifted a torch left on the ground and used it to light his way. He knew nothing of the twists and turns or how many chambers and passages he would have to navigate before finding the men—if he found them.

He stopped at a branch where two tunnels met. Screams echoed off the walls, making it impossible to determine down which passage they came from. Charles closed his eyes and listened. When the shouts resounded once more, he hurried down the larger of the two, using his hands to remain upright while he ran, hunched over as the ceiling gradually descended.

Without warning, the tunnel opened up to a chamber, small and round. It held nothing and connected to another chamber. Charles checked for any other escape route and slipped into the next chamber—except it was something else. He looked around the narrow space and up the dark stairway.

Charles tossed the torch onto the wet ground and proceeded up the narrow staircase, only to be halted by a door. The latch gave and he pressed it open, pushing aside the heavy tapestry that hung between him and the room beyond.

"That's far enough, Blackwood. We're leaving."

Charles pushed the door closed

behind him and inched forward, his arms outstretched and his hands splayed, showing them he held no weapon.

"Not with her you're not." His eyes never moved from Rhona until he raised his gaze to look at the man holding her. "We've not met, yet you look familiar."

"You should have kept your distance from the Order."

"I despise all men who prey upon the innocent, but most especially Englishmen who obviously know better. You're not lowborn or you wouldn't be accepted in your despicable club." Charles studied the man more closely. "Alden Kitchener. You got the lower end of the gene pool, but I see the familial resemblance." Charles ignored him now to address the other two men.

"You're mad, Davidson, if you think you're leaving here with her. Let her go and you may live. I don't want to kill you any more than you wish to die."

"Ye killed me sons!"

"One of them, and I'd do it again." Charles prayed the tears falling over Rhona's cheeks were for the death of her brother or the disappointment in the man she once called her father, and not from fear. He needed her to stay strong. Alden held a pistol to her side while the third man supported Davidson. Charles now saw that Devon's final shot had hit a target— Davidson's leg. "You'll bleed out soon."

Davidson's eyes narrowed to cold and dangerous slits. The older man knew he was defeated but refused to admit the fact. "I'll bleed, ay, but so will ye, as will she."

"Do you wish to leave behind no one after you're gone, not even a daughter?"

"Ye think to fool me, Blackwood, but she is me daughter. Me adulterous wife had a child not me own, but Rhona is my blood, more's the pity."

Rhona broke her silence. "Alistair called me a bastard. I thought perhaps—"

"Thought Crawford was yer father, too? Nae, yer mine, and yer a whore like yer mother, and I want nae part of ye, but ye'll pay fer their dishonor."

Charles moved forward another step, slowly closing the distance between him and the man holding Rhona. "You mean your daughter was to pay for what he did. What did you plan, Davidson, to marry her to your wife's lover and kill them both, or kill Rhona and make Crawford live with losing her? I know it wasn't all about the money. You were willing to risk Wallace in order to gain her compliance."

Davidson's surprise told Charles his words resonated truth. "All of this killing to spite the man who loved your wife. Did you kill her?"

"Ye bluidy bastard! I would ne'er. I was nae a good husband, but I loved me Lara." Davidson gave up and dropped into a chair. "I loved me Lara."

Rhona stared in disbelief at her father. "If you hated me so much, why allow me to stay all those years?"

Charles interjected. "You planned Rhona's marriage to Crawford long before you needed his money."

Rhona's gaze shot to Charles, but

he shook his head and returned her gaze, silently asking her not to say anything.

Charles saw Davidson drop the hand he held against the bullet wound, too weak now to fight. "It was her duty, and she failed me."

Charles listened to a familiar sound and did his best to distract the men before him. "Is your final act of vengeance to be her death?"

Davidson looked first at him and then to Rhona as though contemplating Charles's question. To the other men he said, "Let her go."

Alden pressed the gun closer to Rhona. "They won't allow us to leave without her."

"You won't leave with her," Charles said. "Davidson, you already tried to kill me once when you sent your driver on the journey south to Crawford. He failed, and I promise you will, too."

Davidson appeared genuinely surprised. "I dinna ask me driver to kill ye, but I should've."

Charles didn't have a chance to ask Davidson for an explanation. The door to the room inched open and Tristan stepped inside, gun in hand and aimed at Davidson. "Next time, Rhona, please bar *all* the doors."

Rhona choked back something between a laugh and a sob.

Charles took advantage of the distraction, pulled his own gun, and aimed it at Alden. Charles cast his eyes to Davidson. "Not everyone has to die today."

Davidson wobbled to his feet with the help of the man who had remained silent, a young man who only recently left behind the blush of youth. Charles abhorred the recruitment of young men and women into organizations they couldn't possibly understand, and the practice was a travesty that only increased with each passing year.

"Yer a disgrace, Blackwood. Yer family was once of Highland blood. Do ye remember nothing of yer heritage?"

Charles was astounded by Davidson's interpretation of history. "My Highland blood runs deep and blends with my British ancestors. I do not choose a side, Davidson, nor do I use my country as an excuse to commit grievous acts against my people." Davidson had no response, and Charles saw him weakening, his complexion pale from the loss of blood. Charles turned back to Alden. "I can kill you without harming her.

You will not leave this room alive unless you release her now."

Alden, despite his arrogance, appeared to consider Charles's threat, and in the end he chose life. He pushed Rhona away and into Charles's arms. Without lowering his pistol, Charles held Rhona close for a brief moment and then pushed her behind him. Alden hesitated, watching Davidson for instructions, but the older man was too weak to lift his head. Alden lowered his gun, then reached into his robe and pulled out a long blade, dropping it on the floor, too.

Charles remained with Rhona and watched all three men while Tristan picked up the dropped weapons and relieved the others of their guns.

Rhona stepped from around Charles. "He carries a dagger in his left boot."

Tristan looked at Rhona, then lifted the hem of Davidson's robe away to reach his boot and pulled out a deadly knife, six inches long and sharper than a sword tip. "And what need would an honest man have for this?"

Tristan deposited everything on the other side of the hidden door, then walked over to open the main door. Stooped on the other side, but no longer unconscious, Devon waited.

"I despaired of ever seeing any of you again." Devon looked into the room. "That was too easy. Perhaps next time we ask for an assignment with a little more excitement."

Charles gently propelled Rhona toward the door. He and Tristan searched the room for anything they could use to tie the men, but in the end cut lengths of cloth from their robes. They secured their hands, and with Tristan in the front, they walked the men from the room. Outside, in the open air, Charles inhaled deeply and spent a minute looking around at the darkness. His eyes focused and settled on the most wonderful sight.

"Are you well, Charles?" Rhona pressed a hand gently against his chest and leaned into him. He welcomed her touch.

"I have a secret, my dear." He leaned in close to whisper in her ear. "I've never enjoyed enclosed spaces."

She looked up at him, surprise in her eyes. "The catacombs?"

Charles nodded. "If I never see another, I will die a happy man." He guided her through the abbey courtyard and across the frost-covered lawn.

"That man, Alden, Lord Kitchener's nephew. I saw him before. He met with my father before he told me about Crawford. Everything was a lie from the beginning."

Charles breathed in the scent of her hair and pressed his lips to the top of her head. "Not everything, love."

They walked across the frost-covered grass toward the coach.

"Oh dear, I'm afraid your driver is . . . Alistair killed him."

Charles released her and walked to the driver's body, growing stiff from the cold. He removed a lap blanket from the coach, then knelt beside the loyal servant, and covered the top of his body. "He must be buried. His body should be left here until the police can be summoned." Charles stood and motioned for Rhona to join him. "You should wait in the coach. It's grown colder and—"

Davidson collapsed to the hard ground, Tristan unable to reach him. His robed companions stood and watched.

"Charles!" Rhona pushed passed the others and fell to the ground. "Please, is there anything to be done?" She looked up at him with pleading eyes. "He's still my father."

Charles swore lightly and hurried to lift Davidson's head. He tore another strip of cloth from the robe and handed it to Rhona. "Here, press this against his wound." He pointed to the source of the blood on his leg. "He lost too much blood before he made it out of the tunnels."

"We have to try."

"I know." Charles nodded to

Tristan who tied the other two men to the wheel of the coach. He then handed his pistol to Devon before leaning down to help lift Davidson into Charles's arms. Carefully, with Charles holding most of the man's weight, they managed to set him inside the coach.

"Rhona." Charles held out his hand for her. "Sit beside him and try to slow the blood flow."

"Where are you going?"

"To dig a grave."

"Charles, what was his name?"

Charles looked down at the covered body. "Harry Scott." Charles walked to the front of the coach and lifted the small shovel from underneath the driver's bench.

"You shouldn't do this alone." Tristan grabbed his arm. "Devon can stay and watch over things here."

"He was my responsibility." Charles knelt down and lifted Harry's head. "Besides, I'll be carrying you back if you lose any more blood from that wound."

Charles eased the driver's body onto his shoulder and carried him the short distance from the coach back to the cathedral courtyard.

"Did he have any family?" Tristan asked.

Charles shook his head. "He grew up an orphan and was half-starved when he showed up at Blackwood Crossing." Charles smoothed the last of the cold dirt over the fresh grave. "Harry was always one to seek adventure, nearly killed himself a time or two. He'd be pleased to rest here." He stood and brushed away the dirt and snow from his pants.

"Do you have any words for him?"

Charles looked at Tristan. "None

that would make his death all right. Come, we have a long ride."

Back at the carriage, Tristan helped Devon into the coach beside Rhona, then pushed the other two men into a seat.

"I'll drive."

Charles declined. "You're not healed well enough and still bleeding."

"Which is why you need to be inside." Tristan pulled Charles aside. "If anything goes wrong, you're the best last option."

Devon removed his coat and handed it to Tristan, accepting no argument. "Bloody warm in here already."

Rhona watched her father grow weaker but knew her pleading

glances to Charles and Devon wouldn't stop Calum Davidson from dying. She pulled away a blood-soaked cloth only to replace it with another that Tristan cut from a robe, leaving the outer garment ragged. Charles and Devon both offered to replace her and minister to her father, but she would not leave his side. His actions were deplorable, but if death planned to take him that day, Rhona thought it was her duty to be by his side.

She needed the distraction to tear her thoughts from the two brothers she would never see again. One brother whose final thoughts of her were of contempt rather than love and another whom she had failed to protect and would miss to the end of her life. Rhona's chest tightened and she inhaled a few deep breaths to calm her rising emotions. The coach picked up speed and jostled the passengers. Rhona fell forward, but Devon reached out to keep her from falling against the men on the other bench. Charles braced himself and looked out the window.

"What's happening?"

Charles shook his head. "I don't see anything yet."

Rhona waited with the others while Charles continued to look outside the coach, and it wasn't a minute later when he pulled his head back inside.

"We have company, and not the kind we want." He leaned forward and looked at her father. "I'll wager those are your men?"

Rhona watched in amazement as her father raised his head and smiled. Charles swore and looked to Devon. Rhona didn't understand what silent communication took place, but whatever it was spurred them both into action. Devon, limited more than Charles by his wound, merely nodded when his fellow agent and friend opened the door on the moving coach.

"Charles, you're mad."

He held onto either side of the door, his smile frightening her for she guessed what he was about to do. "I have to, Rhona." He turned his body around and climbed outside, propelling himself up and out of sight."

"He knows what he's doing."

Rhona glared at Devon. "He didn't have to look happy about doing it."

"There are easier ways to die, Charles."

"I have no intention of dying

today, friend." Charles glanced at Tristan's side where the coat flayed opened from the wind. "Damn, man, your wound is bleeding again." Charles reached out and pulled the leather reins from Tristan's grip. "There are only four behind us, but we're still two miles from Bankfoot and carrying too much weight."

Tristan braced against the coach and looked back. "We can't fight them."

"And we can't outrun them." Charles urged the horses to a faster pace. "Wait, ahead there."

"The innkeeper won't be pleased."

"No help for it." Charles began to slow the horses a little at a time and felt a slight shift of the coach wheels.

"Ice?"

Charles nodded. "They'll make it."

"The riders have slowed down, but

they're still coming."

Charles brought the horses to a stop a few feet from the front door of the inn. "Get Rhona and Devon inside. I'll deal with the others."

"Alone?"

Charles climbed down before looking back up at his friend. "Need I remind you about our first assignment together? There were five of those blokes alone with you. Come." Charles assisted Tristan down from the carriage, a helping hand he knew his friend didn't appreciate needing. Charles opened the coach door and hurried Rhona outside.

"Charles, what is happening?" He tried to shield her view, but the approaching men drew closer. "They're still coming."

"Yes, hurry inside with Tristan."

"What are you going to do?" Rhona

tried to shake off Tristan's grip.

"Stubborn woman." Charles pushed her against Devon. "Get her inside."

Devon propelled her from behind and Tristan guided her through the front door. A few seconds later, Devon returned.

"You'll both bleed to death, and I'll be the one who has to explain it to Alaina."

Devon held a pistol in the hand not affected by the gunshot wound. "Rhona will see to Tristan. My wound is fine."

The three riders stopped a dozen yards from the inn and waited, staring at them.

"Rather anticlimactic of them. Do they think we're going to let their friends go?" Devon looked into the coach and pointed his gun at the two men in good health. One pushed back his coat and reached a hand toward his hip. Devon shook his head shouted, "That's a foolish choice you're about to make."

Charles looked around Devon to see what the man had done and swore. "I'll put a bullet in each of you before you get away. You're bound for Newgate, unless you manage to negotiate with the British government."

Devon climbed into the coach and retied the men, this time linking Alden and the young man together behind their backs. Charles continued to watch the three riders, but it was Calum Davidson who concerned him most. The man lay slumped on the seat with his hands limp against his side. The bleeding appeared to have been stopped by a makeshift bandage.

"Is he still alive?"

Devon turned in the confined space and checked Davidson for breath and pulse. "Barely." He climbed from coach and closed the door. "Time to invite the chaps over."

Charles nodded and walked a dozen feet before stopping and waving the men in. None of them moved. "Your choices are few, gentlemen. Come forward peacefully and join your companions in prison, leave and never return to British soil, or come forward and be killed."

One of the men finally spoke. "Ye'll send them out, unharmed."

"No, we won't." Charles backed up a few paces until he stood close enough to the coach in the event he required shelter from bullets, but none of the men appeared to be carrying weapons.

"We have to get Davidson inside."

Charles spoke once more to the riders. "Davidson is badly wounded. A conflict will ensure his death."

"Give him to us, and we'll be gone."

"They don't seem to understand."

Charles swore. "Enough of this."

"Charles!" Devon fired a shot, and the sound echoed in Charles's ear.

The riders had pulled their weapons and advanced. An older man stepped out from the inn, and one of the shots hit the door above his head. He shouted something Charles couldn't hear, backed up, and hurried inside.

"They'll wake the bloody village." Charles hit one of the men in his arm, causing him to drop the gun. Devon hit another and the man fell to the ground. The third man held his gun but did not fire. With a shaky hand, he dropped it to the frosted earth and held up his hands.

"Damn fool." Charles nodded to the coach door. "Will you check on Davidson? I don't want to have to go inside and tell Rhona her father died. I'll dispel the robed madmen of their idiot notions."

Twenty-Three

Rhona heard the gunfire cease. It lasted only a few minutes, and the innkeeper rushed back inside and shouted words Rhona was never allowed to use growing up. Her heart raced at the thought of harm coming to Charles, Devon, or even her father. Tristan lay unconscious on a bench, too large of a man for the innkeeper to carry him upstairs. The innkeeper's wife ministered to Tristan's wound and was now re-stitching the threads that tore open. Rhona couldn't imagine how the older woman managed to remain calm during the brief ordeal.

The inn was empty save for a young couple newly married. They were in the common room with the innkeeper when the sound of gunshots first filled the air, and they rushed up to their room. Rhona didn't blame them and wished she could ignore the worry plaguing her mind. Tristan began to move, but Rhona remained standing before the door, praying for Charles to walk in unharmed.

The door pushed open with more force than might have been necessary, but when Rhona saw that Charles nearly carried her father, she hurried forward to help, calling out to the innkeeper. The man hesitated, but when he saw that most of them were injured, he moved to help. Once Charles deposited her father in a chair, he turned to the innkeeper and indicated Tristan.

"Thank you for looking after him."

"Can't turn away a man wounded, but we don't have room for the kind of trouble you've brought to our door."

"My deepest apologies for that, but trouble has left us now."

The innkeeper said, "You're noble."

Charles nodded once. "And you're British from the sound of it. Will you welcome fellow countrymen?"

"Scottish on my mother's side, but my father was as British as you. I prefer the Scots."

Rhona stepped forward to stand beside Charles. "I am Scots, as is my father." She felt uncomfortable under the innkeepers studied looks but held out hope that he would soften toward them.

"You'll not be causing me any more trouble?"

"No, and I will pay for any

necessary repairs to the exterior of your inn."

The innkeeper nodded. "Did they deserve it?"

Charles nodded. "Yes."

"Were they English?"

Charles laughed. "No, Scots."

"Pity." The innkeeper walked back to his registry. "Names, please." "What is this?"

The young rider fought for breath. "Here, my lord. Your man said to get this to you straight way."

"My man?"

"The footman, my lord."

"Who are you? Why did Ellis not send one of my own men?"

"I can't rightly say."

"Will you return to England?"

The young man nodded. "Tomorrow. Do you have a return message, my lord?"

"No, I don't believe so. How did Ellis find you?"

"The footman came to Lord Kitchener."

Charles handed the young man a few coins. "Thank you, and safe journey."

The rider remounted and left as quickly as he'd come.

"Why would your neighbor release one of his men to travel this far north?"

"I can think of no reason." Charles tore open the seal. "Unless one of my own men could not leave."

Robed men have surrounded Blackwood Crossing. Ellis dead. Going to constable after this message has left Lord Kitchener.

The paper crumbled easily in Charles's hand. "It seems your father was right. This is not over."

"Are you certain the message is genuine? And how did that rider know where to find you?"

"The lad likely stopped at half a dozen inns before finding us here, but if Arthur or Tanner managed to get away . . ." Charles raised his hands to set upon Rhona's shoulders. "We will go to Crawford, but if there is any shred of truth to this message, then I must return home, and quickly."

"Not alone?"

Charles pulled her against his body, without a care for who might walk into the hallway and pressed his lips to hers in a brief kiss. "Trust me."

"I do."

Charles left her side and entered the room where Devon and Tristan convalesced. However, instead of resting, both were dressed and playing cards.

"We could dig your graves here and save me the trouble of carrying your carcasses back to England."

"We've had three days and we've all been in far worse condition." Devon laid down his cards on the table and grinned at Tristan.

"Bloody hell man, how do you do it."

Charles walked to end of the bed where his traveling bag sat on the trunk. "I must return to England."

"About time." Tristan stood from the table. "Alaina won't forgive me if I stay away any longer."

"She'd forgive you anything." Devon lifted his coat from a hook in the wardrobe. "What's wrong, Charles?"

He handed Devon the crumbled

paper and finished placing his items in the bag.

"Revenge for what we did at Dunkeld?"

"Most likely." Charles slipped into his coat. "I need to ask one of you to stay with Rhona."

A light knock on the door drew Charles's focus, and he opened it to an unexpected visitor.

"You're dressed to go out."

Rhona nodded. "I'm going with you."

"Rhona, I can't take the coach. It will be a hard ride, and I don't know what will wait for us when we arrive."

"And I can ride." She peeked around him at the others, then lifted the hem of her skirt. "I had my tailor make them before I left home. I can ride, and I won't slow you down, and the skirts will cover the trousers." She dropped her skirt. "I won't be parted from you, not again."

"The lady makes a valid argument."

Charles turned and glared at Devon, but his friend only smiled. He faced Rhona. "How did I not know you rode astride?"

"It's not ladylike."

Charles gave up. "It's too dangerous for you to come with us to Blackwood Crossing. You'll stay with Lord Kitchener. You must agree to that."

"Agreed."

Charles spared glance after glance toward Rhona, watching her breath heat the air. She was true to her word and rode nearly as well as any of them. They left behind everything except what could be carried on horseback. A hefty purse to the innkeeper assured that Rhona's trunk would be sent along and delivered to England. The train journey gave any of them little to do except worry and occupy themselves with talk. Only now, when Charles rode upon English soil with a few miles before they reached Keswick, did he allow his concern to surface.

His concern grew tenfold when the rise of smoke drew their attention to the hill. Flames joined the smoke, and they all spurred their mounts into a run, racing across the land and up the hill where Blackwood Crossing burned.

"Keep her away!" Charles shouted the order, but he did not know which of his friends kept Rhona from moving with him toward the mansion. The east wing burned, but the remainder of the house was still intact. A horse-drawn fire apparatus, manned by half a dozen men Charles didn't recognize, sprayed water onto the flames, but they did little to calm the growing blaze. Charles raced forward, but one of the men stopped him.

"You can't go in!"

"I'm Lord Blackwood."

"I'm sorry, my lord, but it's not safe. You shouldn't go in there."

"I have people in there."

The man shook his head. "We've not seen anyone leaving, and no screams for help."

Devon rushed up. "Where is everyone?"

"I don't know. I have to go in."

Devon held him in place. "The man's right. That water won't keep the fire from spreading. It's too dangerous."

"No one is out here, Devon."

"It's too dangerous to go alone." Devon slapped him on the shoulder and ran beside him to the main entrance of the house. Somewhere far behind him, Charles swore he heard the sound of Rhona's screams as he disappeared into the mansion.

Rhona pushed against Tristan, but even in his weak state, she was not strong enough. "They'll die in there."

"Rhona, listen. There are innocent people in that house. Charles isn't going to let them die."

Defeated, Rhona slumped against Tristan. "Can I trust you to stay here? I should be in there with them."

Rhona nodded.

Soon Tristan was inside, and Rhona now had three people she loved whose lives rested precariously on the edge of death.

Charles stopped and pressed a hand to his chest to help control the coughing. The smoke drifted into the main corridor, but thus far the rooms they checked were empty. He turned to Devon just as Tristan came in through the door.

"Where's Rhona?"

"She's going mad."

Charles blinked his eyes rapidly to bring moisture to them. "I'll check upstairs. Keep looking through the rooms down here." He gave them no chance to argue and rushed through the hall and up the stairs. He shouted and checked in each room down both hallways. The heat grew closer, and Charles knew they did not have much time.

He raced up to the servants' quarters, once again finding the first set of rooms empty. It wasn't until he passed through to the men's living quarters that he discovered the locked room. With what strength he had left, he fought another fit of coughs, then rammed himself into the locked door, once, then twice. It burst open. His entire staff lay on the ground or sat against the wall, all tied and unable to move.

Charles hurried first to Ellis and sliced through his ropes. "I was told you were dead."

Ellis grabbed his chest. "A temporary problem, my lord."

Charles cut through Arthur's ropes and handed the footman the blade. "The women first." He set a hand on

Ellis's arm. "Are they still here?"

"No, my lord." Ellis hunched over coughing. "I can only believe they left once they set the fire."

Charles worked through the knots of a maid and his cook. When everyone was free, he urged them from the room. "Get everyone out, Ellis. The main corridor is open, but it won't be for long."

Ellis nodded and guided his charges from the room. Charles followed behind, searching for Devon and Tristan as he went. Both were in the main foyer helping the others through the front door. A wall crumbled. Charles yelled at them to leave, and he raced into his study. Across the room, he pulled open a false wall he used only as a security measure. Within the wall lay a small room and a safe. Charles covered his mouth and nose with the edge of his jacket and opened the safe. He pulled out a single bag and hurried from the room.

Once outside, he moved away from the mansion and dropped the bag. Folding over, he breathed in the fresh air, only to stumble backward when Rhona rushed into his arms.

"You're crazy and lucky you made it out alive!"

"You didn't think I would make you a widow before the wedding, did you?" Charles bent forward again, unable to control the coughing. "Did they all get out?"

Devon and Tristan stepped up beside them. "Everyone is safe," Tristan said. "What was worth going back inside?"

Charles kicked at the bag and held Rhona close to him. He watched Devon open the carpet bag to reveal papers. "My family's entire record of fortune and properties on paper are in that bag. I don't trust offices of the recorders to keep things in order. I may reconsider."

Charles turned with Rhona in his arms and stared up the dissipating flames. A light rain began to fall, turning most of the fire to smoke.

"Were the men who did this inside?"

"No. Ellis said they left when the fire started."

"Will you go after them?" Rhona asked.

"No, but if I cross paths with another member of the Order of Thoth again . . ."

A coach rolled over the drive at a brisk pace, and the door opened before the driver had a chance to stop the conveyance. Patrick disembarked and hurried toward them.

"Was anyone hurt?"

Charles shook his head. "You were nearby?"

Patrick nodded. "Coming to see you. I heard what happened at Dunkeld."

"You do have men everywhere."

"We all do, Devon." Patrick looked up at the mansion. "It's not all in ruin. Did they get away?"

Charles nodded. "I trust the agency will find them. Come, we have to get out of this rain, and I must secure lodging for my staff."

"You'll not stay here?"

Charles glanced at his home. "There is enough intact, and we'll return and rebuild, but until then, my people need to feel safe. Patrick, if you'll join us at the inn, we have matters to discuss."

Rhona lay asleep and secure in one of the rooms upstairs. Lord Kitchener had walked as far as his front door when his butler informed him of the fire at Blackwood Crossing. Kitchener sent a driver to intercept their coach and inform them that the lord insisted they stay on as his guests.

Charles secured the remaining rooms at the inn, offering a large purse to the proprietor for the late hour and the extended stay. He, Devon, Tristan, and Patrick now sat in Kitchener's parlor. The late hour did not stop Charles from insisting Patrick remain to answer questions.

"Tell us about Emsley Hargrave."

Patrick stared at him, but Charles remained firm in his resolve. "What do you wish to know?"

"How well did she know Calum Davidson?"

"I believe they were intimate."

"Before or after she was hired as Rhona's maid?" Tristan asked.

"I suspect after. She was to see to it that Rhona complied and followed through with the marriage. Two years ago, your relationship with Rhona worried her father, but we never knew how he learned of it until we discovered his close connection to Miss Hargrave."

"And do you know where Emsley went? I secured her passage, but Ellis informed me that she slipped away at the train station."

"It's possible she returned north to Davidson Castle. When did you suspect her?"

"Not until Rhona informed me that Emsley was leaving. I imagine she was there to watch Rhona for Calum."

Tristan said, "We still don't know who tried to kill you, Charles."

Patrick's eyes narrowed. "When was this?"

"Something you don't know?" Charles asked. "Davidson's driver tried to dig his blade into my chest when we escorted Rhona south. Davidson's surprise appeared genuine when I mentioned it. I don't believe he was behind it."

"And you have no leads?"

Charles shook his head. "No. I can only hope that it was somehow involved with this case and that the matter is done. We have enemies aplenty and will always have to watch ourselves."

"Derek and Zachary could ask around if you'd like. They would draw less suspicion than one of us."

Devon leaned forward in the chair. "Calum Davidson is on his way to Newgate. What will happen to his estate?"

Charles said, "If his debts are as great as you've said, Patrick, then there won't be an estate before long."

"You're not coming back, are you?"

Charles smiled. "I will soon be married, and I have family in Ireland who I'd like Rhona to meet. Blackwood Crossing must be rebuilt. I have no desire to return to the agency."

Patrick looked at the others. "Tristan?"

Tristan said, "I'm done now. Alaina and Christian need me at home."

"Devon?"

Devon leaned back in his chair, a slow grin forming on his face. "And give up this life? Not today."

Twenty-Four

"This can wait, Rhona."

She shook her head. "I don't expect my reasons to make sense, but I need to know what happened between my mother and him. Was it love that caused her to give herself to another, to risk everything, even her children? I have to know."

Charles smiled down at her, and when the carriage stopped, he helped her down. A flustered footman greeted them, his eyes darting back and forth and his hands overly eager to work.

"Is all well here?"

The young man looked directly at Charles. "Yes, my lord. Well, no. It's the laird, he's—"

"James, bring in the luggage."

The young footman nodded at the butler, red-faced at being caught for speaking of his employer. Charles waited for the young man to return to the house before addressing the butler. "What's happened to the laird?"

"It is not for me to say, Lord Blackwood."

"Yet I'm asking you."

"Laird Crawford will see you now." The butler stepped to the side, allowing them to precede him.

Sensing Charles's amusement, Rhona shared a small smile with him and linked her arm with his. Her own body trembled and she took comfort in the gentle weight of Charles's hand on her own. The butler led them through a short hallway to a sitting room, dark with the drapes drawn.

"Please, come in." Crawford beckoned them in and offered them refreshment. "Don't mind the curtains. I suffer from deplorable headaches, and the dark helps to ease the discomfort." He pointed to the tea and sandwich setting and looked at Charles. "I prefer a good whisky, but it increases the pain. I can pour you something stronger if you'd like."

"Hot tea will be agreeable after our journey, thank you." Charles leaned forward in his chair and accepted his cup after Rhona had been served.

Now that she knew the truth, Rhona tried to see him as her mother would have. Strong and sure of himself and his place in the world, a handsome and kind man. Rhona understood what drew her mother to this man.

Crawford leaned against the back of his plush chair. "I was surprised when you sent a messenger about your visit. I did not expect to see either of you again."

Rhona's cup rattled in the saucer, and she set it down before it toppled to the carpet. "I've learned something about you, Laird Crawford."

"Please, just Crawford, or Braden, if you'd like."

Braden sounded too intimate for Rhona, but Crawford seemed cold, considering his relationship with her mother. "I want to ask about you and my mother. I know it's deeply personal, but . . . was she happy?"

Crawford smiled, a slow contented smile. "She was, and never was there a dearer soul to me than your mother."

"When you offered for me, why did you not tell me then? I might have understood."

"No, darling girl, you would not have come, and I knew your father's anger ran deep enough to allow you to come. I suspected what he might plan, which is why I could not express my gratitude when you stopped the wedding. Please know that I would have freed you, and we would never—"

Rhona held up her hand. "Charles told me, and I'm grateful for the sacrifice you were willing to make. I wish I had not tried to kill you."

Crawford and Charles both laughed. "A risk worth taking. Love and loyalty tore your mother's heart, and I did not want that for her daughter."

"You had daughters."

Crawford nodded. "Beautiful bairns, though neither survived the birth. When your mother realized she could not bear to lose any more children, she went home."

Rhona sat forward in the chair, her hands gripping the heavy fabric of her skirt. "My father gave her no choice. I was prepared to shower you with my anger for the betrayal and lies. Now, I'm only sorry she lost you."

"But I did not lose her." Crawford hesitated and exchanged a quick glance with Charles before moving to sit in the chair next to her. He reached for her hand and held it gently, the way she imagined a father would. "She lives on in you and in my memories. Our time was brief, but it was beautiful and filled with love."

Rhona automatically looked at

Charles.

Crawford smiled, but the couple missed it. "I watched you over the years, Rhona. I believed it was my duty to your mother. She did not worry for her sons, but she was concerned for you."

Rhona turned back. "Why did she worry?"

"When your father threatened to take away her children, he did not mention your brothers. He thought to send you to a nunnery. Your mother never would have seen you again."

"I didn't realize."

Crawford released her hand and returned to his own chair. "I heard what happened to your father. Will he live?"

Rhona nodded. "He will. Charles saved his life."

"You're to be married."

It was not a question and both Rhona and Charles knew it. Rhona was pleased that she and her future husband could share the good news.

Charles grinned. "I hoped to see the deed done before we returned to Scotland, but time did not allow it. We are to marry upon our return, at Blackwood Crossing."

Rhona hesitated, then made her decision. "Will you come and give me away?"

Crawford stared at her, and she felt an overwhelming urge to hug him. His eyes filled with moisture. "It would be my great honor."

Twenty-Five

On what should have been the most beautiful day in her life, Rhona experienced an overwhelming sense of sadness. Her mother had not lived to see this day. Her father wanted no part of her life for the very reason that he thought she was compromised. Her family was unraveling fast, and she was uncertain what tomorrow would bring, but she was certain about the choice she had made. Charles Blackwood, the man, and not the wealthy English viscount, stood by her side as they reverently repeated the priest's words. An old friend of the Blackwood family, Father

Silsbury, wore an uncommonly wide smile, possessed a gentle nature, and Rhona was certain he winked at her before the ceremony began.

In the presence of God, Father, Son, and Holy Spirit, we have come together to witness the marriage of Charles, Viscount Blackwood, and Miss Rhona Davidson, to pray for God's blessing on them, to share their joy, and to celebrate their love.

Rhona looked around at the few people in attendance. Braden Crawford stood beside Tristan and Devon. His love was the most fatherly affection she'd ever received. Father Silsbury offered her an encouraging smile as he continued to recite words of loyalty, commitment, and joy. He spoke of the love and trust and how they would unite in heart, body, and mind. With each word, Rhona's heartbeat accelerated. Charles gently squeezed her hand, and she closed her eyes. Her heart desired this union, but her mind remembered the agonizing loss she had endured when Charles left. She trusted him and knew he would not abandon her again. Rhona focused her thoughts on all of the reasons why she stood beside him now, pledging to join her life with his.

Charles Blackwood, will you take Rhona Davidson to be your wife?

Will you love her, comfort her,

honor and protect her, and forsaking all others, be faithful to her as long as you both shall live?

"I will." Charles declaration broke through her worries.

Rhona Davidson, will you take Charles Blackwood to be your husband?

Will you love him, comfort him, honor and protect him, and forsaking all others, be faithful to him as long as you both shall live?

It was her moment of truth, and she'd never been more certain. "I will." She heard the words spill from her lips, and her certainty became absolute. From this day and beyond her last breath, she was bound to Charles, willingly and unconditionally.

Those whom God has joined together let no one put asunder.

Cheers and congratulations rose forth from their friends. Tristan moved stiffly but managed to embrace Charles. Alaina came forward and pulled Rhona into her arms. She kissed each cheek, and her smile warmed Rhona's heart. A true friend, unlike any she'd ever known, stood before her.

They shared light touches and glances during the celebration dinner. Rhona wondered if Charles's heart fluttered as strongly as hers. The afternoon turned to night as the sun descended and its final rays glistened over the water. Charles pulled her aside, held her close, and lifted her chin so he could look into her eyes. He pressed his hand to her heart. "Your beauty astounds me, my love."

Rhona glanced around, then slipped her arms around her new husband. "In my heart, I was always yours, and you were always mine. Thank you for finding me."

"I lost you, but it will never happen again. I was a fool."

Rhona laughed. "Ah, but my love, you are now a reformed fool."

Charles silenced her laughter with a kiss and surrendered his heart to her forever.

Brannon Cottage, County Wexford, Ireland

They lay in comfortable silence, their bodies resting beneath the bed coverings. A fire burned strong, heating the room, though Charles had no need for the extra warmth. His wife's head rested against his bare chest, her long hair caught beneath his arm as he stroked strong fingers up and down the center of her back.

"Thank you for showing me Ireland, Charles. It was kind of your friends to lend us their cottage."

"I helped them out of a difficult situation many years back. They are now among the few I call friends." He brushed his hands through her long, soft hair. "Tomorrow we'll meet my cousins."

"I imagined all your relatives would be Scottish or English."

"They used to be, but I have no

immediate relatives left, only my distant cousins here. I rarely see them, but I want them to know you."

Rhona shifted until she half covered his naked body with hers. "Won't you miss the excitement?"

Charles pressed a kiss against the top of her head. "I only returned last time for you. All I want now is in my arms." He pulled her closer to him, as though it were possible for two people to be more connected than they already were.

"What will I do with you all to myself?" Rhona grinned and nipped at the skin on his chest.

"I can think of better places for your lovely lips." Charles laughed when she inched her fingers down. "I was thinking up here." He dragged her body up along his until he could capture her lips.

The bell secured at the front of the

cottage rang loudly in the night, drawing Charles and Rhona apart.

"It's well past midnight."

Charles slipped into the closest pair of trousers and a previously discarded shirt. Rhona slipped from the bed, naked until she covered her long body with a heavy robe. "I want you to stay here," Charles said.

"Be careful."

Charles moved quickly to the window, pulling the wool fabric aside. "My God." He removed the latch and opened the door. "Anne, whatever are you doing here?"

"I'm sorry, Charles. You sent word you'd be here, and I know we were to meet tomorrow."

Rhona stepped into the front room, still clad in her robe. "I heard you open the door. Is everything all right?"

Charles motioned her forward. "This is my cousin, Anne Doyle. Anne, this is my wife, Rhona."

Rhona reached out and welcomed the younger woman into her arms. "You're shivering and cold. Come sit by the fire."

Charles helped her into a chair and covered her with a blanket. "What are you doing out alone on a night like this?"

Anne's eyes welled with tears. "Something terrible has happened, Charles. I need your help."

The End

Continue reading for a glimpse of the third British Agent novel, *Clayton's Honor*.

CLAYTON'S HONOR
Book Two of the British Agent
Novels

**Journey to Ireland and England in
Clayton's Honor, a dazzling story
of danger, honor, and undeniable
love.**

Would you give up duty for the sake of
your honor?

On the windswept shorts of Ireland,
Anne Doyle lost her father to a foolish
war and her mother to madness. Left
with debt and an ancient family home,
she struggles to keep the rest of her
family together even as an enemy
attempts to take them away. After
witnessing a brutal murder, Anne must
enlist aid from the only family she has left
if she is to save those she loves.

Devon Clayton had no intentions of

leaving behind his life of adventure and danger, but when he is charged with protecting a witness and her family, he must choose between duty to the country he serves and a woman who tests his honor and willingness to change.

Together they will discover that nothing is what it seems and that without honor, love and life are for nothing.

Clayton's Honor is historical romance at its best—a captivating adventure set in the rolling hills and crumbling castles of Ireland.

Excerpt from *Clayton's Honor*

County Wexford, Ireland
February 4, 1892

Could they hear her? If she moved deeper into the shadows, could she sneak away? If she loosened the grip on her lungs and took the deep breath she desperately needed, would they find her? The heady stench of copper filled the air of the great hall, the dank stone walls doing little to block the scent of death. The carpets beneath her slippered feet masked her first step. Back one, and then two. She ducked behind a heavy tapestry, one of the few left in the old castle.

Masked under a cloak of clouds and desperation, she escaped out the servants' entrance, confident that the cook and single housemaid would not see her. Wet slush and rain combined to make her retreat difficult. She could not risk discovery by hailing someone and beseeching them for a ride. Her own two feet must carry her the miles to Brannon Cottage.

The noise of the carriage wheels competed with that of the storm, but she did not mistake the sound of the small rocks as they ground and rolled over one another. She hurried behind a nearby copse of blackthorn and waited. Lights from the carriage lanterns broke through the darkness as the conveyance approached. The man in the driver's seat sang "She Is Far from the Land" faintly heard through the wind. After he passed, Anne set one foot in front of the other and paused. Her fear overpowered her desire for warmth.

She could do this. It was only four miles.

One worn slipper almost fell from her foot when she stepped in a small slush of wet snow. Colder now, she pressed forward. One mile. Two miles. Three. She must reach him before they realized she was gone. Anne flailed and her body lurched to the ground. Her arm scraped over a sharp stone that sliced through her cloak. The faint clatter of bottles in her satchel managed to reach her ears over the harsh howl of the winds.

Anne rose to all fours and then stopped and knelt on the sodden road, choking back a trail of tears as they coursed down her already wet skin. She tucked soaked locks of her long hair beneath her wet bonnet. Drawing on pure need, Anne pushed up from the ground and continued down the dirt road. She did not know the Brannons well. They visited Ireland once or twice a year, and yet the only person on this earth she could hope to trust was currently on holiday and using the Brannons' cottage. Ten years had passed since she'd last seen him.

The tidy two-story stone structure appeared as though from the fog. Soft, white flakes fell in time with her heavy breaths but lasted only the time it took for her to reach the front door.

End of Excerpt

Read an extended excerpt on the book page at mkmcclintock.com.

Thank you for reading
Blackwood Crossing

Visit mkmcclintock.com/extras for more on the British Agents.

If you enjoyed this story, please consider sharing your thoughts with fellow readers by leaving an online review.

Never miss a new book!
www.mkmcclintock.com/subscribe

THE MONTANA GALLAGHERS

Three siblings. One legacy.
An unforgettable western romantic
adventure series.

Set in 1880s Briarwood, Montana Territory, The Montana Gallagher series is about a frontier family's legacy, healing old wounds, and fighting for the land they love. Joined by spouses, extended family, friends, and townspeople, the Gallaghers strive to fulfill the legacy their parents began and protect the next generation's birthright.

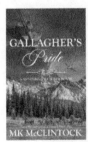

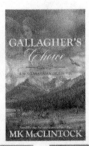

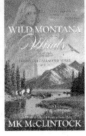

THE WOMEN OF CROOKED CREEK

Four courageous women, an untamed land, and the daring to embark on an unforgettable adventure.

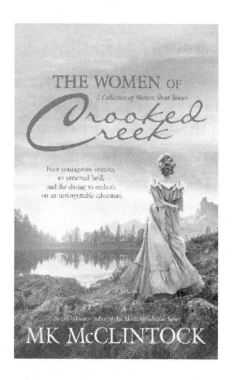

If you love stories of bravery and courage with unforgettable women and the men they love, you'll enjoy the *Women of Crooked Creek*.

MCKENZIE SISTERS SERIES

Historical Western Mysteries with a Touch of Romance

 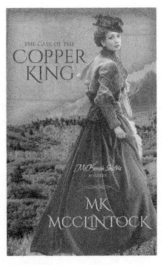

Cassandra and Rose McKenzie are no ordinary sisters. One is scientifically inclined, lives in Denver, and rides a bicycle like her life—or a case—depends on it. The other rides trains, wields a blade, and keeps her identity as a Pinkerton "under wraps."

Immerse yourself in the delightfully entertaining McKenzie Sisters Mystery series set in Colorado at the turn of the twentieth-century.

THE MONTANA GALLAGHERS

Three siblings. One legacy.
An unforgettable western romantic
adventure series.

Set in 1880s Briarwood, Montana Territory, The Montana Gallagher series is about a frontier family's legacy, healing old wounds, and fighting for the land they love. Joined by spouses, extended family, friends, and townspeople, the Gallaghers strive to fulfill the legacy their parents began and protect the next generation's birthright.

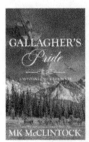
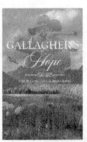
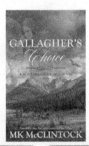
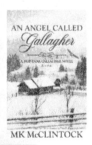

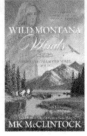
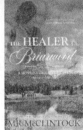

THE WOMEN OF CROOKED CREEK

Four courageous women, an untamed land, and the daring to embark on an unforgettable adventure.

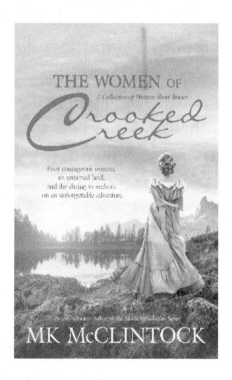

If you love stories of bravery and courage with unforgettable women and the men they love, you'll enjoy the *Women of Crooked Creek*.

MEET THE AUTHOR

Award-winning author MK McClintock writes historical romantic fiction about chivalrous men and strong women who appreciate chivalry. Her stories of adventure, romance, and mystery sweep across the American West to the Victorian British Isles, with places and times between and beyond. With her heart deeply rooted in the past, she enjoys a quiet life in the northern Rocky Mountains.

Visit **www.mkmcclintock.com** for more.